HIPPO
in a
TUTU

HIPPO

in a

TUTU

DANCING IN DISNEY ANIMATION

Mindy Aloff

EDITIONS

New York

Editor: Christopher Caines

For information please address Disney Editions, 114 Fifth Avenue,
New York, New York 10011-5690.
Editorial Director: Wendy Lefkon
Senior Editor: Jody Revenson
Assistant Editor: Jessica Ward

The following are some of the trademarks, registered marks, and
service marks owned by Disney Enterprises, Inc.: Disneyland®;
Disney's Hollywood Studios.

Walt Disney's *Bambi* is based on the original story by Felix Salten.
Dumbo is based on the Walt Disney motion picture *Dumbo*, suggested
by the story *Dumbo, the flying elephant*, by Helen Aberson and Harold
Pearl. Copyright © 1939 by Rollabook Publishers. Mary Poppins
is based on the Walt Disney motion picture *Mary Poppins*, based on
the series of books by P. L. Travers. Roger Rabbit characters © Walt
Disney Pictures / Amblin Entertainment, Inc.

Academy Award® and Oscar® are registered trademarks of the
Academy of Motion Picture Arts and Sciences.

Library of Congress Cataloging-in-Publication Data on file
Reinforced binding

ISBN 978-1-4231-0079-9

First Edition
10 9 8 7 6 5 4 3 2 1
Printed in Singapore

PAGE 2: *The animator and inventor Ubbe ("Ub") Iwerks, a friend of Walt Disney's from boyhood, produced brilliant animated short films during the Disney company's earliest years. In* The Barn Dance *of 1928, Iwerks included a scene in which Mickey Mouse mangles one of Minnie Mouse's legs while they dance: Iwerks's artful drawing of Minnie's pain elicits a pang of empathy in the viewer, even though Minnie is "merely" a cartoon.*

OPPOSITE: Springtime, *layout drawing. From an undated Disney studio document: "Released in 1929. The first animated picture in which flowers were used to interpret a ballet."*

For my daughter, Ariel Nikiya Cohen,
wise and kind, with whom I saw many of these films

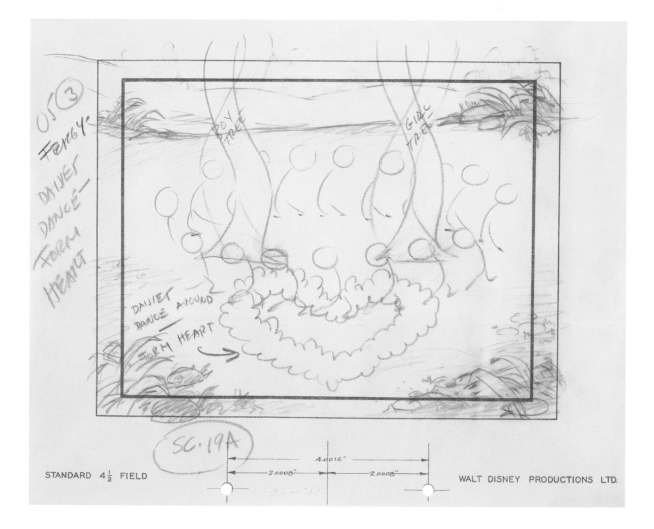

OPPOSITE: *A cel from the 1959* Sleeping Beauty. *The animator and storyman Burny Mattinson, who was an assistant to animator Marc Davis on the picture, has explained that the animators had difficulty "grounding" the figure of Prince Phillip—that is, of giving his body the illusion of gravity and physical purpose as he moved. More than two decades before, the animators of the Prince in* Snow White and the Seven Dwarfs *had had the same trouble.*

A scene from Mark Morris's version of Jean-Philippe Rameau's opera Platée (1997), surrounded by images from Disney's Water Babies (1935). Platée, a singing frog diva, believing herself to be loved by Jupiter (at far right), lounges in a pool, surrounded by other creatures of her aquatic world. Sets by Adrienne Lobel; costumes by Isaac Mizrahi. Photo: Bill Cooper.

I am often asked for a list of choreographers who have most influenced me in my own work. Along with George Balanchine, Merce Cunningham, and Busby Berkeley, I invariably mention Walt Disney.

And in naming Disney, I mean the teams of directors, animators, composers, reference models, and background artists involved.

For my entire career, I have been accused of the dreaded sin of "Mickey Mousing" the music (as if music itself contained an embedded dance that needed only a cryptographer to release it to the world). I figure that somebody brilliant taught us all how to watch dancing and music and to recognize the bond between the two. I love it when sound and sight are saying the same irreducible thing. The inevitable. That's what Disney does. From the very early Silly Symphonies (my favorites) through *Cinderella* and *The Jungle Book* (not my favorites) via the great *Fantasia*, I marvel at the variety of choreographic invention and aptness. What a remarkable resource of whimsy, fantasy, art!

What a trip! Take *Water Babies* (1935): I first saw *Water Babies* when I was young enough to think that it was some kind of documentary. It is a strange, amazing pastoral fantasy that features naked babies (distinctly male and female although they have no genitals) who sleep in water lilies, harness the power of birds and bugs, and can pray in English. There's even a bullfight with a bullfrog. Seeing it again as an adult gave me a kind of melancholy. That's when I realized that I actually believed in that world. It is where I come from.

It is not just the place where I first heard Rossini and Mendelssohn and Schubert, where I first encountered W. C. Fields and ZaSu Pitts and Cab Calloway. It is also the place where I came to believe, without question, that everything—people, the moon, spiders, animals, trees, clocks, even fire—had a spirit. And usually a personality and a face. Flowers can not only walk, they also prance and mince and swagger. Hens can gather up their skirts daintily to escape a fox attack. Skeletons play xylophone on each other's ribs using femurs for mallets. How do they do it?

Everything is alive. Everything is animated.

In my own work as a choreographer, I happily and purposely observe a direct, symbiotic relationship of music and action. I call it dance.

It is where I come from.

MARK MORRIS was born on August 29, 1956, in Seattle, Washington, where he studied as a young man with Verla Flowers and Perry Brunson. In the early years of his career, he performed with Lar Lubovitch, Hannah Kahn, Laura Dean, Eliot Feld, and the Koleda Balkan Dance Ensemble. He formed the Mark Morris Dance Group in 1980, and has since created more than 120 works for the company. From 1988 to 1991, he was director of dance at the Théâtre Royal de la Monnaie in Brussels, the national opera house of Belgium. Among the works created during his tenure were three evening-length dances: *The Hard Nut*; *L'Allegro, il Penseroso ed il Moderato*; and *Dido and Aeneas*. In 1990, he founded the White Oak Dance Project with Mikhail Baryshnikov. Morris is also much in demand as a ballet choreographer. He has created six works for the San Francisco Ballet since 1994 and received commissions from American Ballet Theatre and the Boston Ballet, among others. His work is also in the repertory of the Pacific Northwest Ballet, Dutch National Ballet, New Zealand Ballet, Houston Ballet, English National Ballet, and the Royal Ballet. Morris is noted for his musicality and has been described as "undeviating in his devotion to music." He has worked extensively in opera, directing and choreographing productions for the Metropolitan Opera; New York City Opera; English National Opera; and the Royal Opera, Covent Garden. Morris was named a Fellow of the MacArthur Foundation in 1991. He has received honorary doctorates from the Boston Conservatory of Music, the Juilliard School, Long Island University, Pratt Institute, Bowdoin College, Bard College, Bates College, and George Mason University. In 2006, Morris received the New York City Department of Cultural Affairs Mayor's Award for Arts and Culture and a WQXR Gramophone Special Recognition Award. He is the subject of a biography by Joan Acocella (Farrar, Straus & Giroux) and Marlowe & Company has published a volume of photographs and critical essays entitled *Mark Morris' L'Allegro, il Penseroso ed il Moderato: A Celebration*. Morris is a member of the American Academy of Arts and Sciences. In 2007, he received the Samuel H. Scripps/American Dance Festival lifetime achievement award.

ABOVE: *Kathryn Beaumont, who provided the live-action reference model and voice for Alice in* Alice in Wonderland *(1951), in a scene from the reference footage with Jerry Colonna as the March Hare and Ed Wynn as the Mad Hatter.* LEFT: *This frame from the reference footage, with a sketch of Alice's animated figure superimposed on the live model, shows how the rotoscoped images were used.* RIGHT: *A figure from a large sheet of "clean-up suggestions" for Alice's character. Such drawings guided the animators as they refined their work in a later stage of the process.*

Dance and animation—a pas de deux choreographed in heaven.

Animators have often been called actors with pencils (and, in this computer age, pixels), but in many ways we also resemble dancers. Dancers and animators both carve out movements in time, rhythm, and space; and both utilize pure motion to tell stories, delineate characters, and communicate moods and emotions. Indeed, the spirit of Terpsichore hovers above each of these art forms.

From its earliest days, the animated cartoon has displayed an affinity for dance. In Emile Cohl's 1908 short *Fantasmagorie*, stick figure Fantoche performs a naughty absurdist miniballet that prefigures Léonide Massine's surreal *Parade*, premiered by Serge Diaghilev's Ballets Russes in 1917, and the modern morphing forms of Pilobolus.

Gertie, a childish dinosaur animated brilliantly by Winsor McCay in 1914, performs (despite her girth) a dainty gavotte that appears completely believable and holds its own against the later comic vaudeville brio of eccentric dancers such as Charlotte Greenwood and Ray Bolger, or nondancer comedienne Fannie Brice spoofing *en pointe* a hoity-toity ballet dancer.

Felix the Cat often assumed a pantomimic succinctness and personality modeled on the balletic Charlie Chaplin; but this 1920s feline jazz baby also moved with an explosively joyous, body-contorting exuberance later seen in the Nicholas Brothers.

Abstract animators, who dwell exclusively in a free-form universe, share a dancer's timing and rhythmic sensibility, too. Early on, there was Walter Ruttman's Opus series, featuring undulating organic and architectural forms sensually rising and falling; and Oskar Fischinger's white chevrons, arrows, and dots dart and caroom through jet-black space, as eloquently nonrepresentational as a Merce Cunningham "chance" dance.

Then there are the dance—animation connections and accomplishments produced by the cartoon world's own Diaghilev: the extraordinary Walt Disney. His Silly Symphony shorts often featured rhythmic dance movements performed by impossible creatures. *The Skeleton Dance* (1929), the first film of the series, is a mock-macabre performance by a bunch of bones who break up and reassemble with alarming élan and without missing a beat.

Later Sillies showcased more sophisticated animation, dance knowledge, and study: in *Cock o' the Walk* (1935) a rooster and hen perform a barnyard version of the carioca backed by a chorus of poultry (including peacocks) forming Busby Berkeley-like patterns amid the chicken coops.

Woodland Café of 1937 stars dance-mad insects who punish the parquet by Truckin' and dirty dancing (in addition, a spider and a fly perform a deliciously zany apache); and 1938's *Merbabies* (a saltwater remake of the 1935 *Water Babies*) contains an underwater ballet to make both Billy (Aquacade) Rose and Esther (*Neptune's Daughter*) Williams hold their breath and turn sea green with envy.

The Silly Symphonies were made possible by the phenomenal success in 1928 of Mickey Mouse, the rhythmic rodent whose movements so closely resemble dance that Graham Greene once famously observed that Fred Astaire was "the nearest we are ever likely to have of a human Mickey Mouse; he might have been drawn by Mr. Walt Disney, with his quick physical wit, his incredible agility."

Mickey's basic happy-go-lucky double-bounce walk is itself a kind of dance. It reminds me of Astaire in *Funny Face* when his stroll down the Avenue des Champs Elysées begins with an unassuming, ordinary walk that through a subtle change in emphasis and energy placement quickly and magically becomes—a dance!

In fact, Mickey directly impersonated Astaire's top-hat elegance and movements in the memorable 1936 short *Thru the Mirror*. By then the Disney animators were constantly studying film footage of dancers and attending live theater performances (everything from burlesque to ballet), and also bringing dancers into the studio for even closer scrutiny.

Many dance figures posed for Disney's artists and cameras, among them versatile Marge Champion, who was a model for Snow White; the Blue Fairy in *Pinocchio*; and a hippo, an ostrich, and an elephant, *à la* Sally Rand, in *Fantasia*; the Jackson Brothers, whose imaginative improvisations were transferred by animator Ward Kimball to *Dumbo*'s famous crow quintet's raffish song and dance; Irina Baronova and Tatiana Riabouchinska of the Ballets Russes de Monte Carlo, who, though both lithe and slender, posed for an ostrich and a hippo, respectively, for the brilliant "Dance of the Hours" sequence in *Fantasia*.

Some of my favorite moments in Disney films involve either formal dance movements or dancelike choreography within the staging of scenes or sequences. *The Adventures of Ichabod and Mr. Toad* (1949) showcases the agile moves of schoolmaster Ichabod Crane, principally animated by Frank Thomas, who was inspired by eccentric dancer Gil Lamb. In one memorable sequence, the tall, gangly Ichabod multitasks at a country dance: he simultaneously woos the fair Katrina and nonchalantly thwarts his bumptious rival Brom Bones while devouring a cartload of food—a tour de force of personality definition, conveyed through carefully planned choreography.

Disney's version of the flight to Never Land in *Peter Pan* (1953) is arguably more satisfying than Jerome Robbins' stage and television productions of the same period.

Unhampered by flying harnesses and the limitations of gravity, each of the animated characters performs highly choreographed visual gags, culminating in an exhilarating, dizzyingly thrilling flight over London atop cumulus clouds as they head toward Never Land.

Fantasia, as mentioned, contains a veritable treasure trove of dance imagery from beginning to end. The gorgeous "Nutcracker Suite" choreographs season-specific dancing fairies and flora, including a midair adagio of falling sycamore leaves, milkweed ballerinas, and (on the ground) shape-shifting hallucinogenic fungi.

Mickey Mouse has a star turn as the Sorcerer's Apprentice. Using only dance and pantomime, he gives perhaps his greatest performance.

The "Night on Bald Mountain" sequence gathers the spirits of the dead in a writhing bacchanal with a deeply emotional climax that demonstrates animator Vladimir Tytla's mastery of acting through animation: as a church bell tolls, the giant demon Chernabog expresses through subtle movements of his face, upper body, and arms a quicksilver array of emotions—annoyance, puzzlement, anger, fear, despair and, finally, exhausted resignation.

Chernabog's movements reveal his innermost feelings frame by frame and, as Martha Graham often said, "Movement never lies"—a dictum that applies well to dance and animation.

Mindy Aloff explores all of the above and more in this most welcome addition to the study of Disney animation.

On with the dance!

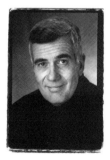

JOHN CANEMAKER is an Academy Award–winning independent animator, animation historian, teacher, and author. His films are in the permanent collection of the Museum of Modern Art in New York and are distributed by Milestone Film & Video (*John Canemaker: Marching to a Different Toon*). Canemaker won a 2005 Oscar for his twenty-eight-minute animated short *The Moon and the Son: An Imagined Conversation*, and also created animation for the Oscar-winning documentary *You Don't Have to Die* (HBO), the Peabody Award–winner *Break the Silence: Kids Against Child Abuse* (CBS), and *The World According to Garp* (Warner Bros.). He has written nine books on animation history that are considered to be among the most important and thoroughly researched in the field, on subjects ranging from Winsor McCay and Felix the Cat to Tex Avery and numerous Disney artists. He is a full professor and director of animation studies at New York University's Tisch School of the Arts, Kanbar Institute of Film and Television. John Canemaker was awarded a 2006 Emmy Award for outstanding television graphic design (for *The Moon and the Son*); an honorary doctor of fine arts degree from Marymount Manhattan College in 2007; and, for his work as an animation historian, a special award from the 2006 Zagreb Animation Festival and the 2007 Jean Mitry Award from Italy's Le Giornate Del Cinema Muto. In 2008, he received the Winsor McCay Award from ASIFA–Hollywood in recognition of his career contributions to the art of animation. The Museum of Modern Art featured Canemaker's 1998 short film *Bridgehampton* in its 2008 Jazz Score show, with screenings throughout the day and original animation art from the film on exhibit in the gallery.

The Disney inspirational artist Mary Blair produced memorably wonderful color combinations for the animators of Peter Pan. THIS PAGE: *Blair's own scene showing the dance of the Indians.* OPPOSITE: *From the film: Peter Pan, the Darlings, and Tinker Bell in full flight. Their cruciform flying position, which turns them into planes or gliders, is reminiscent of the animated history of aviation from Disney's 1943* Victory Through Air Power.

The first time my folks took me to see a movie in a theater, I was five years old. The Korean War picture featured June Allyson, in a terry-cloth bathrobe, dodging live ammunition on a muddy battlefield. The events enacted seemed very real, and I thought we were all going to die. Afterward, I had terrible nightmares and didn't want to go to any more movies. But my mother had faith in Hollywood, and, a few months later, she and my dad offered me another picture. It was Walt Disney's feature *Peter Pan*, and the visual charm—largely a product of the delicate colors and gentle wit of the Disney inspirational artist Mary Blair, I learned many decades later—opened the door for me to a lifelong fondness for animated films in general and Disney pictures in particular. While in elementary school, I was treated often to Disney animated features in theaters: *Cinderella*, *Sleeping Beauty*, and *Lady and the Tramp*, re-releases of the 1937 *Snow White and the Seven Dwarfs* and the 1942 *Bambi*, as well as *20,000 Leagues Under the Sea*, *The Living Desert*, and other live-action Disney films. I also loved the animated Disney shorts starring Mickey, Donald, Goofy, and Pluto that sometimes preceded theatrical features; they were so funny and marvelously drawn, and although their characters weren't as cool as Bugs Bunny and Daffy Duck of Warner Bros., they seemed more physically substantial and, ultimately, kinder.

We had a television set, too, which only transmitted images in black and white and with a screen half the size of the computer monitor I'm now looking at as I type. Still, wonderful things flowed out of it: George Balanchine and the New York City Ballet in *The Nutcracker*, Sid Caesar's *Your Show of Shows* and *Caesar's Hour*, *The Ed Sullivan Show*, *The Hallmark Hall of Fame*, *Mr. Rivets*, *Crusader Rabbit*, Max Fleischer cartoons—and Disney productions. On weekday afternoons, I'd race home for *The Mickey Mouse Club*, and on Sundays there was *Walt Disney Presents*, a variety hour whose unpredictable programming I always enjoyed. As with the animated films, there was a special spirit to these Disney shows; outgoing and optimistic, even when times were hard or situations threatening. They suggested that the next day would be better. For the kid I was, that message was a gift.

Disney's output was part of the larger magic of my childhood, in which all the arts were available, affordable, and encouraged, and few, if any, distinctions were made between art for children and art for adults, or between true art (which originates deep within individuals, who may be working in concert) and commercial cultural product (which originates in an effort to benefit from market forces), or between originality and kitsch. Everything was for everyone—an impossible ideal, but one my family tried to realize at home. At the Free Library, my parents took out on their library cards all the novels, biographies, and plays I wanted from the adult section and wasn't permitted to borrow with my children's card. The radio in the kitchen was always on, and the music I heard included both the hit parade and the Saturday afternoon broadcasts of the Metropolitan Opera. My folks had a well-worn collection of big-band as well as classical records, and my babysitters, as well as my

A scene from Dances of Hungary *(about 1961), a Disney film intended for television but never aired. Hungary enjoys one of the richest folk-dance traditions in Europe, especially for men, with an unbroken chain of strong and complex dances for warriors going back many centuries. During the nineteenth century, the French composer Hector Berlioz, visiting the country, noted that Hungary also offered the most sumptuously appointed* grand bals *on the continent.*

Ballerina Kirsten Simone and principal dancer Henning Kronstam, both beloved stars of the Royal Danish Ballet, in the feature-length film Ballerina, televised in two parts during 1966 on Walt Disney's Wonderful World of Color. The cast included the young dancer Mette Hønningen, who also became a ballerina with the Royal Danes, as well as the young actress Jenny Agutter. LEFT: Kronstam with Simone (far upstage) and corps de ballet. BELOW: Simone and Edwin Thiemroth, playing a theater manager, watching Mette Hønningen. Written by Casey Robinson (erstwhile husband of ballerina Tamara Toumanova), the film was coproduced by Disney, who hired Norman Campbell to direct it. Campbell—who would go on to direct more ballet for television—closely observed his boss early in the production process: "I remember Walt Disney as I screened our first tests in Hollywood," Campbell has been quoted as saying. "I was told to watch out for his fingers. I did. As the scenes unraveled on the screen I could see his fingers, perfectly still. This was the 'Good Sign.' He loved it."

mother, would teach me dances to some of the songs, such as the Charleston and the Big Apple. In the early 1950s, people still did dances like these, with steps you had to learn, for fun; my second-grade teacher taught our entire class the rumba and cha-cha she was learning in her Arthur Murray classes. For years, I was put to sleep with 45 rpm records of the original cast of *South Pacific*, of operettas such as *The Chocolate Soldier*, and operas such as Flotow's *Martha*, along with "The Syncopated Clock" and Lee Hayes singing "The Little White Duck." Occasionally, the pianist who accompanied my ballet classes would suddenly play a musical theme from a movie. Philadelphia in the 1950s was also a live-theater town, the site of Broadway tryouts, and I was regularly taken to musicals and plays, as well as to world-class classical dance and music performances. Neither of my parents was involved in the arts professionally: my mother taught history and accounting in a public high school and my dad was an electrical engineer. Still, both of them were enraptured by the theater, music, film, and the ballet—anything that *moved*, either figuratively or physically. The only distinction that mattered was between what was riveting and what wasn't: on weekends, when my mother would play her recordings of Artur Rubinstein by day, she would wake me up to see Mickey Rooney and Judy Garland, directed by Busby Berkeley, on the Late Movie. Financially, our family struggled, but in terms of the arts I was given a millionaire's education, much of it free or very inexpensive. You didn't learn to be a connoisseur in such an environment—to say "No!" You learned to be curious and tolerant—to say "Yes."

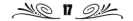

The 1950s was the era when the words *highbrow*, *middlebrow*, and *lowbrow* were thrown around in the press, and yet, as far as arts and culture were concerned, I didn't know any snobs, although I met kids who certainly had the bona fides for snobbery. When I was ten, one of my classmates at the Quaker school I attended for a couple of years was a gifted pianist who played a concert repertory for us at school assemblies and who has gone on to a highbrow, international career as a powerhouse interpreter of Liszt and Beethoven. Away from the keyboard, though, his tastes were just as wide-ranging as everyone else's. At Halloween, as an expression of his identification with a Disney live-action hero, he dressed himself from head to toe in black—boots, jodhpurs, loose shirt, cape, mask, and gaucho hat—and his obsession lasted for the rest of the school year. I still have the spring autograph book where his page is signed *André Watts—Zorro!* My parents and those of my agemates belonged to the generation that had come through the Great Depression and World War II and was reaching for something utopian

for themselves and their children in peacetime: a combination of high standards and freedom of choice. I saw my first ballet on television—Margot Fonteyn as Aurora in *The Sleeping Beauty*—and when I was eight, my father, a big football fan, enthusiastically squired me to Sergei Denham's Ballet Russe de Monte Carlo at the sumptuous mirrored-and-gilded Academy of Music. By the time I was in the fifth grade, I was avidly collecting pop songs on 45 rpm records and also attending Friday afternoon student concerts by the Philadelphia Orchestra. The Ice Capades and the Ice Follies—so elegantly produced and performed—were as much a part of my childhood as the great doo-wop groups on *American Bandstand* (produced right in Philadelphia and televised each afternoon immediately before *The Mickey Mouse Club*) and the Handel oratorios in which I sang as part of the chorus at my Hebrew school. I and my schoolmates were brought up with a richness of genre and media and a democracy of excellence in the arts, and we came to take it for granted, as our birthright.

OPPOSITE: *Although* The Little Mermaid *was released by the Disney studio in 1989, Walt Disney had begun to plan an animated version of it during the late 1930s as part of a projected film combining live action and animation about Hans Christian Andersen and his works. The great Danish illustrator Kay Nielsen (1886–1957), who produced some concept art for the* 1940 Fantasia *and inspirational drawings for a planned second installment of* Fantasia *that was never produced, contributed inspirational sketches and storyboards of such delicate beauty for* The Little Mermaid *in 1939—such as the example here—that the finished film a half century later credited him for his visual development. Nielsen left the Disney company in 1941, unable to adjust to its deadlines and methods; moreover, at the time his art was considered old-fashioned. By the late 1950s, both he and his wife, Ulla, had died in penury; today, his works bring small fortunes at auction.*

ABOVE: *Ariel, the Little Mermaid, from the 1989 film. Although Andersen's story emphasizes the mermaid's desire to dance with legs on land, the Disney film's most spectacular dance scenes take place underwater and suggest the aquatic choreography for Esther Williams in her Busby Berkeley movies. Ron Clements and John Musker, the co-directors of* The Little Mermaid, *brought their affection for Broadway and 1950s Hollywood musicals, including the happy ending (quite different from Andersen's), to this fantasy.*

Disney's 1991 Beauty and the Beast—*melodious and beautiful, with complex characters—contains two ballroom-dance scenes: one for the title characters (shown here in a preliminary sketch) and one for Beauty (named Belle) and the Prince into whom the Beast is transformed by Belle's devotion. The first, more detailed dance was animated specially for the film; it looks like a waltz but the music is in 4/4 time rather than a waltz's characteristic 3/4. The second, shorter number was recycled from the ballroom dance in the 1959* Sleeping Beauty, *using animation from the final waltz of Prince Phillip and Princess Aurora, though the music—a reprise of the title song heard in the earlier ballroom sequence—remains in 4/4.*

For me, the pre–World War II animated Disney films, especially— musically distinguished, magnificently designed, and driven by artfully shaped stories and memorable characters— held their own with many other images to which I was exposed, including Old Master drawings in the cases of *Snow White*, *Pinocchio*, and the 1940 *Fantasia*. And they still do. Indeed, thanks to what I've learned about their joys and their technical detail from my daughter, Ariel, who grew up studying them on VHS as well as in theaters, I'm even more appreciative of them now than when I first encountered them as a child. As it happened, my Ariel was born four years before the release of *The Little Mermaid*, the Disney musical whose heroine bears the same name. Ariel's father and I had named the baby for one of the Jewish angels (in Hebrew, *Ariel* means "lion of God"), and when this movie, one of the most brilliant animated features ever produced by the Disney studio, arrived on the scene, we took our daughter to see it, along with *Beauty and the Beast*, *Aladdin*, *DuckTales the Movie: Treasure of the Lost Lamp*, the live-action Disney animal picture *Homeward Bound* (a story of friendship that gathers resonance as one ages), and a few enduring live-action musicals and comedies from other studios. Meanwhile, I attempted to offer Ariel the performing arts, too; however, by the late 1980s, that was a rather expensive mission. Routine Broadway shows, ballet, and musical concerts were out of the question. (Although I was given pairs of seats to performances I was reviewing, I didn't put pressure on Ari or the artists by taking her to the theater as part of my work.) Puppet shows weren't predictably to her liking, and her Hebrew schools did not perform Handel. Even art museums had become costly, and we chose the shows we attended with care. When she was still in a stroller, I introduced her to the Metropolitan Museum of Art by way of a huge retrospective of the Belgian Surrealist René Magritte. American cartoons of the early 1930s from the Disney and Fleischer studios, or the illustrations of Clement Hurd for the classic children's books of Margaret Wise Brown, evoke aspects of Magritte's somewhat buttoned-down version of Surrealism, with recognizable elements from the everyday world fantastically isolated or recombined. One small, mysterious Magritte canvas, the 1925 *Nocturne*, of a bird flying out of a painting-within-the painting, where a miniature house was on fire, which my daughter noticed before I did and didn't want to leave, is something she remembers to this day, possibly because it was

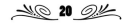

The dance scene in the 1940 Pinocchio *for the title character and the French, Dutch, and Russian puppets is possibly the only such dance scene made under Walt Disney's guidance in which the act of dancing is not meant to represent joy or well-being but rather an enforced facsimile of those feelings. In recent decades, critics have charged Disney with anti-Semitism for the way the tyrannical puppetmaster Stromboli has been represented, suggesting that his oppressive dominance of his marionettes is a covert reference to the way Jewish heads of major studios controlled the actors tied to them. However, in the late 1930s the Disney animators were attending the de Basil Ballets Russes and might well have seen its production of Michel Fokine's* Petrouchka, *which features a cruel, bearded puppetmaster and his enslaved marionettes.* Pinocchio's *Stromboli was animated by Vladimir (Bill) Tytla, a master at drawing fearsome villains.*

evoked for her hundreds of times by the working fireplace in the bedroom that Hurd conceived for *Goodnight Moon.*

Images in museums are one thing; images on television or film are something else again. As a new parent in the 1980s, I listened to all the arguments then in the press about whether or not young children should be permitted to watch television at all, and, after considering the various positions on the matter, I decided that the thing to do was to permit *a little* television (*Sesame Street* and *Reading Rainbow*), along with all the videocassettes I had to watch for work as a dance critic or that Ari's dad and I chose to watch for enjoyment. The household rule was that Ari couldn't watch them alone: we had to watch *with* her until she was old enough to operate the VHS machine without mishap. That meant that, in Ari's early years, we ended up conversing constantly about moving pictures—analyzing the stories and characters, or the styles and techniques of the acting or dancing or moviemaking,

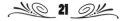

Various preliminary ideas of Sleeping Beauty's *Princess Aurora, sketched by Disney artists during the pre-production process. Note that the artists did not draw her as a dancer; in the film, however—for which the live-action reference model for Aurora was the ballet dancer Helene Stanley—the character, though barefoot, is shown dancing in the forest on high 7/8 pointe.*

and, on occasion, addressing issues outside the film that events within it might raise. One of the videocassettes I had to study for work when Ari was a year old was the Walt Disney Silly Symphonies anthology, with the now-classic 1920s and 1930s cartoons *Flowers and Trees, Music Land,* and *The Skeleton Dance.* It became one of her immediate favorites, which she chose to revisit often over the next decade, giving me ample chance to examine (and to wonder at) the craft of the Disney artists, composers, and directors. As complements, I bought or taped some comedies for us from the same, interwar period as the Sillies: movies by Charlie Chaplin, Buster Keaton, the Marx Brothers, Laurel and Hardy—pictures that the original audiences for the Sillies would also have known and that helped to stretch both Ari's and my historical imaginations. For my dance articles, I frequently watched the RKO movies that Fred Astaire and Ginger Rogers made in the 1930s and the Nicholas Brothers and Gene Kelly made in the 1940s, so Ari grew up with first-rate examples of live-action screen musicals. She learned to recognize what choreography is, to distinguish between technique and charisma in a dancer, and, in cartoons, to evaluate how well the animators have captured the illusion of life in dancing. Thanks to the screen scores of Irving Berlin, George and Ira Gershwin, and Jerome Kern, which set a standard of excellence in songwriting

and dance orchestration, she was also able to appreciate how good the Disney composers were, even though their names are less well known.

As I write, my daughter is a senior in college, studying to be an elementary-school teacher. By this time, she has seen thousands of movies from many genres, including hundreds of animated films from all over the world. And yet, she not only continues to revisit the Disney pictures from her childhood but she also continues to teach me about them. Like many of her technologically sophisticated peers, she has memorized those Disney movies, studied the documentaries on the DVDs, expanded her knowledge of them on the Internet, compared them with animated shorts and features from other American animation studios and with such international animation genres as Japanese *anime*. And because she and I have the habit of watching movies together, I've benefited tremendously from her comments. This book could not have been written without her.

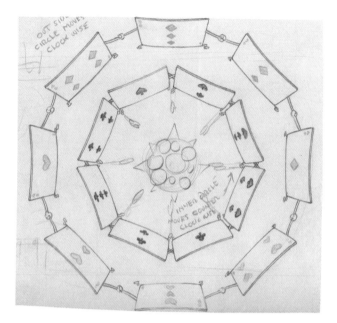

ABOVE: *A ballet of playing cards—an animation drawing from Disney's Mickey Mouse cartoon* Thru the Mirror. *Courtesy the Cowan Collection, Jenny and Robert Cowan.*

ABOVE: *In the 1936 animated short* Thru the Mirror, *Mickey Mouse falls asleep while reading* Alice in Wonderland *and dreams that he passes through a mirror into a fantastical and often surreal world where inanimate objects come to life and nothing is predictably safe from transformation. A publicity shot of this scene from the film bears the caption: "Mickey has the gloves in stitches as they toe the line with their fingers. 'I've got to hand it to you,' he shouts." The short owes less to Lewis Carroll's Alice books than to the studio's earliest animation experiments.*

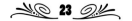

By all accounts, Walt Disney (1901–1966) was not a connoisseur of music or of dancing. He liked both, but admitted that he would sometimes fall asleep at concerts; and although he and his wife, Lillian, apparently took some lessons in ballroom dancing together early in the 1930s, Walt Disney's leisure activity of choice through much of that decade was polo. However, what seems to have been most important to him throughout his career in animation was his perfectionism, and in that he shared a lot with serious dancers and choreographers of all enduring traditions. One example of how dancing served him to explore this perfectionism: at the beginning of the 1950s, Walt Disney decided to expand his beloved model-train layout into a replica of an entire turn-of-the-nineteenth-century American village and tour it around the country. He scoured miniature shops in the U.S. and Europe to furnish the project, but eventually he decided that the figures inhabiting the village couldn't be still: they had to move. And so, in 1951, as a way to study how miniature mechanical figures of farriers and other tradesmen might be brought to simulated life, Walt Disney hired the actor and dancer Buddy Ebsen to perform a tap dance in front of a grid and had him filmed by a 35-mm camera. A curious choice of model, perhaps. Disney and his assistants, a sculptor and a sketch artist, discovered in studying the film that Ebsen never repeated his steps exactly and that it wasn't possible for them to imitate the precise way his pants cuffs rose and fell in the course of his tapping: they couldn't perfect a mechanical facsimile. Yet, as Disney's biographer Neal Gabler put it, "they made the man dance . . . and Walt entered a new territory that further extended the metaphor of control." The exhibition, called Disneylandia, ended up comprising only one scene, briefly exhibited in Los Angeles, and that was it. Nonetheless, as Gabler notes, Disney knew very well why he did it. Beyond the psychological benisons of control and the tactile exhilaration of his own craftsmanship, beyond the way it preoccupied him while the studio seemed to wobble, he did it because he harbored an even larger, more audacious plan—a plan for which Disneylandia was only a trial run and a plan that seemed to sustain him even as he was losing interest in the rest of his company.

Disco Mickey, an unmistakable reference to John Travolta's famous Hustle in the 1977 movie Saturday Night Fever, *first appeared on the record jacket for the 1979 album* Mickey Mouse Disco, *released by Disneyland Records. Among its selections: a song entitled "Macho Duck," for Donald.*

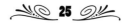

Drawings for the "Pink Elephants" dream in Dumbo, *a musically driven procession in undefined space that borders on surrealistic abstraction.*

It is impossible to say exactly when, but Walt Disney had decided to build an amusement park. And so Walt Disney's study of how one dancer moved became an integral step toward the creation of Disneyland.

Dancing wasn't crucial to the Disney enterprise, but it was intrinsic to it. Bodies moving in periodic rhythms to music—either while executing choreographed dances, or while engaging in physical activities that verge on dance, or, occasionally, while creating abstract designs (such as the surreal marching-and-floating-in-space patterns of the "Pink Elephants" ballet in *Dumbo*)—were hallmarks of Disney's animated films during the studio's golden age and continued to enliven many of the studio's cartoons through the 1960s.

In researching this book, I presumed that the most vigorous dancing in Disney animation would be found in pictures made prior to 1941, a watershed year in which the Disney company suffered a bitter animators' strike that incurred painful financial losses and resulted in key artists being fired or resigning. The studio suffered further from its loss of access during wartime to the European market for its films; a third blow—both financial and, for Disney and many of his most trusted collaborators, emotional—was the commercial failure upon its initial release of the elaborate 1940 *Fantasia*, the most dance-driven animated feature that the Disney company has ever made. Although the studio produced beautiful and virtuosic animated films for general audiences between the end of the war and Disney's own death—and although some of those shorts, featurettes, and feature films contain exquisitely conceived and observed dance and/or dancelike sequences—I presumed that the energy of dancing would no longer be identical with the vitality of living in the animated imagery, that dancing as an expression of well-being and joy would no longer reliably represent the life force itself.

But then I watched the feature-length animated 1945 *The Three Caballeros*, essentially a samba-and-gaucho ballet about a world where the most wonderful as well as the most horrifying transformations can occur in an instant: a tour of South America from inside the unregulated brain of Donald Duck! Everyone dances, constantly, even when they're immured inside flowers. On the surface, it may

look like kitsch, but it doesn't feel like it. There is so much complexity in tone: the smoldering footwork in a flamenco-like solo for one of the live-action ladies is presented as coolly as if the dancer is simply typing—for sheer complexity of steps, the moment is breathtaking. (It turns out that one of the choreographers for the live action on the picture was the fabled classical phenomenon Carmelita Maracci, teacher of ballerinas Allegra Kent and Cynthia Gregory. Maracci was also a virtuosa of Spanish dancing, and my guess is that she staged that remarkable solo.) As Walt Disney himself telegraphed to Nelson Rockefeller about this film, which is as exhausting as it is exhilarating to watch, "IT MOVES WITH THE TEMPO OF AN EXPRESS TRAIN."

Okay! So Disney was dancing *throughout* the 1940s. Like *The Three Caballeros*, the three mid-1940s anthologies of musically driven cartoon shorts (the 1943 *Saludos*

Publicity drawing of Mexican dancer Carmen Molina (1920–1998) with Donald Duck and a corps de ballet of saguaro cacti in the "Jesusita" Chihuahua dance during the "La Piñata" section of the 1945 Donald Duck vehicle The Three Caballeros. *Both Molina and Donald are merrily wielding riding crops. This astonishing percussive dance, performed by the dancer live in heeled boots in the company of the animated cacti, is executed through precise, flamenco-like taps with the feet close to the floor.*

Amigos, the 1946 *Make Mine Music*, and the 1948 *Melody Time*) give the effect of disciplined energy. Their component cartoons variously tender a valentine to ballet ("Two Silhouettes"), a juicy *hola* to Latin dancing ("Aquarela do Brasil," "Blame It on the Samba"), and a wry fan letter to the jitterbug ("All the Cats Join In").

Even so, by the early 1950s, Disney's animated dancing had largely evolved into an extension of high-style social deportment and good manners rather than a projection of spontaneous enthusiasm and vigor that could pour out of a character anywhere, anytime. The characters now seldom just got up and danced: they required a predefined, socially acceptable dance situation to get started and looked as if they had needed lots of lessons. One reason for the gentrification was probably Walt Disney's increasing remoteness from the animation division of the company as he shifted his focus to live-action productions and, even more intently, to the development of Disneyland. Another reason, perhaps, may have been that Disney's artists had mastered the animation of dancing figures, which now provided few stimulating challenges to their ever-advancing technique.

Furthermore, the key emotional and social elements that made dancing on the screen magnetic during the 1930s—that grain of lust embedded in the oyster of romance and the resulting equality between the sexes (think of Astaire and Rogers), or even the elevation of the woman to a privileged status—were no longer central to the moods of many of the postwar cartoons, whose stories, perhaps coincidentally, frequently concern the friendships and fantasies of solitary daydreamers. Yet, even taking into account that many of the 1950s features had been in development for a decade or longer, compared with earlier Disney films, the pictures as a whole are more ruminative or tempered than purely joyous: when a dozen bonneted baby oysters trip the light fantastic with a ferociously hungry middle-aged Walrus and a salivating Carpenter in the 1951 *Alice in Wonderland*, they are tiptoeing along a downward path to wisdom from which there is no happy escape. The scenes in *Alice* with the true vigor of dance focus on utilitarian action, such as the lovely sequence, accompanied by harp glissandos and scraped piano strings, in which that most enterprising of solitaries, Alice, falls through the rabbit hole, or, later, when the deck of gardener-cards cuts and deals itself into choreographic patterns during a parade.

Even in a traditional "princess" picture, such as the still-popular 1950 *Cinderella*, the scene with the most romantic magic—the Fred-and-Ginger buoyancy and sense of brimming anticipation—is not, as we would expect, Cinderella's waltz with the Prince in the ballroom. That we only get to glimpse from behind the

Some of the jitterbugging teenagers from "All the Cats Join In," one of the animated shorts in the 1946 anthology, Make Mine Music. *The orchestral music for the dancers is provided by Benny Goodman and his orchestra. Hollywood dance director Dick Barstow (choreographer for Judy Garland in* A Star is Born*) adapted the animated jitterbug-swing in the Disney film to invent several popular versions of the dance for amateurs to try in local ballrooms and dance halls.*

Ballerina Tatiana Riabouchinska of Col. de Basil's Ballets Russes in a Disney publicity photograph. Riabouchinska was one of the distinguished dancers who served as live-action reference models for various characters in Fantasia. *With David Lichine, also of de Basil's company, she performed a balletic pas de deux in the "Two Silhouettes" section of the 1946* Make Mine Music.

courtiers watching it—during those moments when the dance isn't interrupted by comic business for secondary characters or by the couple themselves breaking off the dance merely to drink in each other's shadows. The accent is on their private discovery of their feelings, not on the public celebration of their newfound romance. The real dance energy, rather, surges forth in the designing, cutting, and assembly of the heroine's dress in her lonely bedroom by an exaltation of singing mice and birds: a solitary girl's fantasy. The Disney inspirational artist for *Cinderella*, as for many animated features of the 1950s, was the brilliant and thoughtful painter Mary Blair. Although Blair was frequently heartbroken by what she viewed as the mistranslation of her concepts in the finished films—a feeling that seems to be embodied in the moment when Cinderella's wicked stepmother and stepsisters tear her dress to shreds—throughout the picture you can still see evidence of Blair's deeply unconventional ideas of how stories can be told through synecdoche (key details made to stand for a larger whole) and emotions represented through color and shifts in proportion.

After working with Blair's elliptical sensibility, it must have been a short step for the animators to go from showing a mere fragment of a dance that invoked the whole to the removal of all visible traces of dancing to invoke, paradoxically, the art's ineffable grace. By 1959, Disney had spent six million dollars on a sumptuous full-length animated version of *Sleeping Beauty* that used excerpts from Tchaikovsky's great ballet score of the same name, yet intentionally bypassed any direct reference to the ballet itself. This is the more surprising, since *The Sleeping Beauty*, choreographed in 1890 by Marius Petipa for the Russian Imperial Ballet (and

generally regarded as his masterpiece) was arguably the best-known incarnation of the fairy tale for late-'50s audiences, after the 1955 nationwide U.S. television broadcast of the then-current Royal Ballet production (somewhat streamlined), starring Margot Fonteyn as Aurora. Fonteyn, the leading British ballerina of her era,

Actor Grant Williams as Peter Tchaikovsky, conducting an imaginary orchestra in a reverse shot for The Peter Tchaikovsky Story, *a featurette televised on January 30, 1959, on the ABC show "Walt Disney Presents." The sequence, which included about five minutes from a Soviet film of prima ballerina Galina Ulanova dancing Odette in the Bolshoi Ballet's production of* Swan Lake, *was a promotion for the Disney animated feature* Sleeping Beauty, *which drew on the Tchaikovsky ballet score and which had just been released on January 29.*

of course performed in tutu and toe shoes; Disney's Aurora, for whom the ballet dancer Helene Stanley served as live-action reference model, first appears to her prince as a barefoot peasant. The animation's palette, iconography, and draughtsmanship were based on illuminated manuscripts from the Late Middle Ages. The film was fueled by a sophisticated graphic vision (traceable to the inspirational art of Eyvind Earle), but dancing isn't at the heart of its action or text; instead, dancing serves as a referent that's everywhere present and nowhere visible, as the *subtext*. (Perhaps this explains the mixed reception of the film to this day; general audiences have always been indifferent to the picture, finding it static, while it remains the object of a devoted cult following among animation aficionados.)

Ironically, thanks largely to the MGM unit led by Arthur Freed that produced musicals during the 1950s, theatrical dancing, including ballet, enjoyed prominence in live-action Hollywood feature films at several studios. Nor was dance absent as a live-action subject from the Disney enterprise. To promote *Sleeping Beauty*—a project in which Walt Disney took a special interest and which was the last animated fairy tale to be produced by the studio in his lifetime—on January 30, 1959, about half of ABC's *Walt Disney Presents* was devoted to *The Peter Tchaikovsky Story*, which included a five-minute excerpt from a Soviet film of the Bolshoi Ballet's *Swan Lake*, with Galina Ulanova as the enchanted swan maiden, Odette. (Walt Disney's obsession with high-quality sound for the music of his films was also in evidence here: the program was simulcast in stereo, and it included a scene of Disney demonstrating to us viewers how we could set up our televisions and AM radios in our living rooms to achieve the stereo effect.)

Disney also went out of his way to include other live ballet and dance performances on his television shows. In a recently published memoir by Harry Tytle—assistant to Walt Disney, who kept a daily diary of his boss's doings during the forty years that Tytle worked for him—we learn that on a trip to Europe in the 1960s, Walt Disney visited the Paris Opéra Ballet and was quite taken with *les*

petits rats ("the little rats"), as the youngest dancers at the school are called. Although his plan to film them fell through, he persevered with the concept, turning to the Royal Danish Ballet. The Danes performed for him in a feature film, *Ballerina*, for which Walt Disney was the uncredited producer and which was first televised in two parts during 1966 on *Walt Disney's Wonderful World of Color*. Among the dancers you can see in the excerpts of classical choreography from various ballets in the film are Kirsten Simone, Mette Hønningen, and Henning Kronstam, stars of the Danish Ballet during the 1960s and '70s. (Among the film's writers was Casey Robinson, married at one time to ballerina and movie star Tamara Toumanova.) Also prepared for telecast by Disney was a program called *Dances of Hungary*, but it was never aired—a pity, since the traditional Hungarian dances for men, especially the warrior dances, are intricate, very fast, and fierce.

A poster for Saludos Amigos *from around the time of the picture's initial 1943 release.*

The postwar years at Disney saw the production of several lovingly conceived and realized feature films that mixed live action and animation, and all of them contain vivid dance sequences: *The Three Caballeros* (1945) noted above, the much-criticized yet exquisitely acted and crafted *Song of the South* (1946), and the smash hit *Mary Poppins* (1964), which gave stellar dance opportunities to both humans (Julie Andrews and Dick van Dyke) and animated creatures (Ollie Johnston and Frank Thomas's penguin waiters). Gene Kelly's dance turn with Jerry the Mouse in the 1944 *Cover Girl*—whose story is based on the early career of cover girl Jinx Falkenburg—is often cited as the first Hollywood dance for a human being and an animated figure together. However, as Disney historian and composer Alexander Rannie has observed, it's worth remembering that "throughout Walt Disney's *Alice* pictures of the 1920s, starting with the first one, *Alice's Wonderland* (1923), the live-action Alice almost always dances at some point in the cartoon. One sequence that

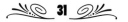

stands out is a brief piece in *Alice Gets in Dutch* (1924), in which Virginia Davis, as Alice, dances what appears to be a variant of the Charleston hand-in-hand with a cartoon cat. Another popular example, from 1927, is the nine-minute black-and-white short *Alice the Whaler*, in which child actress Lois Hardwick is matched on shipboard with jigging and horn-piping cartoon characters. The team of animators on that (and many other) early Walt Disney pictures reads like a roll call of pioneers: Ub Iwerks, Isadore ("Friz") Freleng, Hugh Harman, Rudolf Ising, Ben Clopton, Les Clark, and Norman Blackburn. And before that, there were the live-action-and-animation glories of Max Fleischer and his cavorting creation, Koko the Clown, in Fleischer's Out of the Inkwell series, which inspired Disney (and for which a clown-suited Dave Fleischer, Max's brother, served as the live-action reference model).

When Walt Disney died, many projects were left unfinished or only sketchily envisioned. One of them—possibly the most unlikely—was a collaboration with the surrealist artist Salvador Dalí, a projected ten-minute cartoon short entitled (by Dalí) *Destino.* According to interviews conducted by Disney historian Jeff Kurtti with studio archivist Dave Smith and animation historian and filmmaker John Canemaker, Walt Disney met Dalí in 1945, at a party given by Jack Warner, during the time that Dalí was designing the sets for Alfred Hitchcock's *Spellbound.* The two men got along well, and Walt Disney put Dalí on staff, installing him in an office, to make art toward the goal of producing an animated film. Walt Disney also assigned animator John Hench to work with Dalí on translating the artist's drawings into art that could lead to animation. *Destino* was never completed, and the drawings—both Dalí's and Hench's—were stored away in a basement. At some point during the subsequent decades, some of them were stolen and sold. (To make the sale, all were authenticated as being by Dalí, even though some forty percent were by Hench.) After Dalí died in 1989, the remaining art in the basement was reexamined; later, Roy E. Disney contacted the director Dominique Monfery about reconstructing a film from the *Destino* materials. Monfery worked on the project with a team for a couple of years; in 2003, it was screened at the Dance on Camera Festival in New York, where I saw it. *Destino* doesn't resemble anything else from the Disney studio: it's much more Dalí than it is Disney. As Monfery told Kurtti, "We tried to take every idea from Dalí's art and put as many as possible in the movie, keeping clarity and readability in terms of timing and editing." Among the enigmatic events, though, is an unmistakable love story between a baseball player and a ballerina. It hardly seems a stretch to think of those figures as, together, representing the ideals of the Disney enterprise.

THE LEGACIES OF DANCE AT DISNEY ● The most important legacy of historic Disney is the best of contemporary Disney. During the 1990s, the studio produced a bevy of feature-length animated pictures with original song scores. These were designed and animated with a knowing nod to the classics, and they helped to revive both the company's fortunes and its prestige. Some of them actually show figures dancing—*The Hunchback of Notre Dame* from 1996 (see feature, pages 42 to 43), *Hercules* from 1997 (whose "Zero to Hero" number paid homage to tapper Cholly Atkins's iconic choreography for the Supremes and other Motown groups), and *Lilo & Stitch* from 2002 (whose story, located in Hawaii, showcased hula dancing, for which the studio hired Kunewa Mook, a hula master, as choreographer). When Belle dances with the Beast in the ballroom scene of the 1991 *Beauty and the Beast*, the couple, whose animation is hand-drawn, advance their relationship through dancing: this element of storytelling through dance—rather than the frequently discussed computer-generated animation of the rest of the scene—is what makes the moment enjoyable. In other Disney films of the 1990s the dance qualities are a matter of design, timing, and meaning in context. Many of these sequences are also, in effect, conversations with Disney and Hollywood achievements of the past. The indelible, nearly abstract image of the stampeding wildebeests in 1994 megahit *The Lion King* evokes the experiments in abstraction in *Fantasia* and the falling sequence in *Alice in Wonderland*. The irrepressible number "Be Our Guest" in the 1991 *Beauty and the Beast* evokes both the overhead shots of Busby Berkeley's Warner Bros. musicals of the 1930s and *Dumbo*'s "Pink Elephants." The underwater extravaganzas of the exuberant 1989 *Little Mermaid* evoke memories of *Pinocchio* and *Fantasia*'s "Nutcracker Suite." And surely many more historic influences, intended and serendipitous, contribute to the resonance of these films.

However, influence also streams the other way: Disney's historic animated films have had effects on stage choreographers. In a 2008 public "TimesTalk" interview with *New York Times* reporter Daniel J. Wakin, Mark Morris—one of the most imaginative and knowledgeable choreographers now at work—pronounced Walt Disney the greatest choreographer of the twentieth century. Morris's own experiences with Disney films are noted in his foreword for this book; for an observer of his dances like me, the links between them include a certain tolerance, even indulgence, toward the vulnerability and openness associated with small children, an element of human nature we used to call innocence. In addition, it seems to me, Morris demonstrates toward Disney's achievements a theatrical choreographer's fascination with images that magically and efficiently (and logically) turn into other images purely through

ABOVE: *A choreographic moment from Mark Morris's dances for Jean-Philippe Rameau's opera* Platée *(1997), which the choreographer also directed. Sets by Adrienne Lobel; costumes by Isaac Mizrahi. Photo: Bill Cooper.* OPPOSITE: *Mark Morris dancing his 1992 George Gershwin solo,* Three Preludes, *originally made for Mikhail Baryshnikov.*

the deployment of the artist's chosen language—in Morris's case, purely through dancing.

Transformation in general seems to be what attracts dancemakers to Disney—when they *are* attracted. Not all are. When George Balanchine was brought out to Hollywood in 1937 to choreograph dances for *The Goldwyn Follies*, he not only learned about camera angles from the cinematographer Gregg Toland but his experiences with the moviemaking process also led him to develop thoughts of his own about the possibilities of dance in cinema. In 1937, perhaps with editing by Lincoln Kirstein, cofounder with Balanchine of the New York City Ballet, the choreographer wrote down some of those thoughts in an essay that *Dance News* ultimately published in full in December 1944. Balanchine's aphoristic observations included these paragraphs:

> The importance of ballet for motion pictures is the element of pure fantasy.
>
> Although motion pictures have known quite a lot of fantasy, it has been limited to the field of comedy as exemplified by the Chaplin and Marx Brothers films. The average picture seldom deals with free fantasy, but is tied up closely with real life. The fairy tale type of unreality has up to now been employed in the field of animated cartoons. This field, through the medium of the technical tricks of the camera and the freedom it has over imaginative conceptions, is most suitable to the motion picture and, as yet, remains completely unexplored.
>
> People have gotten into the habit of going to the movies to see reenacted their own lives or the lives of people they envy, but the world of make-believe and of pure fantasy is still only a by-product of present day production. Naturalistic theatre has always bored me, as I think that essentially theatre art is based on the audience's desire to escape rather than to relive reality.

In addition to visiting the Disney studio with Igor Stravinsky in December 1939, while the "Rite of Spring" section of *Fantasia* was being prepared, Balanchine also seems to have considered the rationale and mission of the films, and, at the time he wrote his essay, found them wanting. However, even artists can change their minds. From the Balanchine ballets that have survived—and the descriptions of some, particularly from the 1930s, that haven't—it is clear that he was profoundly involved with issues of transformation on every level, insofar as dancing, alone, could achieve it: transformation of mood, of character, of imagery, of tone, and even of dance technique itself and the palette of steps that an expanded technique

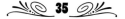

version of Snow White,
with Elie Chaib as the prince
(and wicked stepmother),
Cathy McCann as the
title character, and other
members of the Paul Taylor
Dance Company as "Some
Dwarfs." The evil stepmother's
severed head (a mask) lies
on the floor at the lower
left. Costumes by Cynthia
O'Neal. OPPOSITE: *Lisa Viola,*
Robert Kleinendorst, and
other members of the Paul
Taylor company in Taylor's
2001 Mary Poppins*–like*
suite, Antique Valentine,
to a score of pieces by Bach,
Chopin, Mendelssohn, and
others played on music boxes,
player piano, and mechanical
organ. Costumes by Santo
Loquasto. Photographs by
Johan Elbers.

could offer him. Balanchine's interest must have predated any encounter he had with cartoons and animated features by Disney or any other producers. And yet, given his meetings with both Walt Disney and the Russian-speaking Disney animator Bill Tytla (described in chapter 4), it is possible that Balanchine stored away images and ideas and used them later on, as he stored away and later used images and ideas from every place and art he ever encountered. And so, after looking closely at "The Nutcracker Suite" in Disney's *Fantasia* and then revisiting Balanchine's "Waltz of the Flowers" in his 1954 production of *The Nutcracker*, I begin to superimpose the diagonals for some of the animated fairies onto the diagonal entrances for Balanchine's Dewdrop Fairy, or the overlapping ballerina-flowers rushing down the river onto the corps de ballet of stage flowers, with their overlapping poses and rhythms. Is this a kind of legacy? Is it a coincidence—two giants who thought alike? Is it a product of a zeitgeist that affected many artists who were active in the anything-can-be-anything 1930s and '40s? We do know that Lincoln Kirstein was a Disney fan from his 1940 article "Mickey Mouse Goes to the Ballet," but Kirstein and Balanchine often disagreed in aesthetic matters. (Choreographer Jerome Robbins, long associated with New York City Ballet, apparently looked at animated pictures, but he seems to have been a Warner Bros. fan, as suggested by the vaudevillian/cartoonish flavor of some of his early works. Take for example, the sideways, one-legged chug-chug-chug–pause–and-away-we-go! phrase danced by each of the three sailors in turn in Robbins's 1944 ballet *Fancy Free* as they take off down the street in pursuit of a hot blonde—pure Tex Avery.

More direct examples of the connection between Disney and concert dance can be found in the repertory of the modern dance master Paul Taylor, who has directly referred to Disney classics in his comic works *Snow White* (1983) and *The Sorcerer's Sofa* (1990). Taylor has also set scores famously associated with Disney pictures in his magisterial *Promethean Fire* of 2003 (the Stokowski orchestral transcription of the Bach Toccata and Fugue in D Minor for organ that opens *Fantasia*) and his comic

Troilus and Cressida (Reduced) of 2006 (Ponchielli's "Dance of the Hours," used in *Fantasia* for the ballet of the elephants, alligators, and hippos in tutus).

In an interview, Taylor once spoke of the impression that *Fantasia* made on him in childhood. It's difficult to imagine that, while he was growing up and attending the movies in the 1940s, he wouldn't have seen other Disney pictures, notably the animated shorts, in addition to *Snow White*. Taylor's thought process is elusive, and it's possible that some of his dances—especially certain comic pieces that appear to have no connection to Disney pictures at all—may, in fact, incorporate choreography whose details were prompted by memories from popular culture of all kinds. Taylor is, moreover, fascinated by various kinds of transformation. In *Snow White*—in which the costumes by Cynthia O'Neal specifically refer to the clothes worn by Disney's characters and the theater-within-the-theater set, by David Gropman, creates a little movie-palace proscenium—the references are part of the fun. Taylor analyzes the characters and re-accents their visual allure and moral qualities, bending them away from their animated incarnations; and although the dance works if you only know the gist of the fairy tale, the choreographer depends on our having seen Disney's version to appreciate the wickedly charming glosses on the film. The Prince is transformed into the Wicked Stepmother (a detail that lingers in the audience's mind when he and Snow White embrace for their happily-ever-after . . .); Taylor's Dwarfs are tall male dancers who locomote in a continuous rolling crouch accented by goofy, squatting acrobabtics; the Bad Apple is a vamping, dancing seductress with a tangle of scary long red fingernails. Donald York's made-to-order score contributes to the sense of connection with the movie.

(A book could be written about the oeuvre of Paul Taylor, and, as it happens, at least two are in process: one by dance historian Angela Kane and an authorized biography by dance critic and historian Suzanne Carbonneau.)

The Sorcerer's Sofa, in which Taylor relocates the setting to a phrenologist-psychoanalyst's den and transposes the threatening brooms hauling water into devouring female monsters of Freudian id, is not alone in its debt to "The Sorcerer's Apprentice" section of *Fantasia*. Prior to Disney's version, Michel Fokine was the only choreographer of stature to make a ballet (in 1916) to *L'apprenti sorcier*, Paul Dukas's symphonic poem of 1897, based on a poem by Goethe that was, in turn, based on an episode from a story by Lucian. In the Goethe poem, when the apprentice attacks the brooms, he merely splits one into two; it was Disney who multiplied the brooms into a horde. By this criterion you can easily tell when a choreographer is referring directly to the Disney film rather than to the Dukas score by itself.

However, filmmaker Michael Powell—who, with Emeric Pressburger, made the hit ballet films *The Red Shoes* and *Tales of Hoffmann*, as well as other admired films on other subjects—both wrote in his memoirs and spoke in interviews of his great admiration for Disney. And yet his 1955 film of a balletic version of *The Sorcerer's Apprentice*, first performed onstage in Frankfurt (with guest star Sonia Arova on pointe as the first broom), does not multiply the brooms into hordes: like Goethe, he stops at two. Perhaps Disney, rather than inspiring Powell's choreographic imagery, affirmed the choreographer's intent to follow his own intuitions regarding the story's implacable logic, rooted in his understanding of the characters' pyschology.

Did founder-choreographer Peter Anastos and his original colleagues at Les Ballets Trockadero de Monte Carlo, the New York–based male travesty ballet company, consult the cast list of *Fantasia*'s "Dance of the Hours" when they began to craft the comic names of their company's prima ballerinas? ("Ida Nevasayneva" and "Olga Supphozova," for instance, appear with the company today.) Some of the Trocks' brilliant parodies of nineteenth-century ballets also seem to owe a debt to the choreography for Hyacinth Hippo and Ben Ali Gator in *Fantasia*. And what about the earnest full-length *Snow White* ballet from Spain, choreographed in 2005 by Ricardo Cué to an original score by Emilio Aragón (and available on DVD, with the Royal Ballet's ballerina Tamara Rojo in the title role and a supporting cast of students from Spain and recent conservatory graduates from all over Europe): is this a Disney legacy? The dance is a generic fairy-tale ballet with opportunities to showcase the cast's technical abilities, but the dress Rojo wears as Snow White appears to refer to the Disney heroine's dress.

These days you can't help but wonder sometimes what audiences really want: works that rub our faces in reality or those that provide an escape from it? Balanchine—who, by 1937, had suffered tremendously in ways physical, emotional, and professional—voted for escape. A few years after he composed his essay, a filmmaker also addressed the question on-screen—perhaps the only auteur of the period to take it on directly. In the 1941 Hollywood movie *Sullivan's Travels*, by screenwriter and director Preston Sturges, a successful picture director (played by Joel McCrea) declares that, after a string of hit comedies, he wants to make a movie about the downtrodden called *O Brother, Where Art Thou?* He decides he wants to graduate from being a commercial wonder to becoming an artist. Since his life by the swimming pool doesn't give him much actual knowledge of the poor, he embarks on undercover research as a hobo. Eventually, he's arrested somewhere in the Deep South and sent to an unregulated, swamp-ridden state penitentiary, on the order of Mississippi's notorious Parchman Farm. Initially he tries to resist the guards' orders, and for his insolence is thrown into a "sweatbox," where he spends an uncomfortably educational summer day without ventilation or water. Wised up, he finds himself performing backbreaking labor on a chain gang. One night, Sullivan and his fellow manacled prisoners, filthy and hunched, are taken to a poor yet fastidiously whitewashed and decorated African American church for a recreational movie. Shuffling in lockstep down the center aisle—two by two, as if for a marriage—they arrange themselves on the first three wooden pews, which, at the behest of the congregation's preacher, the families and many small children have cleared for the visitors. Then the lights are dimmed and, projected from a rickety machine on a clean sheet, is a black-and-white cartoon about a befuddled pup who keeps getting himself into sticky situations, first by way of some flypaper, then a chest of drawers. And everyone—children, the elderly, prisoners, and their guards—are brought together in increasingly raucous laughter at the foibles and perils of a creature so far beneath them in the social hierarchy that it makes them able to laugh—even Sullivan, who, up to this point, has kept a sense of distance from the people around him. That a "mere" cartoon can elicit belly laughs from this artiste-in-the making who is already Hollywood royalty signifies that the filmmaker has gone about as low as he can in his undercover research: his joining in the general merriment serves as his diploma from the school of human misery.

Sullivan's Travels, a movie about moviemaking and the maturation of a director, offers a storyline that is easy to follow, yet its haunting character studies and visual effects bespeak tremendous complexity of tone and message (almost every scene

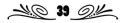

can be taken both earnestly, in terms of the story, and ironically, as a parody of particular moviemakers and classic images from both silents and talkies). The cartoon screened in the church is a real Walt Disney animated short that was shown to real Depression-era audiences: a Mickey Mouse picture from 1934 called *Playful Pluto*, with a focus on the title character, Mickey's pet hound, who always gets into scrapes and is permitted sometimes to show anger, unlike his unvaryingly good-natured master.

Pluto never demonstrates an understanding of periodic rhythm in his movements; he represents chaos pure and simple, which is inimical to dancing. Mickey Mouse, on the other hand—especially in the black-and-white shorts of the late 1920s and early 1930s—bubbles over with dance rhythm, as does his significant other, Minnie Mouse. Take their appearances on-screen in 1934. Although *Sullivan's Travels* cuts *Playful Pluto* down to a single segment that shows Pluto in chaos, if you watch the entire cartoon, you can see that, from the very beginning, Mickey walks with a dancer's bounce, and a jazz dancer's at that; his body percolates with rhythmic energy on the verge of boiling over into dancing. Life—the substance of the short—consists in Pluto's interruptions, but the energy that provides Mickey with a psychic metabolism optimistic enough to address the disasters and put things right, or as right as he can, is represented as the physical order of dance rhythm. In another 1934 Mickey short, *Mickey Plays Papa*, in which a poor mother leaves a baby mouse in a basket on Mickey's doorstep with a note asking that the infant be taken care of, Mickey and Pluto are delighted with the orphan, and, when he cries, Mickey tries to entertain him by dressing up as Charlie Chaplin's Little Tramp. Complete with Chaplin's exaggerated turnout of the feet, he performs a little hop-skipping dance—his ideal of comic entertainment, as Chaplin was Walt Disney's ideal. In fact, the story goes that Preston Sturges wanted a clip from a Chaplin picture to be shown in the church, but Chaplin wouldn't give permission, and so he went with Disney. As it happens, the flypaper episode of *Playful Pluto* is considered by some Disney historians to be a landmark—the first "personality" cartoon. But it's also funny; it does what dancing does at its best: put the observer and the dancer fully in the moment. In fact, if the Chaplin story is true, then Sturges was lucky. By 1941, Chaplin was not exerting the magic on movie audiences that he had a decade earlier. Disney, who adored Chaplin, was ahead of Sturges in this insight: the baby in the 1934 *Mickey Plays Papa* gives Mickey's Chaplin imitation a big yawn, followed by a raspberry.

SHORTS (STARRING STANDARD CHARACTERS)

The Barn Dance, 1928 (Mickey Mouse)
Mickey's Follies, 1929
Jungle Rhythm, 1929 (Mickey Mouse)
The Jazz Fool, 1929 (Mickey Mouse)
The Shindig, 1930 (Mickey Mouse)
The Birthday Party, 1931 (Mickey Mouse, Minnie Mouse)
The Delivery Boy, 1931 (Mickey Mouse)
Mickey Steps Out, 1931
Blue Rhythm, 1931 (Mickey Mouse)
Mickey's Revue, 1932
The Musical Farmer, 1932 (Mickey Mouse)
Trader Mickey, 1932
The Whoopee Party, 1932 (Mickey Mouse)
Orphan's Benefit, 1934 (Mickey Mouse, Donald Duck,
     Goofy, Clarabelle Cow, and friends)
Thru the Mirror, 1936 (Mickey Mouse)
Hawaiian Holiday, 1937 (Mickey Mouse)
Mr. Duck Steps Out, 1940
Golden Eggs, 1941 (Donald Duck)
The Nifty Nineties, 1941 (Mickey Mouse)
Orphan's Benefit (remake), 1941
     (Mickey Mouse, Donald Duck, and friends)
Mickey's Birthday Party, 1942
Donald Gets Drafted, 1942
Springtime for Pluto, 1944
Donald's Crime, 1945 (Oscar nomination)
Clown of the Jungle, 1947 (Donald Duck)
How to Dance, 1953 (Goofy)
A Symposium on Popular Songs, 1962
     (Ludwig Von Drake, Oscar nomination)
Mickey's Christmas Carol, 1983

SILLY SYMPHONIES
(NO STANDARD CHARACTERS)

The Skeleton Dance, 1929
Spring Time, 1929
The Merry Dwarfs, 1929
Summer, 1930
Autumn, 1930
Frolicking Fish, 1930
Midnight in a Toy Shop, 1930
Winter, 1930
Mother Goose Melodies, 1931
Egyptian Melodies, 1931
The Clock Store, 1931
The China Shop, 1934
The Grasshopper and the Ants, 1934
Cock o' the Walk, 1935
Woodland Café, 1937
The Night Before Christmas, 1941 (Oscar nomination)

FEATURES

Snow White and the Seven Dwarfs, 1937
Pinocchio, 1940
Fantasia, 1940
Saludos Amigos, 1943
The Three Caballeros, 1945
Make Mine Music, 1946
Fun and Fancy Free, 1947
Melody Time, 1948
The Adventures of Ichabod and Mr. Toad, 1949
Cinderella, 1950
Peter Pan, 1953
Sleeping Beauty, 1959
Mary Poppins, 1964
The Jungle Book, 1967
The Aristocats, 1970
The Great Mouse Detective, 1986
The Little Mermaid, 1989
Beauty and the Beast, 1991
Aladdin, 1992
The Lion King, 1994
The Hunchback of Notre Dame, 1996
Hercules, 1997
Fantasia, 2000
Lilo & Stitch, 2002

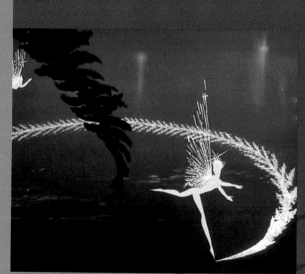

LEFT: *A Frost Fairy in a figure-skating spiral—an arabesque on ice—during the "Nutcracker Suite" section of* Fantasia.

DISNEY ANIMATED FILMS THAT INCLUDE DANCING

LEFT: Hunchback *choreographer Naomi Goldberg with her company around the time of the Disney film's making. Goldberg is at the far right; Susan Castang, the dancer who served as Esmeralda's live-action reference model in Goldberg's choreography, is second from right. Photo courtesy Naomi Goldberg.* OPPOSITE: *Esmeralda in her pole dance during the Feast of Fools in* The Hunchback of Notre Dame *(1996)*

During the 1990s, the Disney studio turned out a handful of animated features with music, most of which proved to be hits and all of them containing passages that deal with tragedy and/or rage. A couple of the films had to alter the stories derived from their literary sources in order to provide the hopeful endings commensurate with the ultimately optimistic storytelling tradition of the studio's founder. The most astonishing example is the 1996 animated feature of Victor Hugo's tragic novel *The Hunchback of Notre Dame.* Not only does the Disney version include a blissful reunion for the Gypsy Esmeralda and her true love, Phoebus, as well as ticker-tape-parade celebrity for the hunchbacked bell ringer, Quasimodo, but in 2002 Disney went on to produce *The Hunchback of Notre Dame II,* a fantasy sequel, which opens with the news that Esmeralda and Phoebus have a son named Zephyr.

To be fair, the Disney features of the 1990s omit act-one scenes of a book being opened and pages turning to establish a literary source—which the features made in Walt Disney's lifetime usually included. These later films are not really based on literary works; rather, they just use a well-known story as a platform for the filmmakers' purposes. The *Hunchback* sequel was a flop, at least critically, while the first feature remains controversial because it is in some ways so dark despite the happy ending. Some viewers give Disney credit for even attempting to animate such dire material for a family audience; others also note that by 1996 cartoons from Japan and Europe that explore dark subjects were readily available through VHS, that comic books—not to speak of video games—had become much more edgy if not violent, and that the Internet was bringing a much expanded spectrum of imagery to children.

Perhaps the most dramatic departure from Hugo in the 1996 *Hunchback of Notre Dame* is in the tone of the animated film, a mixture of irony (bordering on sarcasm) with the exuberance and innocence we expect in the Disney tradition. The first scene in Disney's *Hunchback* infused with this disturbing mixture of tone shows the public crowning of the "King of Fools" in an annual world-turned-upside-down festival during which the poor are permitted extraordinary liberties (a European Eastertide tradition dating back to Medieval times). The crowd chooses Quasimodo precisely because his disfigured face is his own rather than a mask, but then proceeds to torment him while he is strapped to a wheel. Early in the scene, Esmeralda comes out to entertain the mob with an acrobatic dance that picks up the motif of jumping around poles, which has been introduced previously by other characters. These days, suburban housewives learn pole-dancing routines at their local gyms as a welcome change from aerobics; in 1996, however, the practice was rather closely associated with exotic dancers and strippers, and so the theme of suspended social protocols is underwritten by the dance.

The choreographer for this, as for all the dancing in Disney's *Hunchback,* was Naomi Goldberg, who today directs a New York–based company of seniors and professional dancers called Dances for a Variable Population. At the time she worked for Disney, she was choreographing shows for the Mark Taper Forum in Los Angeles. (Roy Connelly, the production manager for the Taper, brought her onboard at Disney.) "I think my experience both as a concert choreographer, with a company of excellent dancers, and in the storytelling necessary for theatrical work was useful for Disney," Goldberg told me. For her Esmeralda dance model Goldberg chose one of the members of her company, the Los Angeles modern dancer Susan Castang, distinguished by her athleticism and her marvelously wild long hair, a feature retained in the character design for the animated Esmeralda. Goldberg's background includes study at the School of American Ballet, performance with Pacific Northwest Ballet, and appearances with postmodern choreographers Randy Warshaw and Stephen Petronio. As Goldberg described the process of working with the Disney staff in a 2008 phone interview and subsequent e-mail, the studio gave her quite a bit of latitude within the boundaries of specific directives.

"At the first meeting, they gave me a bunch of pages of things that were drawn," Goldberg said. "They also described the scene and gave me the music on a cassette. They had videotaped

the pages [storyboard drawings] and they explained how they went with the music: 'It's a festival in the streets, with dancing and sliding down poles.' I asked them how about transitions, how the dancer would get up onto the pole. 'This is a cartoon: that's no problem,' they said. 'We can make anything happen,' or something like that. What they needed most of all was a way to draw actions of dance—the movement of the skirt and hair as it twirled, actions of the wrists, hips, etcetera. As a whole, I felt that they were very collaborative. They really knew, in an incredibly thorough way, what they wanted. There are so many productions where the directors don't know what they want, and you [as a choreographer] spend so many hours trying to make something and don't get the credit. With Disney, they said, 'You're the dancer person; figure this out.'"

The films of Susan Castang jumping up onto street sign poles and swinging around them with her hair flying wildly in tangled skeins until you just get dizzy watching can be found at Disney's Animation Research Library in Glendale, California. Goldberg

explained that they were shot on one day at a playground, "somewhere in the Valley." A second day of rehearsal took place in the Disney studio, and that was also recorded: sequences of movement, choreography that was matched to the planned action. "It was just like in film or theater choreography," Goldberg added. "We got to get the story told. The action supports the story." But the process was also "very satisfying. They had much of it planned. The storybook on paper was then translated, with the music, to a VHS tape I could watch on a TV. For a choreographer, it was like coloring in the pictures with movement to move the story along." Goldberg remembers that both she and Castang were paid standard rates for the theatrical industry.

Unlike the choreography for the older Disney features, which was often changed for the goals of the animation, Goldberg's here seems to have been adopted more or less as she made it. When she and Castang saw what the *Hunchback* animators had finally made of her work and Castang's performance, she found it, she said, to be "just what we did."

Throughout the 1940s and 1950s the Disney studio produced a series of hilarious educational shorts starring Goofy, all directed by Jack Kinney, a member of the Disney staff since 1931, who became indelibly linked with Goofy's pictures. Many of the early how-to shorts had a sports theme, such as the 1942 *How to Fish* and *How to Play Baseball* and the 1944 *How to Golf*, but later on there were some one-offs as well: the 1952 *How to Be a Detective* and, from 1953, *How to Sleep* and the wryly engaging, six-minute-long *How to Dance*. Narrated by Art Gilmore, well-known for his radio-announcer–style narrations of such comic live-action shorts in the 1940s as *So You Want to Keep Your Hair* and *So You Think You're a Nervous Wreck*, *How to Dance* sends its star to take ballroom-dancing lessons to save him from being one of those people who are, as the narrator says, "so inhibited they no longer have the ability or instinct to dance away their cares" and the sort of clueless simpletons who get stuck with everyone else's checks in nightclubs. Dancing, the narrator suggests, will make Goofy debonair, cosmopolitan, and smarter—a real man about town.

The first thing Goofy sets out to learn is not, however, "how to dance," but rather *what* to dance—that is, choreography—and he tries to learn it from a book. This is not as outlandish as it might sound. During the early 1950s, ballroom dancing was still a popular form of recreation among ordinary people and an expected social skill at many celebratory occasions; it had not yet become dominated by professional competition and celebrity culture, as it is today. Publishers of how-to-dance books insisted that it was possible to learn ballroom dances by yourself, from the printed page alone, along with the manners and deportment that go with them.

The artists at Disney during Walt Disney's lifetime were pranksters, and sophisticated ones, as pranksters go, even when compared with the pranksters at Warner Bros. and other animation studios. Among their favorite pranks in their comic short films were embedded references to contemporary entertainers, movies, and books, both famous and obscure. For instance, there is an episode in *How to Dance* in which Goofy practices partnering with an undressed hollow dressmaker's mannequin, slipping his own arm through one of its armholes to form a ballroom "frame" (that is, a stylized dance embrace) with his "partner." (Later, while sitting out a dance together in the moonlight offscreen, Goofy even

Goofy and his dance partner approach the dangerous punch bowl, whose contents will stimulate the Goof to try to deepen their intimacy.

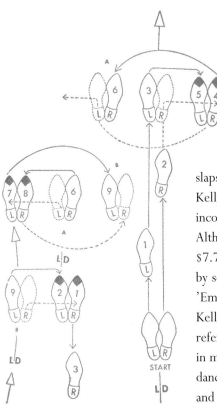

The foot pattern for the man's part in the "double twinkle," a special syncopated maneuver in the foxtrot from How to Dance, *a popular how-to book in the 1940s and '50s. Footprints with dotted outlines indicate that the foot glides through the position shown without bearing weight; footprints with darkened tips show steps with the weight on the toes and heels lifted. Goofy's confusion in trying to follow dance diagrams like this seems a reasonable response for a novice trying to learn complex steps from a book!*

slaps himself for trying to get fresh.) Just one year before, in 1952, the Gene Kelly–Stanley Donen movie *Singin' in the Rain* had presented Donald O'Conner incorporating an almost identical gag into his bravura "Make 'Em Laugh" number. Although *Singin' in the Rain* was a modest box-office success in its first year, earning $7.7 million worldwide while costing only $2.5 million to make, it was panned by some prominent critics: for Hollywood insiders, then, the reference to "Make 'Em Laugh" in Disney's *How to Dance* effectively takes a stand on the side of the Kelly–Donen picture. I have little doubt that this one Goofy cartoon contains other references as well, especially to books. One figure I think the animators surely had in mind is Arthur Murray, who, with his wife, Katherine, "taught America how to dance" with their weekly TV show and their nationwide dance-studio franchises— and who published a small volume called *Ballroom Dancing* in the same year that *How to Dance* was released. Or perhaps the Disney staff knew of another book from 1942, reissued in 1952 (one year prior to the release of the Goofy short) and called, like the film, *How to Dance*. The authors, much less famous than the Murrays, were Anita Peters Wright and Dexter Wright ("of the Peters–Wright Studios"); their handy book explains the basic figures of the rumba, waltz, foxtrot, Spanish dancing, etiquette, and much else that Goofy tries gamely to learn. For each dance, they include meticulous written step-by-step descriptions and matchstick-figure drawings that show the appropriate stances and "frames." Most important, diagrams of footprints and arrows show the floor patterns of how each dance moves through space. The book even includes outline footprints at the back "which you can cut out and use on the floor while learning and practicing the different steps."

A gag of particular charm in Disney's *How to Dance* is based on such foot-pattern diagrams: Goofy lays the cutout footprints on the floor to start practicing; in an instant, a gust of wind blows them into a chaotic blizzard. And yet, taken earnestly, as the Wrights do, these patterns and diagrams can be viewed as choreography transcribed, direct descendents of the symbols for recording movement in various dance notation systems extending back in time, at least in Europe, to the Renaissance, and elsewhere in the world to much more remote periods. (The Disney short, incidentally, is introduced by a slam-bang tour of world dance history that opens with a Stone Age stomp and jumps around to several dance traditions: a Native American buffalo dance, hieroglyphs in Egyptian tombs that come alive to simultaneously dance and crush grapes for winemaking, a Hawaiian maiden in a

sensuous hula.) Of course, the overarching joke of the short is that Goofy's efforts to learn the rhythms, steps, and gestures—the forms of a given dance—will make him a dancer. "Thus we find in a simple design the basis for the dance," the narrator intones reassuringly. "It's merely a matter of following the diagrams."

Eventually, Goofy abandons self-study to attend "Atencio's School of the Dance," one of the in-jokes about the staff common to many Disney films—in this case, a tip of the hat to animator Xavier Atencio, whose very nickname, "X," could represent the floor-pattern diagram for a dance. (Atencio, who began his Disney career as an animator on the dance-rich *Fantasia*, later went on to become a leading Imagineer.) At Atencio's—in what may well be a knowing reference to the second act of the ballet *Coppélia*, during which the ballerina displays the steps of several dance traditions one after another while trying on the national costume appropriate to each—Goofy attempts, in appropriate outfits and with various

A scene from the Goofy short How to Dance *showing the Goof trying to teach himself ballroom dancing at home.*

mechanical aids, the switchblade kicks of a Russian *kazatchka*, an athletic Cossack folk dance; the volleys of footwork in Irish step dancing (his speed assisted by bullets shot at his feet from a mechanically activated revolver); the light-footed, swordlike flicks of a Highland fling; classical ballet's *grand jeté* (big leap) and *entrechats* (rapid aerial crisscrossings of the feet); and the heel–toe fusillades of the Mexican hat dance. All the dance steps are rendered by the animators knowledgeably, even while they're being lampooned.

Finally, Goofy, in white tie and tails, and a coiffed partner, in a Cinderella-at-the-ball gown, attempt a waltz, although an X-ray view of the lady's skirt reveals her to be seated on a stool with casters that Goofy is steering around the floor—a partnering gambit also popularized by Gene Kelly. Goofy is doing the steps, but he remains a figure of fun. For even a general audience can enjoy Goofy's misunderstanding of what he needs in order to dance well. His acquisition of steps is crucial, of course, and eventually, for a few seconds, he actually waltzes with suavity and style; through dint of practice and determination, he overcomes his inhibitions. But the real impediment to his dancing is his innocent self-absorption, the very aspect of his personality that makes him Goofy. He gets so wrapped up in trying to dance accurately and with grace that he has no awareness of other people. In trying to match his foot to one of the cutouts, for example, he kicks a neighbor in the rear end, on which the cutout has landed. Even more amusingly, Goofy does not notice when the dressmaker's dummy he partners with has managed to poke one of her casters into an electrical outlet; he embraces her, to explosive effect. Nor does he suspect that the Cinderella he waltzes around the floor is seated on a wheeling stool—that she has no faith in his ability to lead the dance (and since he can't tell the difference between a dancer on her feet and one on wheels, she's probably right). Ballroom dancing requires two people working closely—known in dancers' parlance as the leader and the follower: Goofy practices as if he were responsible for both roles, as a soloist, with his ladies as mere props, and so, predictably, he runs into disaster. He fulfills the demands of the choreography but not of the dance: he remains trapped in his own bubble and so is never completely free. For it is physical, imaginative, and emotional freedom that is always appropriate to the restraints of a given dance style or tradition that makes dancing *dancing*.

Perhaps the finest compliment one can offer a dancer—or an animator of dancing—is that he, or his dancing character, appears to be making up the dance on the spot, as it's being performed. Sometimes live dancers are, indeed, making it up, as in the improvisations of rhythm tappers such as the late Jimmy Slyde, of Flamenco dancers, and of advanced practitioners of the Argentine tango. In the case of most live theatrical dancing, however (including the elaborately configured and synchronized

tap routines of the Nicholas Brothers and other "flash" acts), dance freedom, or spontaneity, emerges from the dancer's security in knowing exactly what the steps and gestures are and, if they are set to a musical score, of knowing that score so well that the dancer feels liberated to play a little in each performance with the way the movement addresses the music, to make each performance different while keeping the choreography the same—to be himself or herself in the midst of a movement design while also maintaining an intimate bond with other dancers. Of course, in the case of animated films, the illusion of spontaneity, like the illusion of life, is a product of intensive labor at every stage: concept, story conferences, conferences among the composer(s) and the writer(s), perhaps inspirational art to suggest mood and palette (as at the Disney studio), sometimes live-action reference film of real dancers, sometimes input from real choreographers, and test drawings—all this before a single cel or image of animation is drawn.

For Walt Disney, dancing—or ice hockey, or piano playing, or bare-knuckle boxing, or any physical endeavor found in the films made under his personal direction—first and foremost offers a window into the personality of a character in the course of telling a story. That is, dancing in Disney films is not offered for its own sake, and the films are never in any sense excuses for dance numbers. In the early animated shorts, which, rather like today's so-called "reality TV" shows, consist of characters dropped into this or that situation—a graveyard, a Christmas party, a

Carefully observed and accurately rendered scenes of characters dancing are peppered throughout the Disney studio's short animated films of the 1920s and early 1930s. In the 1928 Gallopin' Gaucho, *Minnie Mouse stars as a cantina dancer.*

In both versions of *Orphan's Benefit*, the enthusiastic cartoon characters put on an improvised stage show to raise money for orphaned kids. OPPOSITE: The 1934 "circles-and-rubber-hose" version features a lively balletic pas de trois, in the course of which Horace Horsecollar and Clarabelle Cow execute a lift of considerable virtuosity. This first *Orphan's Benefit* also featured the debut of Clara Cluck. ABOVE: The short was remade in Technicolor in 1941 in the more sophisticated "squash-and-stretch" style with Goofy and Clarabelle as a couple of swells (note Goofy's clownlike pants). The fancy maneuver shown here appears to be a direct reference to the final pose for Fred Astaire and Ginger Rogers in the "Let's Face the Music and Dance" number from their 1936 RKO hit *Follow the Fleet*.

Hawaiian island—and then required to deal with various sorts of mayhem, the dance scenes (and there were many in the early days) served as opportunities for satire, gags, and other interruptions of the story that display the characters' eccentricities or the feelings bubbling up uncontrollably within them. Eventually, as the storytelling mission of the feature-length films began to dominate the shorts as well, the dances became more detailed and were often structured with real narrative arcs—with beginnings, middles, and ends. However, the most successful of the shorts subscribe to Disney's vision: no matter how intricate the patterns of stylized movement—the *choreography*—every sequence is guided by another, larger pattern of caricature or humor that results from the conjunction (or collision!) of a character's personality and an obstacle or frustration. This, in the most essential sense, is what *choreography* means for a Disney animated picture: a pattern of movement set to music that incorporates nondance asides and reactions, as well as the dance steps and gestures.

To establish the distinction between dancer and dance in an animated film—especially a Disney film—it is quite helpful to know the overarching goals that guided the team that produced the animation, and the logistical details involved in how they chose every step and gesture, invented the characters' physicality, devised the timing and pacing of the action, settled on the background and colors (color, in animation, can be crucial to how an audience both perceives and responds to imagery), and then realized their vision through film technology and art. In the case of Walt Disney, that kind of behind-the-scenes analysis goes against the grain of everything he believed in concerning entertainment—the reason he made animated films in the first place. Even so, we can find in the Disney catalogue superb examples both of dancing as a spontaneous expression of personality, when the dancers appear to invent the moves as they go along (as in the bravura "I Wan'na Be Like You" number in *The Jungle Book* of 1967) and of dancing as a performance of learned steps, gestures, and maneuvers worked into a movement design—of choreography in its conventional definition (as in the minuet that Ichabod Crane dances with Katrina Van Tassel in the 1958 animated featurette "The Legend of Sleepy Hollow"). I will examine both of these scenes in detail below.

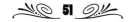

CHOREOGRAPHY: Steps and Effects ● Despite many unbridgeable differences between live dance and animation, there has been cross-pollination between them. However, live theatrical and social dance has had a much more powerful influence on animated dance than vice versa, both in terms of movement itself and in the look of dancers' bodies doing that movement. As the twentieth century unscrolled and theatrical dancing acquired increasing prominence and prestige, there were corresponding changes in the way animators depicted dancers in their films, especially at the Disney studio. Classical ballet, for instance, became important as an emblem of cultural aspiration during the studio's "golden age," when its ambitions for filmmaking were most lofty. Ballet dancers from the Los Angeles area—which was at the time an important metropolitan center for dance training, since many dancers were employed in Hollywood films—served as live models for the intensive art classes given to the Disney animators beginning in the early 1930s. These classes, taught by Don Graham from the nearby Chouinard Art Institute and later by other master teachers, became more intense—longer and more frequent—during the mid-1930s in preparation for *Snow White and the Seven Dwarfs*, the studio's first full-length animated feature, released in 1937.

The Hawaiian hula has made appearances in Disney animated films of several eras. BELOW, TOP LEFT: *In this publicity drawing, Minnie hulas as Mickey plays a steel guitar in the 1937* Hawaiian Holiday. BOTTOM LEFT: *In the 1952* Hello Aloha, *Goofy ponders the allure of the gentle hula style.* BELOW RIGHT: *For the 2002* Lilo & Stitch, *a Hula master was engaged for the choreography. Here, Stitch plays the guitar for dancing Lilo.*

But the live-dancer models were only a small part of the story. Between the antic yet comparatively simple animated shorts of the late 1920s for Mickey Mouse and other characters and the sophistication of the shorts and animated features of the late 1930s, culminating in the 1940 *Fantasia*, the jolly effects of dancing mice, cows, and horses "making it up as they went along" gave way to the detailed, highly sophisticated portrayals of animals and the occasional human being in genuine dances, with steps and gestures that a practitioner of the dance tradition in question would unfailingly recognize. The element that began to emerge was dance itself, and it has never entirely, so to speak, walked off the set. By the twenty-first century, a feature-length animated film such as *Lilo & Stitch* (2002), set in Hawaii and featuring a character who studies and performs the hula, would base its dance scenes on the action of a real hula expert whom the animators filmed as a live reference model so that they could accurately depict his style. The dancer contributed ideas and influenced the way the animated version of the dance proceeded from beginning to end.

Dancer Helene Stanley, in a practice tutu, models a classical fourth position for the animators. The studio walls boast the fruits of their prior attempts to capture balletic poses on paper.

By the second half of the twentieth century, audiences had learned to look at *what* dancers did onstage as well as at *how* they did it, and animators took note. At the Disney studio, where the mission of the animated films was to tell a story and, with *Snow White* and subsequent animated feature films, to stimulate audiences to empathize with characters created from mere line and color, the representation of dancing developed from bouncing steps mechanically repeated (as in Walt Disney's own earliest animated shorts), to dance phrases that grew longer and increasingly included syncopated movement (as in the Silly Symphonies), to complete dances that, like the stories of films, had proper beginnings, middles, and ends (as in *Fantasia* and the shorts of the 1950s). The dancing characters are shown full figure, as Fred Astaire demanded in his films. In a parallel development, what might be called dances for the camera—that is, discontinuous bits of imagery drawn from various contexts and given a dancelike continuity by being rhythmically sequenced to music—were also included in some of the Disney features, beginning with *Dumbo*. Such sequences turned elements of dance into abstract or surreal inventions, as in the spectacles that Busby Berkeley devised for Warner Bros. films in the 1930s.

Although written theories concerning how dances should be designed can be traced back as far as about 1,000 BCE, to the *Natyasastra* of India—an elaborate treatise concerning the aesthetics of solo dancing and the strictures for devising performances that will bring an audience to a desired state of jubilation—the English word *choreography* wasn't invented until the end of the sixteenth century, when grandly scaled and elaborately appointed French and Italian court ballets and horse ballets became popular with royalty and their retinues. The term *choreography* is derived from two Ancient Greek words, *choreia* (dance) and *graphein* (to write). Implicit in the very word for a dance design, then, is the idea of its notation—of some form of "writing" that fixes the sequence of movements so that the dance can be remembered and reproduced. Well into the twentieth century, we can find the expression "to write a dance" used to refer to the act of devising choreography for the stage. The outdoor sixteenth- and seventeenth-century ceremony-pageants for human beings and mounted steeds—luxurious precedents for the formations of marching bands and cheerleaders at today's football games—were arranged so that the royal audience looked down on them from an elevated position. Consequently, the choreography featured intricate spatial patterns for masses of bodies that would be legible when viewed from a distance and primarily from above; and it was that element—the floor patterns or geometric paths of the pageantry's movements— that were most easily notated. Three centuries later, stylized patterns of animated figures can still sometimes lend a dance quality to dramatic, nondance scenes, as in the harrowing stampede of computer-generated wildebeests in *The Lion King* (1994).

Dance patterns for dukes, ducks, and drums! LEFT: *Twelve choreographic figures for an equestrian ballet, performed by night in 1652 for the Archdukes Ferdinand Charles and Sigismund Francis and the Archduchess Anne of Tuscany in the arena next to the Grand-Ducal Palace in Florence, Italy. According to the catalogue of the New York Public Library, in whose Lincoln Kirstein collection at the Library for the Performing Arts at Lincoln Center this etching resides, "The horse ballet followed a sham equestrian battle, both composed by Tommaso Guidoni; verses recited by Benedetto Rigoli; costumes and scenery by Alfonso Parigi." One of four images to illustrate the text of the entertainment (30.8 x 22.8 cm), by printmaker Stefano Della Bella (1610–64), from Parte delle Fiure del balletto; Foglio III. Courtesy Jerome Robbins Dance Division, The New York Public Library for the Performing Arts, Astor, Lenox and Tilden Foundations.* ABOVE, TOP: *A publicity drawing of choreographic geometry for the 1935 Silly Symphony* Music Land. ABOVE, BOTTOM: *Partial layout drawing for a choreographic figure for ducks, part of the spectacular barnyard ballet in the 1935 Silly Symphony* Cock o' the Walk.

In the twentieth century, the movies—with their close-ups, their capacity to record motion, their tolerance for discontinuous images through jump cuts and other editing, and their capacity to synthesize a "perfect" performance from footage of many flawed attempts—affected theatrical dancing in ways too numerous to enumerate. One aspect of this pervasive influence: performers' faces. If you browse through the thousands of theatrical dance photographs from the nineteenth century—whether from the United States, continental Europe, or Russia—you find a very wide range of faces for both men and women. With the technical perfection of Hollywood filmmaking, which glorified actors through the close-up (and through the studios' elaborately produced still photographs of stars in close-up) and the worldwide distribution of those images, the standards for beauty and handsomeness in a face became increasingly defined according to standards of design: symmetry, amount of space between the edge of the eye and the bridge of the nose, the relationship between the nose and the chin, and so on. Even with these restrictions, the range of beauties was remarkable: they could be girlish, vampish, sluttish, glamorous, highfalutin, noble. Actress Lillian Gish was one of these early screen deities, her face an icon of the intelligent-innocent end of the spectrum.

In a dancer's face, however, beauty is more than a question of design: it is a matter of how the face a dancer was given genetically looks in motion. Some dancers—such as ballerina Alexandra Danilova, a star of Diaghilev's Ballets Russes—are striking in person, yet transformed into goddesses on stage by the way that the life of their dancing lights up their faces. Yet some dancers whose looks may be traffic-stopping offstage lose their distinctiveness on it, owing to a certain lack of vitality in their dancing or their inability to "open themselves up" to the audience in performance. Nevertheless, when we look at photographs of dancers in the United States and Europe during the 1930s, we see that they had, in Hollywood parlance, "Faces!" Although Fred Astaire was able to overcome his offbeat handsomeness through a gift for dancing and choreography of such a high order that George Balanchine called him America's greatest dancer, he was one of the exceptions who proved the rule. It took four decades for dance audiences to be retrained by stage

Courtesy George Eastman House Motion Picture Department Collection

dancers and choreographers to look at the achievements in motion of the dancer's entire body when evaluating beauty in stage dancing.

Hollywood's standards of beauty influenced all the cartoon studios, such as the Fleischer studio, whose superstar Betty Boop was partially modeled on images of the actress Louise Brooks. And the animators from different studios influenced one another. Indeed, Grim Natwick, a Disney animator who worked on the figure of Snow White, had drawn Betty Boop at Fleischer before joining Disney. The studio's Herculean efforts to configure the face of Snow White (LEFT)—the result, with her cel cheeks tinted with real rouge, was the most beautiful face of any female character in Disney history—are detailed in Neal Gabler's recent biography of Walt Disney, and J. B. Kaufman's forthcoming study of the film will surely cover this point, too. The model sheet shown here (RIGHT), indicating how an artist has begun to take a rotoscope tracing of a live dancer and then to submit it to myriad geometric adjustments, represents a tiny portion of the labor on behalf of Snow White's iconic beauty. The dancer was Marge Champion (see page 127) whose face can be clearly discerned in the initial tracing. Ironically, the heroine ended up looking almost exactly like Marguerite Clark (seated, ABOVE, with Dorothy Cumming as Queen Brangomar), the Snow White in the 1916 silent film, distributed by the Famous Players–Lasky Corporation, that Walt Disney saw and loved as a teenager.

ROTO

SNOW WHITE
MODEL SHEET 4
F1 ©W·D·P 1936
1151-154

In the "El Gaucho Goofy" segment of the 1943 Saludos Amigos, *Goofy is transported to Argentina where, among other activities, he demonstrates local dances with the assistance of his horse. The animators have distinguished here between the human anatomy of Goofy—whose legs are set in his hip sockets so that he can achieve complete turnout of the hips—and of his obliging steed, whose equine hind legs cannot turn out fully. The director of this segment was Jack Kinney, who directed many of the observant Goofy "how-to" shorts, including the 1953* How to Dance.

In 1662, Louis XIV of France, himself a virtuoso exponent of the baroque form of ballet dancing from childhood, founded the first conservatory of classical ballet to train professional dancers; eventually, they went on to perform in theaters that were open to the paying public. In a theatrical context, the vocabulary of ballet dancing (developed in part in aristocratic ballrooms and in part derived from the maneuvers for military horses that were featured in exhibitions of dressage, or equestrian ballet) began to evolve so that audiences in 1,200- or 1,500-seat houses could perceive the dancers' actions. Technical virtuosity, especially in aerial steps, took wing during the late eighteenth and nineteenth centuries, with the rise of ballerinas and star male *danseurs* and of an audience that was seated on a level with or below the stage, as well as in balconies and boxes above it. Choreographers for opera houses effectively became architects, responsible for entertaining the eye through the hierarchical distribution of principals, soloists, and framing corps de ballets—this all in addition to their responsibilities to tell stories through pantomime and pure dancing and to otherwise keep the audience focused on the stage.

How much dance history Walt Disney or most of his artists thought about per se on a day-to-day basis is unclear; their interest in dance was practical, not academic. Furthermore, many of the major points could simply be intuited from watching the films of Astaire and Busby Berkeley and one or two ballet performances, and Disney's intuition was formidable. In the event, during the years between Disney's own Alice Comedies, with the live-action four-year-old Virginia Davis cavorting in a comparatively simple cartoon world, and the bravura animated films produced by the Disney studio into the early 1940s, the Disney artists managed to reproduce the broad trajectory of Western dance history, from an emphasis on floor patterns observed from above to subtleties of phrasing for individual dancing figures. The reason for this development is probably not that Disney had any special interest in the imagery of dancing over other athletic action. Rather, Disney and his animators got dancing right because of the master's intense, even obsessive concern with traditional storytelling, with accuracy of anatomical and contextual detail, and with fastidious representation of cause-and-effect logic. This last point is crucial to the Disney studio's depiction of dancing, for Disney insisted that, no matter how fantastical or exaggerated a character's action might be, it must show plausible muscular initiation and effort (as when the lifting of an arm is registered initially in motion at the shoulder), and a perceptible psychological origin as well.

In The Barn Dance *(1928) Mickey Mouse's feet undergo a spontaneous (and embarrassing) growth spurt while he's dancing. When he stomps on one of Minnie's dancing feet with one of his gigantic clodhoppers, stretching out her leg like a strand of spaghetti, she's in agony: her comic disfiguration represents her pain. The short is among the most inventive that Ub Iwerks animated for Disney during the studio's early years.*

Dancing in a Disney animated film is invariably associated with joy and well-being, as it is in the pre–World War I, Edenic masterpieces of Henri Matisse. However, as the studio's film-development process grew increasingly sophisticated, it became possible to give nuances to joy, to shade it with underlying layers of other emotions rooted in the plot. Indeed, efforts at such shading are present even in the black-and-white shorts of the 1920s. In one Mickey and Minnie Mouse cartoon of 1928, *The Barn Dance*, a product of the inimitable solo animator Ub Iwerks (who insisted on drawing "straight ahead," rendering not only the major initial and final poses of every action but also all the "in-between" drawings that represent the transitions between those poses), we see the couple dancing a one-step number (a kind of walking dance in ballroom frame) in the course of which Mickey's shoes unaccountably begin to grow bigger and heavier. Inevitably Mickey steps on Minnie's feet, and then—this being an Ub Iwerks cartoon, in which absolutely anything can happen to a character—he tromps on one of her rubber-hose legs, stretching it to an egregious length, as if it were a piece of chewing gum. A conventional icon of pain (little radiating lines) pops up where her knee would be. The leg, now twice

as long as her other one and completely limp, is unusable. Minnie, who is nothing if not enterprising, ties up her wounded leg in a bow, finds that the loop is still so long it impedes her dancing, takes out a pair of scissors, and cuts it down to a knot. She then merrily and disdainfully one-steps off with another partner as Mickey, who adores her, hangs his head in misery. It is impossible to watch this passage without wincing at both Minnie's physical injuries and Mickey's unhappiness, a sign of Iwerks's gift for bringing a viewer into immediate identification even with figures so simplified in their design as to be almost abstractions. In many Disney histories, it is the seeming death of Snow White in 1937, with the Dwarfs gathered in mourning around her, that is usually credited as the first passage in a Disney film (and possibly in any commercial animation, ever) to stimulate an audience to feel compassion for an animated character. However, the conditions for both physical and emotional empathy were already put in place by the pioneering Iwerks nearly a decade earlier. The choreography for *The Barn Dance* is rudimentary as dance goes; however, if, by *choreography*, we include the entire sequence with the shoes, the stretched-out leg, the tied bow, and the scissors, then we're speaking about a more complex situation altogether, in which the dancing precipitates deformity, pain, self-assertion, and, in several senses of the word, determined severance. Within the joy of dancing we feel something much more painful, darker.

Jumping from the Disney studio's infancy to the ultimate screen achievement of its founder, let us turn to the "I Wan'na Be Like You" scene from *The Jungle Book* (released in 1967, one year after Disney died), the last animated feature for which Walt Disney, already fatally ill, made key decisions. Again, in pure dance terms, it is almost impossible to spot a conventional choreographic design in the song-and-dance number on one viewing. The song (by frequent Disney collaborators Richard M. and Robert B. Sherman), much of it jazz scat, is sung onscreen by King Louie the orangutan and, on the sound track, by the band leader Louis Prima, who provided the physical model as well as the voice for the animated character. The action, like the song, consists of gags, spats, parades in the manner of age-old New Orleans bands, a bit of partnered dancing, and lots of what might be called bodily timekeeping, sometimes interspersed with jazz dance steps that can be named and sometimes with simple hops and rocks in place. The entire sequence slopes along with a drawling nonchalance, and the great fun of it looks, at first, almost unplanned. The narrative situation, though, is complex.

Mowgli, the boy in the jungle (who is being intermittently guarded by the panther, Bagheera, and who has adopted as his mentor the dancing-fool bear, Baloo) has just been kidnapped by a band of monkeys—mean characters, though funny ones, too—who take him to their home, one of the grand, ruined ancient temples of India, where they live essentially as squatters, like hippies. Here Mowgli

encounters King Louie, who, strangely, uses his feet as hands; at one point, he even cradles Mowgli's face with all four paws. This is not quite disturbing, but almost: a world in which hands can become feet—and feet, hands—is a destabilized world of surrealistic dreams, an Alice-in-Wonderland place where you have to be on your toes in order not to get tricked. So we know, from the complexities of the location alone, that we are not seeing everything that can be *felt*, that there are hidden layers to the life the monkeys lead in this place. Dramatically, those layers might almost be called Machievellian. King Louie, so warm and charming—rather like the Sportin' Life character in George Gershwin's 1935 opera, *Porgy and Bess*—is telling the boy he has had kidnapped, through song, that he, the king of the monkeys, wants to be like Mowgli, to walk like him, to talk like him. But King Louie's true intention is, first, to bond with Mowgli in the way that Baloo has in the earlier song-and-dance number, "The Bare Necessities," on which some of the monkeys had spied and which they rudely interrupted. To reinforce the parallel, King Louie even gives Mowgli a banana, as Baloo has. In the course of bonding with him, Louie wants to remind the boy through suggestion that it was he, Mowgli, who had wanted to be like Baloo, which should stimulate Mowgli to imitate King Louie in an unconscious

Jazzman Louis Prima, who provided both the voice and the physical reference for the singing and dancing character of King Louie in the 1967 feature The Jungle Book.

reversal. And Mowgli does this, dancing the same two-footed stomp with the orangutan that he has danced with the bear. Psychologically speaking, King Louie's devious manipulativeness is anything but simple. His ultimate goal is purely selfish: to get Mowgli to reveal the source of fire, an element possessed by the humans back in Mowgli's home village. So "I Wan'na Be Like You" incorporates layer upon layer of intention, in the manner of E. M. Forster's novel *A Passage to India*, whose presentation of the mysteries of India and the confrontations of Westerners touring there with ancient verities they don't quite understand bears a closer relationship to many of the elements in the Disney version of *The Jungle Book* than do Rudyard Kipling's collection of Mowgli stories on which the film is based.

Indeed, there are layers to the song itself. Although it sounds offhand, casual, in the spirit of the 1960s, and the strutting and shaking that King Louie and, later, Baloo perform to it have the unstructured look of a 1960s Frug, if the tempo were sped up, we would see a Charleston, a dance from the Roaring Twenties. And it turns out that one of the monkeys—a white-haired veteran, whose job it is to hold a palm umbrella for King Louie—sings with the diction of the pre–big band era singer Rudy Vallee and actually dances one of the Charleston's iconic steps, little chugging kicks with the arm opposite the kicking leg flung forward. At one point, the old monkey makes a megaphone of his hands and sings in a nasal voice, too. (Vallee sang that way and used a megaphone to project his singing.) For Disney enthusiasts, another 1920s reference is the quartet of monkeys on the top of a stone wall who gleefully gambol sideways in a grapevine step—the very phrase that four skeletons perform in the first Silly Symphony, *The Skeleton Dance*, from 1929. Inside the obvious visual details of the number seems to be another network of references, as if to say that inside the music of the 1960s is another kind of music from an earlier time. In fact, the documentary on the making of *The Jungle Book,* included with the DVD edition of the film, explains that the five vultures who sing as a barbershop quartet yet also sound like the Beatles were originally supposed to be an obvious satire of the lads from Liverpool, but that Walt Disney asked for the change from Beatles to barbershop, from satire to metaphor, because he feared that a direct topical reference would date the movie. Indirect references are another matter. John Grant, historian of Disney characters, has observed that the vultures' dialogue is nonetheless reminiscent of the dialogue in the Beatles' movies.

The same sense of one era nesting inside another obtains for the dancing. The monkeys pair up into ecstatic athletic partnering that could be Lindy Hop (1920s), swing ('30s), jive ('40s), or jitterbug ('50s and '60s). In an effort to try to rescue Mowgli, Baloo comically masquerades as a female orangutan, with a tiny skirt of banana leaves and a half-mask made from a coconut shell: a dance enthusiast can't help but think of the famous, shocking banana skirt worn by the beauteous, nearly naked Josephine Baker in her Paris revue performances during the 1920s. And yet, Baloo's ample (and gelatinous) figure can't be compared with the magnificently

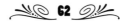

A storyboard drawing of the orangutan King Louie, the boy Mowgli, and the king's jamming courtiers for The Jungle Book. *Even in this sketch, one can see the contrast between Mowgli's forthright character—rendered literally by his grounded stance—and the unbalanced (and so, in this movie, untrustworthy) merriment of the animals.*

proportioned and fit body of Josephine Baker: it is much closer to the body of the hippo ballerina in *Fantasia*—a creature who also wears a tiny skirt that, like Baloo's, has no function as a garment, only as a symbol. And King Louie's prehensile feet-hands, which he slaps down on the earth periodically at first to accent his timekeeping, continue to inject drops of disturbance throughout the number. In the manner of a literary device, the slaps on the ground plant the idea of hitting something, which is then gradually developed. In the course of the dance, King Louie swats his irritating imitator, the old monkey with the palm branch; at the end of the dance, exulting in his powers, he hits the masquerading Baloo to punctuate a musical accent, and the force of the blow causes the coconut shell to fly off Baloo's muzzle, leaving him, in more than one way, vulnerably bare—and bear.

Yet another layer of reference is internal—to the earlier song-and-dance "The Bare Necessities," in which Mowgli, who has just met Baloo (whose endearing baritone belongs to the singing bandleader Phil Harris), imitates the bear's irrepressible bodily timekeeping to a musical pulse, using the same two-footed stepping that he uses later, when imitating King Louie. At one point during the earlier song, Baloo tries to teach Mowgli to box—a sport in which the skittering footwork is often called "dancing"— and Mowgli lands a lucky punch, causing the stunned Baloo to pivot on his heel in a 360-degree pirouette and fall on the ground, all in time to the music. Other elements of this early, extremely affectionate showstopper are repeated, transformed, in "I Wan'na Be Like You," such as a gag in which the tail of Mowgli's fastidious guardian panther, Bagheera (who speaks in the King's English of actor Sebastian Cabot), gets pulled on a musical count while Bagheera is settled on a tree branch. When, in that later number, Bagheera freezes himself by a doorway in the exact imitation of a stone sculpture of a panther on the other side of the door, the plays on art imitating life imitating art are as dizzying as images in two mirrors facing one another.

This particular kind of conceptual and artistic bravura can be found throughout the animated films turned out by the Disney studio prior to the Second World War; its most brilliant example occurs in the 1940 *Pinocchio*, in which the title character, an animation of a puppet pretending to be a "real boy," dances choreographically precise patterns of steps in such a way that we can see: a) the look of wood moving; b) the look of flesh-and-bone moving; and c) line and color that is magicked into "live" action. When the film historian and critic Leonard Maltin wrote that "with *Pinocchio*, Disney reached not only the height of his powers but the apex of what many consider to be the realm of the animated cartoon," he was not exaggerating.

Pinocchio was created in a very different emotional climate from *The Jungle Book*, though: it sailed along on the astounding critical and commercial success of *Snow White*, summarizing numerous mechanical inventions and advances in the Disney artists' technique, and it proved to the world (as well as to Walt Disney himself) that the unprecedented achievement of *Snow White* was not a flash in the pan. *Pinocchio* belonged to a thrilling, no-holds-barred period of creativity rooted in the founder's own artistic origins as an animator, and the virtuosity of the film's dance sequences is but one aspect of a much larger demonstration of animation bravura. Moreover, the Walt Disney of *Pinocchio* was at the height of his physical powers, and his concentration was still entirely focused on producing animated films—unlike the Walt Disney overseeing *The Jungle Book*, who had been through the bitter animators' strike over

unionization in 1941 (which changed forever the Disney studio's naïve—yet also insensitive—paternalism), the fear of bankruptcy during the Second World War, and the Disney enterprise's postwar diversification into theme parks and other extra-animation ventures. However, I doubt that the Disney studio of the 1930s or even the 1940s would have been capable of rendering a sequence with the psychological complexity of "I Wan'na Be Like You." The wisdom in *The Jungle Book* is a result of bitter experiences on an epic scale. That only some of the supporting characters are cynical or evil, and that—as is not the case with a few of the later Disney animated films, which feature irresistible villains—these evil characters are always less magnetic than those who are kind and loyal (Mowgli, Baloo, Bagheera), represents a triumph of the human spirit, separate from any technical or artistic achievement.

As it happens, "The Bare Necessities" is the only song in *The Jungle Book* that the Sherman brothers did not compose, the sole survivor of an earlier score for the picture by Terry Gilkyson that Disney rejected. The song itself was rescued by other staffers, who persuaded the boss that he would be crazy to let it go. Disney buffs will also remember that the entire treatment of *The Jungle Book* had an earlier incarnation, too, by the Disney staff writer and artist Bill Peet, whose darker conception of the story and attempt to be more faithful to Kipling's text than to Walt Disney's own sensibility effected a terrible and irreparable split between the formerly close colleagues, when Peet left both the picture and his job. (According to the documentary about the making of *The Jungle Book*, Disney had left Peet solely in charge of a number of animated features during the 1960s, having pared down the Disney writing staff of some forty men to Peet alone. When Peet left, in effect, the entire writing staff walked out.) Peet's name is nowhere to found in the credits; however, another extra on *The Jungle Book* DVD demonstrates that some of his artistic concepts did, in fact, make it into the final film.

In counterpoint to that salt, however, is the honey of the relationships among *The Jungle Book*'s director, Wolfgang ("Woolie") Reitherman and its directing animators, Milt Kahl, Ollie Johnston, Frank Thomas, and John Lounsbery (all of whom belonged to the studio's venerated third generation of animators, known as Disney's "Nine Old Men"). Johnston and Thomas especially, whose friendship and collegiality as Disney animators stretched back to the studio's earlier years, expressed in all their work a warmth of feeling toward Walt Disney that is palpable throughout the picture. Indeed, I wonder whether it was the collective idea of Reitherman and the four directing animators, who knew that Walt Disney was languishing from cancer, to insert into

The Jungle Book references to the era when the studio was new and to some of its later high points as a kind of bouquet offered to the man whose vision they had worked to fulfill for nearly their entire adult lives. That ancient Indian temple doesn't have DISNEY carved over the main doorway, but it might as well have. For ultimately it is Disney, the man himself, who was the barest necessity behind the studio's gloriously innovative culture—and behind the vast expenditure of treasure and the exertion of brainpower and eye–hand coordination it took to create every frame of animation. In every sense, King Louie's temple is a monument to the great founder who made a self-contained civilization, vanished or vanishing, possible.

It would be a mistake, though, to attribute the beauties of *The Jungle Book* entirely to the personal feelings of some of the master artists who worked on it. Those emotions certainly flowed into the process, perhaps accounting for the picture's peaks of sweetness, yet technique and philosophy of animation are crucial to what made this film an unexpected hit upon its release and an enduring winner with succeeding generations of Disney audiences. Touch, in several senses, is one key to *The Jungle Book*'s effects on our emotions. We as viewers are touched, perhaps unconsciously, by the animators' touch, the residual trace of the hand behind pencil and brush bearing down on page and cel. And we are also touched by the ways in which the characters appear to touch each other—one of the more challenging illusions required to create the illusion of life. As Ollie Johnston noted in a 1985 interview (quoted by Academy Award–winning animator and revered animation scholar John Canemaker in his definitive 2001 study *Walt Disney's Nine Old Men: The Art of Animation*): "It's surprising what an effect touching can have in an animated cartoon. You expect it in a live-action picture or in your daily life, but to have two pencil drawings touching each other, you wouldn't think would have much of an impact. But it does." That is why it is so unsettling when King Louie takes Mowgli's face in his hands and hands-feet during the course of their dance. To touch another's face so intimately is a sign of both trust and trustworthiness, yet Louie, in his calculating manipulativeness, is betraying Mowgli's trust even as he wins it. Moreover, the joyful occasion of dancing together, which unites the characters in seeming friendship, is profoundly compromised by the king's treachery. In a catalogue of films often noted for its achievements in depicting villains, this moment may constitute the most nuanced construction of evil in the Disney canon.

The quality in all departments for Disney's version of *The Jungle Book* cannot be sufficiently praised. Indeed, *The Illusion of Life: Disney Animation*, the 1981 insider's

guide to the subject, coauthored by Johnston and Thomas, compares the film favorably to the studio's revered first animated feature: "*The Jungle Book* was the first picture after *Snow White* to have the personalities and the feelings of the characters be so dominant. The audience understood the characters and identified with what each was trying to do. Every sequence gave new opportunities to see other facets of their personalities. And even though there was very little story as such, these character relationships and interesting personalities made this the most successful cartoon up to that time in our history."

Although the dancing and vestigial pure-dance choreography in *The Jungle Book* would seem threadbare if transferred, untransformed, to the stage, I would argue that the dancing as a vehicle of meaning and the choreography considered as the *whole* of the animated action cued to music are extremely rich artistically. I would argue further that the internal references and embedded codes of gestural meaning in the film's dance sequences work very much the way similar devices function in the ballets of great stage choreographers, such as George Balanchine and Frederick Ashton. However, as an example of how the Disney studio continued to examine the borders between dancing and choreography even in the period when Walt Disney himself was distracted from animated films by live-action features and documentaries, the planning of Disneyland, and the Disney television shows, it seems to me worthwhile to look at a much less heralded featurette (just over thirty minutes long), "The Legend of Sleepy Hollow" (1949), which I saw and loved when I was a kid and which, reissued on DVD, is still being adored by kids today, if the glowing—and surprised—customer responses on Amazon.com are any indication. (As when it was originally released, "Legend" is packaged on DVD with "The Wind in the Willows," another literary featurette, based on Kenneth Grahame's children's classic of the same name, under the umbrella title *The Adventures of Ichabod and Mr. Toad*.)

Narrated by Bing Crosby, "The Legend of Sleepy Hollow" is a faithful retelling, without much dialogue, but with a marvelously supportive score by Oliver Wallace and songs by Don Raye and Gene de Paul, of Washington Irving's immortal story of the same name, from his 1819 to 1820 collection, *The Sketch Book*. Set in the Dutch settlement of Tarry Town, on the Hudson River, circa 1790, Irving's Halloween story concerns a devious and unattractive schoolmaster named, with Dickensian precision, Ichabod Crane, who beats his charges yet also uses his abilities to teach music and French social dancing to court the neighborhood's eligible young ladies and widows—and get lots of free dinners in the bargain. (In the Disney version, he suspends his

In "The Legend of Sleepy Hollow," *schoolmaster Ichabod Crane courts the luscious Katrina Van Tassel in a minuet that evolves into a Lindy during the Halloween frolic at her father's house.*

inclination to brutality in the classroom in order to preserve his relationship with the cooking mothers.) When Ichabod's fastidious manners and dancing abilities make inroads on the affections of lovely, blond, and wealthy young Katrina Van Tassel (who, in the Disney movie, bears a startling resemblance in certain passages to the wide-eyed Marilyn Monroe of the 1955 live-action hit *The Seven Year Itch*), the rough yet ruggedly handsome town bruiser, a daredevil equestrian as well as a bully, who is known colloquially as Brom Bones (according to Irving, his real name is Brom Van Brunt) vows revenge. When Crane leaves a "Halloween frolic" at the Van Tassels' house, where he is certain that he has secured Katrina's affections, he is accosted in the gathering darkness by a horseman who seems to have no head. Crane, already a creature of neurasthenic sensitivity to suggestion, never makes it home and is never seen again, at least in the neighborhood.

The dance scene at the Van Tassels' Halloween party, during which Ichabod and Katrina perform a meticulously correct minuet and contradance and Ichabod cuts loose in a solo jig, is delicately and exactly rendered. It is not, however, the only dance element in the picture. Ballet is everywhere, as far as the principal characters are concerned. When Ichabod walks, he turns out his legs at the hips the way ballet dancers do and pauses with his feet crossed, toes to heels, in a classical fifth position. Katrina also perambulates with her legs turned out, and she runs on her toes in balletic *pas de bourrées*, as we see when she skitters across a meadow. But the most wonderful dance detail secreted in the film is given to none

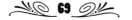

The fair Katrina Van
Tassel, object of Ichabod's
eye, shows off her balletic
tendu *in this cel setup.
The moment is not
actually part of the film,
yet it gives a fine sense of
the character, who, in the
picture, gambols barefoot
across a meadow on pointe
and with de rigeur balletic
turnout of the legs.*

other than Ichabod's nemesis, Brom Bones, who at one peak moment achieves a
mighty leap off a rolling barrel with perfectly turned-out legs and an exemplary
upright carriage of the spine—that is, he performs a classical *grand jeté*, even
though he is wearing heavy riding gear and thick-soled, buckled shoes! In that
one daredevil, Gene Kelly moment, Bones asserts the superiority of his animal
grace—a superiority that is most vividly embodied in his horsemanship, where his
natural athleticism is doubly empowered by his magnificent steed. In the great chase
through the woods and covered bridge that is the high point of the movie in terms
of both its narrative and its animation, the leap that Bones has taken off the barrel
becomes intensified in a moment where, cape flying, the Headless Horseman and
his horse, who together look like a shadow loosed from Hell, take a superheroic
flying leap off a precipice. Ichabod Crane, merely human, and his sweet farm horse,
for all their charm, resourcefulness, and luck, cannot hope to compete with the
fearsome power and well-lubricated ease of motion embodied by the ghost rider
and his stallion, whose Disney bloodlines as a charismatic villain stretch at least
as far back as the spats-wearing boxing champ who served as the title character
in the 1935 short *Cock o' the Walk*—debatably the most brilliant animated dance
film ever produced by Disney—and they certainly pass through the remorselessly
athletic demon Chernabog, rearing up in the "Night on Bald Mountain" section of
the 1940 *Fantasia*. It was somewhat of a tradition in Disney animated shorts that
the best dancer or athlete in a picture would also be associated with the dark side

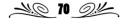

of (human) nature. And yet, faithful to Irving's winking ghost story, in "The Legend of Sleepy Hollow," the Disney team leaves the results of the final confrontation between bully and bullied somewhat complex. Bing Crosby's narrator tells us of the rumor that Crane married a wealthy widow in another county, and we see him happily seated at a laden table with his new family. Meanwhile, at the church alter, Bones looks over paternalistically at his little bride, who suddenly rears up and, to his consternation, kisses him greedily on the mouth as if she were going to devour him: perhaps Ichabod Crane has, once again, proven the luckier after all.

Who produced this little Disney dance treasure? It turns out that the co-directors were Clyde Geronimi, James Algar, and Jack Kinney, the director of Goofy's *How to Dance*—and the directing animators included four of the principals for *The Jungle Book*: Frank Thomas, Ollie Johnston, John Lounsbery, and Wolfgang Reitherman, as well as Milt Kahl and Ward Kimball, another of the "Nine Old Men." (Johnston, Thomas, and Reitherman animated the dance sequences at the Halloween party; and, as it happens, both Geronimi and Reitherman were veterans of *Cock o' the Walk*, too.) In the event, given that many of these dance animators had been thinking for several decades about the implications for character, in a moral sense, of whether a character, in the storytelling sense, is more generously endowed with brainpower or muscular power and grace, one can see how Goofy's attempts to learn to dance were fraught with potential hazards for those who were assigned to oversee him. Would the mastery of dancing transform him into a smooth

Animator Frank Thomas draws Ichabod Crane, the schoolmaster who inserts ballet positions into his daily perambulations, for The Adventures of Ichabod and Mr. Toad.

seducer, even a faithless cad? Or would the mastery of choreography, without the power and grace necessary to dance it properly, leave him a humiliated figure of fun? In learning to dance, might Goofy lose everything about himself that makes him lovable? These are serious, even metaphysical questions, even though their subjects are cartoons and the forms of such ruminations are gags and jokes. For me, the films that display the various efforts to address such issues in changing eras are ever more wonderful each time I look at them. Over the course of many decades of devoted effort, Disney's animators learned something Goofy never quite could: to comprehend the crucial distinction between dancing and choreography, and to master them both.

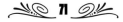

Walt Disney's
SILLY SYMPHONY
COCK O' THE WALK

Produced entirely in TECHNICOLOR • Released thru UNITED ARTISTS

© W.D.P

POLLY PULLET
CHICKEN COQUETTE

Polly, the pretty Pullet of Chicken Town, who makes her debut as a screen star in Walt Disney's newest Silly Symphony, "Cock O' The Walk," adds a new touch to terpsichorian technique. She has planted a new feather in her bonnet by her high stepping with that champion of champions, Cock O' The Walk.

Fame and Fortune await Polly and her fine feathered friends, the dancing Ducklings and the shimmying Chicks, for their rhythmic rendition of one of the more popular dance routines.

All Walt Disney's Silly Symphonies, in Technicolor, are released through United Artists.

Cock O' The Walk In Town!

The Chicken Town beauty shops have been doing a rushing business, literally making feathers fly since the champion, Cock O' The Walk came to town. The Barnyard belles are having their pin feathers curled and putting on Easter finery in their efforts to impress the attractive boxing champion.

"Cock O' The Walk" is the title and name of the star of the latest Walt Disney Silly Symphony, now showing at the............ ....Theatre.

FLIRT OR FOOD

The difference of just one letter means a lot in the life of a new Walt Disney character who makes her debut on the screen in the latest Silly Symphony, "Cock O' The Walk," now showing at the............ Theatre. Polly Pullet, the heroine of this colorful farmyard fable, is a chicken coquette who might easily have been a chicken croquette, were it not for her appearance in this new Technicolor production.

BARNYARD BUSINESS AT A HALT
AS CHAMP GIVES EXHIBITION

RULER
OF THE ROOST

Pictured about is "Cock O' The Walk," a gay young bird-about-coop who is now fluttering through Walt Disney's newest Silly Symphony of the same name. There's nothing chicken-hearted about this domineering dictator of the barnyard, who fought his way up to the championship of the chicken boxing world after a rather inconspicuous youth as a hard-boiled egg.

Rudy, the romantic rooster, and Polly, his pretty Pullet girl friend, co-star with the Champ in this tuneful fable of the farmyard, now on view at the............Theatre.

All Walt Disney productions are released through United Artists.

BASHFUL BANTAM

No one ever saw a chicken blush; probably no one ever thought of the possibility of a chicken wanting to blush, but Walt Disney, in his latest Silly Symphony, "Cock O' The Walk," has his romantic rooster glow and gasp as he stutters or rather cackles sweet sentiments of love to his sweetheart.

Woos Pullet
Symphonically

With a blare of music from h private brass band, Cock O' Th Walk, champion of fistic endeavor and sensational crooning trouba dor, made a spectacular entry in Chicken Town early this mornin For ..... days, this well known ma about-coop will make personal a pearances at the............ Theatre in Walt Disney's late Silly Symphony, "Cock O' Th Walk."

Barnyard society flocked to th barnyard grounds by the hundred and Cock O' The Walk demonstra ed his terpsichorean ability befor the admiring crowd. Polly Pulle a pretty, gay bunch of fluff, one Clucktown's younger set, caugh the eye of our visiting celebrit and he invited her to join him in dance routine.

The "Cock O' The Walk's" cal walk to the carioca was somethin to crow over and we've phot graphed the whole sequence fo your entertainment. See it now, it something to crow over.

FOWL DEEDS

A new dance routine is execute by an ensemble of barnyard hab tues who make up the dramat personnae of Walt Disney's late Silly Symphony, "Cock O' Th Walk," now showing at the............ Theare. The story details much tr love and the frustration of "fowl" deed and is filmed entire in Technicolor. All Walt Disne Silly Symphonies are release through United Artists.

With a wave of his mighty wing, the Cock O' The Walk signals his private orchestra, and the Barnyard Ballad breaks out with a vengeance. The Carioca Chickens introduce a new novelty for the entertainment of Walt Disney fans, at the same time causing much teeth gnashing among the Hollywood dance impressarios. This free mat available from the United Artists Home Office. Ask for mat C. W. 3.

In 1928, with the Mickey Mouse short *Steamboat Willie*—acknowledged in most histories as the first fully realized sound cartoon—Walt Disney proved to himself and the world that the future of animation was music. The idea was in the air—everyone in the business was trying to make sound pictures. Indeed, already in 1924, the Fleischer brothers in New York had in fact achieved basic synchronization of sound and image in their first follow-the-bouncing-ball sing-along series, the Song Car-Tunes, in which the lyrics of popular songs were broken down into syllables and projected onto a theater screen: as the music played on the sound track, an animated ball bounced from syllable to syllable in sync with the music, encouraging the audience to sing the song out loud together; on held notes, the ball lightly bounced in place on top of the sustained syllable—an elementary form of choreography. (For much of the 1930s, the Fleischer studio—inventor of those enduring stars Betty Boop and Popeye and adapter of the animated Superman—was Disney's major competitor.) However, since the Fleischer films initially had only very limited distribution on the East Coast, *Steamboat Willie* reached a much broader audience. Now, together with his growing team of animators and composers, Disney immediately set out in a remarkably methodical way to explore and expand the limits of his art. Along the way, the Disney studio made some extraordinary experiments in animated dance, a few of which, in my view, remain unsurpassed to this day.

Throughout the Great Depression the Disney studio, then located on Hyperion Avenue in the Silver Lake district of Los Angeles, maintained two major series of animated shorts. The first consisted of the Mickey Mouse pictures, to which the shorts that starred Donald Duck were eventually added (Donald even eclipsed Mickey in popularity for a while in the late 1930s and '40s).

The Mickey shorts were driven by gags and personality at first, but eventually encompassed stories that permitted more shadings of emotion. The music for the Mickey films, composed in-house, served mainly as a kind of punctuation—vivid rhythmical underscoring combined with zingy sound effects to punch up the action.

The front page of a four-page newspaper issued by Disney as publicity for the 1935 Silly Symphony Cock o' the Walk.

THE BAND CONCERT(1935):MICKEY MOUSE IN THE MUSIC

A production drawing of Mickey Mouse in the 1935 short The Band Concert---*Mickey's first Technicolor picture---about to conduct the famous overture to Gioachino Rossini's opera* William Tell. Time *magazine reported that conductor Arturo Toscanini, upon seeing the film, exclaimed,"Surely it is impossible! It is magnificent!" and had the film shown again. The virtuosity of the animation in this cartoon is still admired by animators today.*

The Band Concert, a triumph for director Wilfred Jackson and animator Les Clark, stars Mickey Mouse in his first Technicolor short as an earnest early-twentieth-century small-town conductor leading an afternoon concert on a summer's day in what looks, from the flat terrain and a distant windmill, to be someplace near Wichita, Kansas. It's hard work: Mickey has to haul the musical notes almost bodily from the valves and bells in the brass section of his raggle-taggle barnyard band. Nonetheless the audience, made up entirely of male characters arrayed around the bandstand on benches (Disney's animators in mufti?), is appreciative.

At the start of Rossini's *William Tell Overture*, the ambitious conductor's pièce de résistance for the program, ice-cream vendor Donald Duck disrupts the concert by playing "Turkey in the Straw" on a fife while doing a buck dance, a pre-tap routine with roots in mid-nineteenth-century black minstrelsy and vaudeville. Mickey breaks the fife and then has to break a couple more as unflappable Donald keeps producing them out of thin air. Eventually (thanks to the wizardry of Disney composer Leigh Harline), Rossini morphs into "Turkey" played by the entire band, which drives the conductor to distraction. Next, a disruptive bee stimulates a pinball game of grade-school mayhem with the ice cream. Suddenly, the sheet music reads "The Storm," and nature's mayhem, in the form of a tornado, sweeps up the musicians into a giant, whirling pirouette of wind: amazingly, the crisis somehow forces them to focus on Rossini, and the music not only gains continuity but becomes more expressive. As the characters are swept through the eye of the storm, the pirouette reverses direction. When it lets the band members drop, the overture is complete, though only one audience member is left to applaud alone: Donald Duck, who then takes out his fife again.

To see a band of musicians finally compelled to get inside a ballet, literally, is a dancer's dream. And as David Wondrich, author of *Stomp and Swerve: American Music Gets Hot, 1843–1924*, notes, to see a band conveyed into a dance by way of a tune associated with an African American dance tradition is thrilling. If not exactly a dance, *The Band Concert* is a feat of choreography and can be read as an allegory of the empathetic commitment that dancers long for from musicians.

This music can be a lot of fun in its blithe comic opportunism, and is genuinely funny, but it usually lacks much feeling of continuity or wholeness. When people refer to a score "Mickey Mousing" the action onstage or in a film, or when they refer to choreography that "Mickey Mouses" music—even if they have never seen these early Disney shorts—this is the relationship between dancing and music they have in mind.

The second series from the Hyperion period, produced by Walt Disney Productions from 1929 to 1939, was called the Silly Symphonies. From the outset, it was much more serious about music and offered the animators many opportunities to explore dance animation. The Symphonies, which eventually numbered seventy-five titles, seldom featured recurring characters and did not feature cartoon "stars," mainly employing instead characters devised uniquely for each film. (Donald Duck in fact got his start in a Symphony: *The Wise Little Hen*, in 1934.) The absence of recurring characters gave everyone involved great freedom to experiment.

In their encyclopedic *Walt Disney's Silly Symphonies: A Companion to the Classic Cartoon Series* (2006), Russell Merritt, a professor of film at the University of California at Berkeley, and J. B. Kaufman, a historian of Disney animated films, extol the Symphonies as "Disney's Tiffany line: the vital stepping-stones that led to his famous features." The series, they note,

> was the place where he adapted his first fairy tales and the lab that he used for technical innovations (most notably the use of color, intricate musical synchronization, the multiplane camera, in-depth perspective backgrounds, and special effects).

Disney was indeed willing to go to great lengths in pursuit of innovation: in 1932 he even had the sixty-percent-complete *Flowers and Trees* scrapped and redone in three-strip Technicolor, a brand-new full-color process. Experimentation with new processes and techniques proceeded hand in hand with experiments in new approaches to creating believable characters and dramatic story arcs. To the Symphonies Disney

> routinely assigned his best artists and most versatile story people. . . . There is not a scene in any vintage Disney feature that was not worked on by Symphony veterans.

As the name of the series suggests, the cartoons were conceived as musical novelties, and they were driven by their scores, nearly all of which were written by in-house composers—at first by Carl Stalling, Disney's first

Dance critics who wants to disparage a dance whose rhythms, steps, gestures, dynamics, and patterns in space have, they think, been shaped by the choreographer's excessive fidelity to the musical score can be patronizing, but polite, and accuse the dance-maker of mere "music visualization." Choreographers as diverse as Isadora Duncan, George Balanchine, and Mark Morris have all endured this insult, though early in the last century visualizing music was considered by some, for a time, a legitimate approach to dance-making. However, if the critics want to really sting, they will say that the dance "Mickey Mouses the music."

"Music visualization," "Mickey Mousing the music": the idea underlying both terms is that the choreography slavishly mimics the rhythm and accents, even the instrumentation, of the score to which it is set. Implicit is the charge that the choreographer hasn't done enough work—hasn't gone far enough in searching for a way to make dance and music converse or even contradict each other for dramatic purposes. Moreover, as Daniel Goldmark writes in *Tunes for 'Toons*, his landmark 2005 scholarly study of selected composers for Hollywood animated films during the first half of the twentieth century, "Mickey Mousing the music"—which he defines as "the exact synchronization of music and action"—implies also that the score "is telegraphing to the audience too much information: that is, the music is calling attention to itself as it describes what is happening on-screen." In other words, the music is somehow superfluous or redundant. The phrase "Mickey Mousing" can also condemn the opposite of laziness or passivity on a dance-maker's part: it can accuse the choreographer of aggressively misusing the score, neglecting its spirit in order to impose unrelated imagery, meanings, or context on the music. In this sense, the term criticizes the choreographer for dumbing down the music, often for blatantly commercial reasons.

Both usages depend upon the conviction that it is wrong for dance and music to exist in an uneven relationship in which one either unthinkingly mimics or selfishly exerts power over the other. This is surely fair, but the term *Mickey Mousing* has achieved the status of a received idea, such that people use the phrase without thinking of its origin and without considering that it might be unfair to Disney's animators and composers.

"Mickey Mousing" does indeed refer to a kind of musical illustration, in which some aspect of the music—the melody, the rhythm, the instrumentation—seems to duplicate (and therefore to reinforce or amplify) an action we see on-screen. But, as composer Alexander Rannie pointed out to me in an interview:

> Ironically, there is an implication of simplicity, or even worse, simple-mindedness, in the use of the term *Mickey Mousing*, when nothing could be further from the truth. The exact synchronization of music and action in film is an unforgiving science; if a musical "hit" misses the mark of its visual counterpart by more than two frames (often only one!), the effect of synchronization is lost and the magic is broken.

According to Goldmark, the person credited with inventing the phrase was producer David O. Selznick, who was "derisively likening a Max Steiner score [for a live-action feature] to the music of a Mickey Mouse cartoon." As Ross Care, a historian of music for Disney's animated films, explained to me in an interview, Steiner practiced "Mickey Mousing" throughout his film career, as, for instance, in the 1959 movie *A Summer Place*, in which "they're delivering mail to the island, and the mailbag gets thrown off the boat—with a harp glissando." Another often-cited example is the ascending melody that Steiner devised to dramatize the title character's climactic scaling of the Empire State Building in the 1933 *King Kong* (Steiner's breakthrough score). Steiner, sometimes called the father of American film music, was highly influential, and his approach, which is perhaps tailor-made for the narrative priorities of commercial cinema underscoring, quickly became ubiquitous. Moreover, every major cartoon studio practiced some kind of synchronization between image and sound, although with varying degrees of taste, technical resources, and artistic success. Critics might just as easily accuse that hypothetical choreographer of "Bugs Bunnying" or "Betty Booping" the music; that they don't testifies to Disney's dominance of the field in the early years and, of course, to Mickey's evolution from starring character to corporate icon.

Rannie notes too that Steiner, who had long experience in musical theater in Vienna, London, and New York before he began composing for film, relied, as did all the composers in the pioneering days of film, on the centuries-long theatrical tradition of underscoring plays with live music.

A great deal of musical practice had become codified by the advent of motion pictures. (Marches for heroic moments, ballads for tender ones.) Scoring for silent films further strengthened musical prejudices (both pro and con), and these clichés were carried over into film scores of the sound era.

Film underscoring can be more or less original, more or less tasteful, more or less obvious, more or less discreet. There is a clue here to just what it is that critics object to when they say that a choreographer "Mickey Mouses the music": a confusion of genre. The kind of on-the-nose point-scoring that is just right for Bugs Bunny's broad satire or Mickey Mouse's slapstick humor, looks inappropriate in other, noncomedic, musical contexts. "Mickey Mousing the music" isn't inherently bad, but it can be bad in the wrong place.

In any case, regardless of what Selznick may have said about Steiner's music, the quip did his career no harm: Steiner scored 250 films during his Hollywood years (including Disney's 1965 *Those Calloways*) and received twenty-six Oscar nominations, winning three times. Among his hits was the 1939 score for *Gone with the Wind*—produced by Selznick. If anything has been hurt by the phrase "Mickey Mousing the music," it is the prestige of Walt Disney's Mickey Mouse cartoons and their composers, whom the phrase intrinsically, and unjustly, disparages.

OPPOSITE: *A page of the combined short score and bar sheets for* The Skeleton Dance *of 1929, the inaugural Silly Symphony. The composer, Carl Stalling, has made notes of the conjunction between musical moments and the picture's choreographic events, devised by animator Ub Iwerks.*

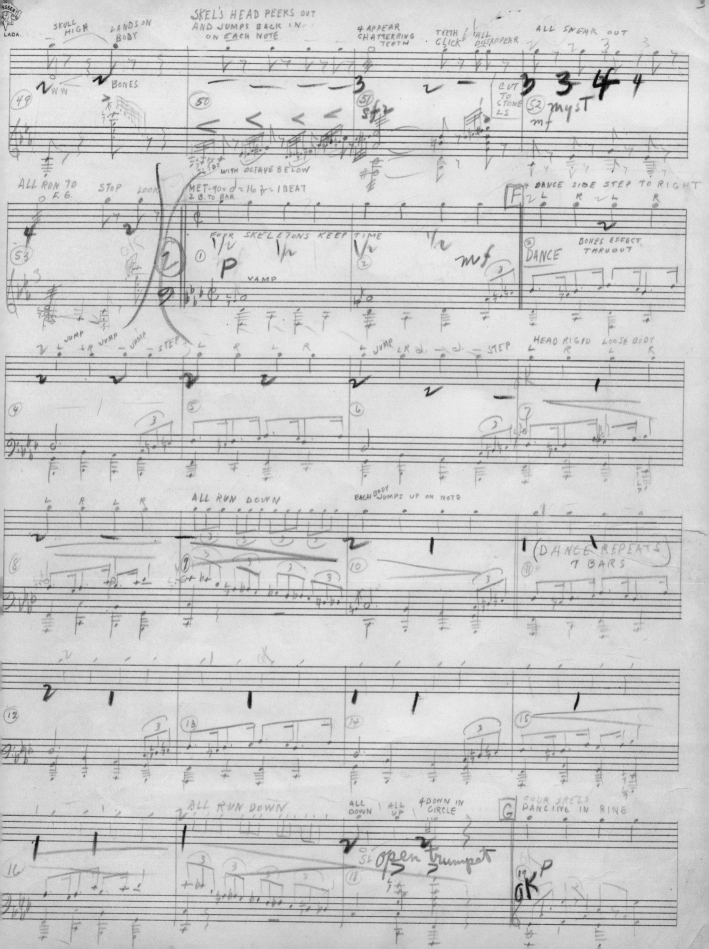

music director and one of the most ingenious arrangers ever to work in animation. Indeed, the series originated in conversations between Disney and Stalling about whether it would be more practical and effective to create animation or music first. For the early Symphonies, Stalling was allowed to compose scores that Disney then handed off to the animators as points of departure. In Stalling's brief tenure at the studio (he left Disney after only two years, but continued to freelance for his old boss until 1936, when he joined Warner Bros., where he remained for the rest of his career), he made several vital technical innovations, all of which gave composers and animators greater control over the element of time.

After Disney animation director Wilfred Jackson in 1928 proposed the use of the metronome to coordinate the musical meters of an animated film score against the unvarying film speed of twenty-four frames per second, Stalling quickly adopted it, becoming the first music director to use the device extensively to time film music. He also pioneered the use of "bar sheets," which allowed appropriate musical rhythms to be developed simultaneously with the action sketched on the storyboards. Stalling is also one of three composers—the others are Max Steiner and Scott Bradley—credited with developing the click track, which enables a conductor to sync music to film during recording, and enables sound and film editors to keep music and image aligned in post-production. Without these three advances, it is hard to imagine ever achieving the precision necessary to render dancing effectively in animation.

Examined closely, the process of composing and recording the music for the Disney films was anything but simple—not "Mickey Mouse" at all. In *The Illusion of Life: Disney Animation*, the indispensable history of Disney filmmaking by revered studio animators Frank Thomas and Ollie Johnston, the authors provide a step-by-step description of what was involved in marrying sight and sound. Far from being a mechanical, assembly-line affair, the work involved was dauntingly complex and exacting. For each film, there were opportunities at many points for the various collaborators—directors, composers, head animators—to make small refinements to the basic musical map of metronomically measured tempos and dramatic accents of the action, refinements that could affect the entire score as well as other aspects of the process, such as the editing.

As Thomas and Johnston present this process, from the inside, it's clear that, although the composers were forced to make many compromises, sometimes

before even a single drawing had been made, the animators had to remain flexible, too. As Thomas and Johnston write:

> It was not an easy procedure for anyone, but that close collaboration was the very thing that produced the new art form. From the advent of sound to the late thirties, music and animation had been one. Wilfred Jackson expressed the general feeling: "I do not believe there was much thought given to the music as one thing and the animation as another. I believe we conceived of them as elements which we were trying to fuse into a whole new thing that would be more than simply movement plus sound."

Thomas and Johnston also make the point that well-defined restrictions may stimulate the creative process, rather than dampen it. Most artists, perhaps even all artists, relish some kind of limitations to keep the terror of the blank page, or the blank stage, at bay. For example, Igor Stravinsky, who composed some of the finest music for dance in the last century for the impresario Sergei Diaghilev and later for choreographer George Balanchine, liked to say that he could not feel excited about a commission until he knew exactly how long the choreographer wanted each section of the music to be. As Thomas and Johnston put it:

> If this close integration of music and action had been a headache to the musicians, it was equally demanding for the animators, forcing them to become more crisp in their thinking and better organized in their statements. They always had been required to get across the story points in the least amount of time, but they had never faced the discipline of working to the rigid pattern of a beat. Where ordinarily they would have taken an extra eight or ten frames to complete an action, stage a pose, or register a look, the music made them search for the absolute essence of the idea—that and nothing more. No frills, no extras; get right to the point. It is doubtful if they ever would have achieved this concise distillation without the constant pressure that demanded they find a way. Looking back on it now, we can see that it was valuable and necessary training. Unlimited footage nearly always lulls the animator into a slipshod performance.

Even if choreography per se could never be the top priority of the series, inevitably, given the Symphonies' musical inspiration, many of the films addressed the problems of how to make animated dancing look physically and emotionally authentic and believable, how to make choreography reveal character, how to exaggerate the contours of dance steps and gestures for comic effect without sacrificing their credibility, and how to integrate dance sequences into a narrative.

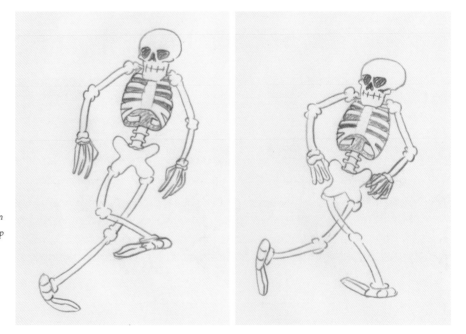

Ub Iwerks's final animation drawings of a skeleton dancing the grapevine step; note the turned-out (even overly turned-out!) supporting leg. BELOW: In the film, four skeletons perform the step in a chorus line, an effect achieved by having the Ink and Paint department trace Iwerks's drawing over and over with the position of the original drawing shifted for each tracing.

THE SKELETON DANCE (1929): ● The vast majority of the Symphonies
Stretchy Bones and Xylophones ● include at least a bit of animated dancing—a phrase, a step, a pose—and some contain much more. *The Skeleton Dance*, the first of the Symphonies and certainly among the most brilliant, feels like a dance from beginning to end, and most viewers remember the entire short as a dance, although in fact the "skeleton dance" as such only occupies about two thirds of its five-and-a-half-minute running time.

The key to this marvelous dance continuity is the way that Stalling's score, which Walt Disney called "a little symphony," is mated to the rhythmically startling and visually unpredictable animation of Ub Iwerks. Stalling came to cartoon scoring with experience dating back to his adolescence as a pianist, conductor, and improvising organist for silent films, and he understood that what serves action in film most effectively is that aspect of music called "gesture"—short, self-contained phrases that evoke something in the real world. In concert with stimulating rhythms and bursts of melody, musical gesture helps to make a score sound danceable, even when the rhythms are not, in any conventional sense, dance rhythms.

For *The Skeleton Dance*, Stalling built his score out of original music (including a foxtrot), special effects (such as the fortissimo choruses of howling cats), and spoofing paraphrases from Edvard Grieg's "The March of the Dwarfs" (from *Peer Gynt*), which Stalling orchestrated to feature the bony rattle of a xylophone. (Stalling's whole style throughout his career was based on quotations from and references to well-known tunes.) Stalling may also have intended the xylophone to evoke Saint-Saëns's "Danse Macabre," which famously showcases the same instrument (he does not, however, as some believe, ever quote the "Danse Macabre" in this film).

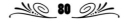

The film opens with a funhouse laugh, the sound of thunder, and strobelike lightning, followed by a scene-setting prelude to an overture filled with musical wind sounds and featuring an owl perched on a tree branch. At first, the owl puffs himself up with the importance of his whistling cry; then, as the tree branches next to him turn into fingers, he grows just a little uncertain. Indeed, it's with the owl—represented at one point only by its eyes filling the screen—that the animation begins to employ its part-for-whole bravura drawing. We hear four sounds, like the tocks of a metronome, as the minute hand of the church steeple clock ticks toward midnight, then twelve soft chimes of the church bell, which we see ringing while bats swarm from the steeple, followed by a goofy-looking spider, which the bell has kicked out of the belfry. A hound bays at the full moon, working its body like a bellows, and two black cats scrap in a graveyard, assaulting one another in a sort of call-and-response rhythm.

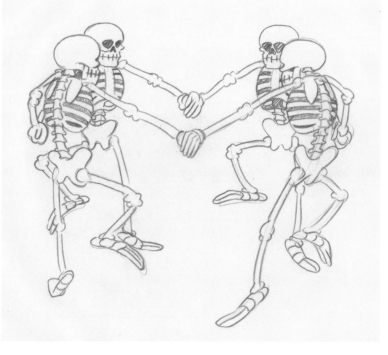

ABOVE: *A moment in the opening sequence of* The Skeleton Dance. BELOW: *Four of Ub Iwerks's skeletons join hands in a round; note that each is in a slightly different stage of transferring its weight from one bony foot to the other.*

But *everything* prior to the appearance of the first skeleton (who pops up and perches on a gravestone like a dog) is setting up the visceral feeling of dancing: the wind, the puffing owl, the teasing tree-branch hands, the claps and the chimes, the baying hound, the brawling cats—all lay down the movement idea of a pulse that will be picked up by the skeletons. A weird little tune accompanies the first skeleton as he walks, lopes, and then—adding a couple of beats on one leg for syncopation—skips, hands on hips. (This melody is another Stalling spoof, paraphrasing a piece of silent-movie mood music, "Mysterioso Pizzicato," attributed to J. Bodewalt Lampe, published in 1914.) The owl scares him, so he takes off his head and pitches it at the bird, which sheds its plumage altogether and yet only looks anxious, not terrified. (You may find yourself thinking of the skeletons as stand-ins for the animator while the owl and other animals represent the composer.) The skeleton opens its mouth and jumps forward, growing huge as it approaches—and then swallows us! Three fellow skeletons, their teeth chattering in perfect synchrony, join the first, and the dance proper begins, accompanied by a minor-key foxtrot. It consists of discrete sections: a vaudeville chorus line in a grapevine step; a swaying dance off the ground in the manner of paper Halloween skeletons (of the kind that Stalling was thinking of from his childhood when he suggested to Walt Disney that the first Symphony be "a skeleton dance"); a merry round, interrupted by pirouettes in

ABOVE: *Les Clark's famous skeleton "xylophone."* BELOW: *A pair of Iwerks skeletons cavorts, one using the other as a pogo stick; note the graceful, balletic hands of the pogo-stick skeleton.*

place while each skeleton "partners" itself with one bony finger on its skull; and a circuslike stunt for two skeletons, who use each other as pogo sticks. A jump cut reveals one skeleton playing another like a xylophone to the paraphrased Grieg melody: the player's knees pump up and down in demi-pliés (half knee bends), his legs turned out in ballet's first position, while the xylophone skeleton crouches on all fours. (This scene is the one passage animated not by Iwerks but by his assistant, Les Clark.) Two of the skeletons perform a big man–little man fun-house act, stretching their limbs and then compressing them (an example combining both "circles-and-rubber-hose" animation and elements of what would become the mature Disney "squash-and-stretch" style). One skeleton plays the tail of a live cat with a shinbone; another performs the waggling hands-crossing step of the Charleston, slapping its hip like an old hoofer.

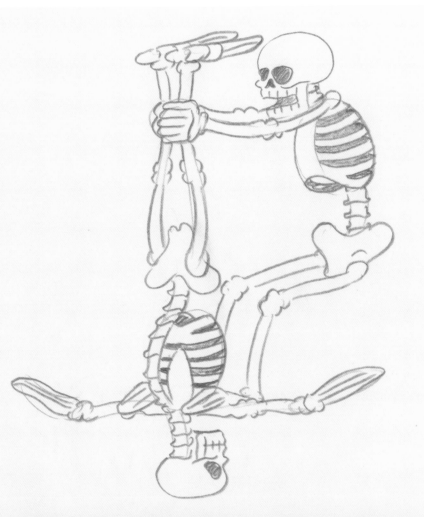

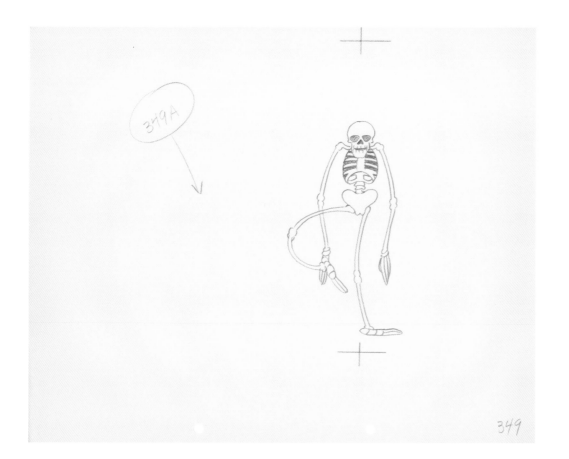

A cock crows, signaling dawn, and the skeletons hectically gallop back into their graves, at one point colliding and collapsing in a mess of bones and, at another, turning themselves into the four horsemen of the Apocalypse, reimagined as a horse with four heads and sixteen limbs. They finally hop underground, although two legs are left jigging plaintively outside the grave; reaching out and pausing for a moment, one bony hand seizes and hauls them back in. Throughout, the whiteness of the bones against the grays and inky black of the other characters and the backgrounds have also been making a case for the world in black and white.

Iwerks, a boyhood friend of Walt Disney's from Kansas City and the animator who first gave form to Mickey Mouse, only stayed with the Disney studio as an animator for a few years before striking out with his own cartoon company (although he did eventually return to contribute pathbreaking technical inventions and special effects during a long career at the studio). However, the cartoons he drew—and Iwerks animated nearly every frame of the pictures he worked on—had a special quality of motion unparalleled by the work of any of the artists who succeeded him. "I did all the animation, but I did it rough, in line form," Iwerks said of his art on *The Skeleton Dance*. "Other guys put in the rib cages and teeth and eyes and bones." And, unlike Disney, who preferred that peak moments of action be held for dramatic accent, Iwerks wanted constant motion. As I noted in

An Iwerks skeleton stretches itself up to bigger than lifesize (or deathsize!); note the balletic turnout of the supporting leg. The lifted, or "working," leg also looks as if it's about to pause in a balletic toe-to-knee (passé) pose; however, in the film, that nearly triangular leg shape is not a held pose but part of a large rippling motion as the limb is lowered again.

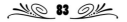

chapter two, while other animators customarily drew mainly the initial and final poses of any motion—the "extremes"—and left their junior colleagues, called "in-betweeners," to fill in the rest, Iwerks always insisted on working "straight ahead," drawing every frame, though he sometimes left the refinements of his outlines to assistants—the "other guys" who had to draw in all those ribs. As his daughter wrote in her biography of Iwerks:

> he reasoned that if he did only the extremes, he would lose the control over the kineticism of his art. . . . The Ub Iwerks style was constant, motivated motion. Ub admired the Fleischer Brothers' concept of moving holds, but he took it even further to an almost balletic level. According to animator Mark Kausler, Ub "created more of a dance. The characters move their arms . . . and they move across and around in perspective. He really figured out how to give a dancelike rhythmic quality to his animation."

The look of the skeletons was apparently derived from several sources: the skeleton scenes of English satirist Thomas Rowlandson, photographs of murals from Etruscan tombs, the paper skeletons that Stalling remembered. However, certain images of the skulls also evoke the skirted helmets of German soldiers in World War I. Walt Disney had driven a Red Cross ambulance in France during the Great War: are the helmet-skulls a delicate remembrance of that confrontation with real death?

Three years after *The Skeleton Dance* was released, the German choreographer Kurt Jooss created the most admired onstage image of a dancing skeleton in the twentieth century: the figure of Death in his ballet *The Green Table*. Jooss's Death is a tall, powerful male dancer in a grey body stocking with stylized bones painted on it in black; he wears terrifying skull makeup, riblike black leather chest armor, flare-topped boots, and a strange crested helmet. He moves rigidly, mechanically, a death machine—or a skeleton without ligaments, like the first skeleton in the Disney cartoon, the one who jumps doglike onto a headstone. Of course, most of Iwerks's skeletons have magical connective tissue, and stretchy bones, too, while Jooss's Death figure ambulates in a stiff stance with his knees bent, shooting out one heel, then the other, sideways. Yet, since the first twelve Silly Symphonies were distributed in Germany starting in 1929, it wouldn't surprise me to learn that, on a day off from researching Germany's rich heritage of medieval dance-of-death imagery, Jooss went to the cinema and saw *The Skeleton Dance*.

38

The Oscar-winning *Three Little Pigs*, perhaps the most well-known animated short that Disney ever produced, begins and ends with dancing by two brother pigs who build flimsy houses. Named for the musical instruments they also play, they are Fiddler Pig and Fifer Pig. The third brother, Practical Pig, who builds the brick house that protects them all from the wolf at the door and grumps that he doesn't have any time to have fun, turns out to be a jazz pianist—who plays a piano made of bricks—but he doesn't dance.

The pig brothers' choreography consists of two jig steps: an evenly metered side-to-side stomp and a syncopated stomp. Representing a state of carefree well-being and meticulously coordinated to the original song by Frank Churchill, "Who's Afraid of the Big Bad Wolf?", the jig and jingle are identically performed several times throughout the cartoon, but they touch the audience differently depending on the scene. Disney made two more shorts featuring the pigs and the wolf: "The Big Bad Wolf" (1934) and "Three Little Wolves" (1936). The pigs dance in all three shorts, and in the second film the wolf disguises himself as "Goldilocks, The Fairy Queen, Spirit of the Woods"—complete with high heels, in which, momentarily, he poses on pointe.

LEFT: *Animation drawings of Fifer Pig and Fiddler Pig. Comparing these drawings with the full-color image of the same pigs (ABOVE) shows the animators' skill in rendering the characters' weight and center of gravity, essential to the illusion of dancing.*

THE GODDESS OF SPRING (1934):

Isadora Duncan Goes to Hell

Ub Iwerks was not the only Symphonies animator to take a playful approach to macabre imagery. Considered a failure by Disney animators as well as by Walt Disney, valued by historians only for the opportunities it offered the Disney artists to experiment in animating the human form as they prepared to work on the studio's heralded first feature, *Snow White and the Seven Dwarfs*, *The Goddess of Spring* offers passages that still fascinate—and puzzle—a dance aficionado with an interest in animation. The cartoon retells a somewhat condensed version of the ancient Greek etiological myth that explains why the earth has seasons. The most complete version of this story is found in the Homeric Hymn to Demeter, composed around 650 BCE, although this version omits some of what are thought to be the most archaic features of the story, which are preserved in various literary fragments. In the mythic tale Persephone (sometimes also simply called Kore, "maiden"), the goddess of what was once perpetual springtime on Earth, is abducted

by Hades, lord of the underworld and god of wealth, to be his queen. Persephone is distraught, and in the end Hades is moved by her pleas—and persuaded by her aggrieved parents, Demeter, goddess of agriculture, and Zeus, father of the gods—to allow her to spend part of the year aboveground (the number of months on earth varies widely according to the telling). Disney eliminates the girls' divine parents from the story, and thus omits the motif of springtime representing Persephone's reunification with her mother.

The Disney story is also retold in a very unexpected way: as a full-blown operetta, although one on the bittersweet side, like something by Franz Lehár, with songs and orchestral music (including a major production number in Hades) by Leigh Harline (best known as the composer of *Pinocchio*'s "When You Wish Upon a Star"), and lyrics by Larry Morey (*Snow White*, *Bambi*). The two "human" characters are Persephone and Pluto (Disney's Hades goes by his Roman name); all the other creatures are either animals, elves, or gleeful little devils with pitchforks (the latter were designed by the great Disney concept artist, Swiss native Albert Hurter,

Persephone's dance on Earth in this Silly Symphony consists essentially of just two skipping steps. OPPOSITE: The upright hop with her leg raised behind her in a low attitude position. BELOW: The forward-bending hop with her face hidden. The birds who carry Persephone's scarf in their beaks, like pages carrying the train of a princess, anticipate the intimacy that Snow White will enjoy with her forest-creature companions.

who would later contribute mightily to the atmosphere, emotion, and stylistic detail of both *Snow White* and *Pinocchio.*) Dick Huemer, the principal animator for Pluto, gives him splendid posture—much better than Persephone's irremediable debutante slouch—and when his figure moves, albeit a little stiffly, he conveys a sense of muscular purpose and grounded weight. All the flamelike tips of his body and costume (ears, fingertips, collar points, demonic horns) look appropriate; only his peculiarly bulbous lower lip seems pasted on. But Pluto, a basso profundo, only sings; he does not dance—the inability to dance seems to be part of his hellish identity. Perhaps Huemer, like Balanchine, believed that evil characters should never dance, only mime.

Persephone, a coloratura, dances before we hear her sing a note. Indeed, she enters dancing in the middle of a musical phrase—a rather sophisticated entrance—amid a procession of blissful animals. Dressed in a version of a Hellenic chiton (tunic), with a chaplet of flowers crowning her honey-blond locks, she performs a dance that consists essentially of one short skipping phrase, step-hop–step-hop: first she springs off her right leg, with her sandaled foot pointed down, her left leg raised behind with knee bent in a low balletic "attitude" position, and her body held upright as her tendril-like arms open wide and her face turns upward; on the second skip, she lifts her attitude leg in front, with her upper body bent forward, hiding her face from view.

Today, we can immediately see the anatomical difficulties that the animator, Ham Luske, had with the figure: the arms have no elbows, the head is uncertainly affixed to the throat, the shoulders don't align. Luske is quoted in some sources as saying that he had trouble because he used his assistant, animator Eric Larson, to model Persephone's movement, and Larson was too bulky and awkward; in another reference, Luske explains that he used his wife as a model, but she didn't work out either.

And yet, despite the problems with his model, Luske somehow managed to depict very clearly a short iconic dance phrase indelibly associated with American modern dance pioneer Isadora Duncan, who included Persephone's skipping motif in one dance after another. Since Isadora created ultimately not just a movement but a whole international climate of inspiration, it is quite possible that Luske encountered her dancing second or third hand: from dancers trained according to her method (such as the Isadorables, six of her best students, whom she adopted as her children, and who toured in the U.S. during the early 1930s); from Isadora's

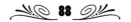

many imitators; or from dancers who absorbed her spirit, such as Russian ballerina Anna Pavlova, who had made five major tours of the U.S. by 1921 and whose many widely distributed photographs made her universally known. Furthermore, those two skips, as well as other poses very close to some Persephone takes, are reminiscent of a still-remarkable series of photographs shot in 1903 of the young Isadora dancing, in peplos and sandals, in the Theatre of Dionysus during her family's first visit to Greece; the photographer was her brother Raymond Duncan, who lived on the West Coast intermittently after Isadora's death in 1927. Did someone involved in trying to conceive Persephone at the Disney studio ever see those pictures, I wonder?

The Goddess of Spring is often noted for playing with the opposition of classical music (for Persephone in her meadow) and jazz (for Pluto's realm), but the film plays just as much with the opposition of nature and the theater. The

floor show in hell takes place on a stage framed by a stone proscenium arch, with a curtain of fire—a witty touch—in a theater that resembles a cross between Radio City Music Hall and the set for a Hammer horror flick. Pluto's house orchestra plays big-band jazz—specifically, the infectiously danceable jazz of Cab Calloway, whose characteristic "Hi-de-ho!" is invoked in Harline's "Hi-de-Hades" number. No female characters dance here—only the grinning little devils; and yet they, too, have choreography that consists of essentially two steps: a two-footed jump and, more arresting, a devilishly fast syncopated heel-and-toe phrase that has clearly been analyzed and reconstructed from some now lost original. Whose dance phrase was that? (Composer and Disney historian Alexander Rannie suggests that the animators must have known the grinning little demons in the films of George Méliès.)

I can't help wondering if Disney wasn't poking fun at himself just a little with this short, too. It is perhaps not sheer coincidence that in 1934, as his biographer, Neal Gabler, recounts, Walt Disney was such a workaholic that his wife, Lillian, was very lonely at home much of the time. When they *were* together, Disney liked to take Lillian out for a drive, but they frequently ended up at the office, where Lillian would curl up to sleep on a sofa while Walt worked through the night, turning back the clock so that Lillian wouldn't know how late it really was. Like the Greek maiden, perhaps she felt doomed to endure her husband's dark realm until he saw fit to let her see daylight again.

The dance of Disney's Persephone in The Goddess of Spring *(1934) was anticipated by Isadora Duncan, here photographed by her brother, Raymond, in 1903 in the Theater of Dionysus at the foot of the Acropolis in Athens. Photo courtesy the Isadora Duncan Dance Foundation.*

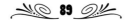

A drawing in colored pencil of a moment from the 1935 Silly Symphony Music Land, *with annotations to guide the Ink and Paint department. The "#49" refers to another drawing of the character's foot: that is, for this drawing, #53, the inker is directed to trace just the foot from #49.*

Romeo and Juliet was a popular theme worldwide for theatrical entertainment during the 1930s. The landmarks included Serge Prokofiev's ballet score (composed from 1935 to 1936, though not produced until 1940, when the Kirov Ballet staged it in Leningrad) and the 1936 Hollywood film starring Leslie Howard, Norma Shearer, and John Barrymore, with much-admired choreography by Agnes de Mille. Prokofiev wanted to give the story a happy ending but was prevented from doing so by Soviet censors; however, George Balanchine (who didn't much like the original story) did get to stage a comic *Romeo and Juliet* that ended happily—a ten-minute version, with the Capulets as a female corps de ballet on pointe, and the Montagues as a female tap chorus, for the 1938 movie *Goldwyn Follies*.

   Had Balanchine seen the 1935 Silly Symphony *Music Land*, a *Romeo and Juliet* with the warring families represented by a classical orchestra who inhabit the Land of Symphony, and a brassy band on the Isle of Jazz? (Disney historian Ross Care has written that the cartoon "springs direct from a musical concept, being a subtle satire of symphonic jazz.") Although *Music Land* doesn't include much dancing as such, the dancing passages are quite charming, if thoroughly inauthentic. We're introduced to the formal court of the cello queen sleeping on her throne in the Land of Symphony while alternating lines of harps and cellos-in-waiting dance the suggestion of a minuet; next we meet the racy court of the sax king, who "sings" and play the drums on the Isle of Jazz in a jam session that includes nubile shimmying ukuleles. (The king is a loving caricature of band leader Paul Whiteman—who was himself called "the king of jazz"—and who, ironically, did much to bridge the worlds of jazz and classical music.) The ingenue violin princess from Symphony is the Juliet character, who sneaks off to meet her Romeo, the young alto-sax prince. Leigh Harline strings together excerpts from nineteenth-century orchestral warhorses and old musicals with such skill that the entire cartoon feels like a jazz ballet. Ten animators realized the inspirational designs of Albert Hurter, whose specialty was discovering personality in unlikely objects and creatures. Duke Ellington and George Gershwin (with whom Whiteman enjoyed a long association), the finest exponents of symphonic jazz, are nowhere mentioned yet everywhere present.

COCK O' THE WALK (1935): The Greatest Dancing Silly Symphony of Them All?

For choreography, elegance, musicality, poetic resonance, and depth of reference, the Silly Symphony *Cock o' the Walk*—created only one year after *The Goddess of Spring*—is one of the most stylish dance films the Disney studio ever released. It's rarely mentioned in Disney histories; however, it had at least one fan. And a great fan, too: Lincoln Kirstein—the man who brought George Balanchine to America and, with him, cofounded the New York City Ballet. In his 1936 essay "Dance and Films," Kirstein issues a call for filmmakers to explore "all the fullest possibilities" of filmmaking in bringing classical dance to the screen; as an example of what they should aim for, he cites this Disney film. "*Cock o' the Walk* was an inspired satire on a Busby Berkeley super-super, but its color and fantasy were incidentally beautiful in themselves," Kirstein writes. It is the sole animated film that he discusses in the essay.

The story for *Cock o' the Walk* is nicely summarized by Merritt and Kaufman in *Walt Disney's Silly Symphonies*:

> The 'cock o' the walk,' a champion prize-fighting rooster, returns to a hero's welcome in the barnyard. A parade in his honor draws dozens of adoring hens, among them a young pullet who abandons her bumpkin admirer at first glimpse of the new hero. She and the champ dance the carioca, triggering an elaborate production number with all the other barnyard fowl joining in. Finally the enraged boyfriend challenges the champ in the ring. He is at the point of losing both the fight and his disinterested girlfriend, when the champ's bag is knocked open and discloses his family portrait: himself, his wife, and a large brood of youngsters! In a rage, the girl returns to her former boyfriend, and gives him a kiss that inspires him to return to the ring and thrash the two-timer.

The source of this Disney story, Merritt and Kaufman explain, was a fable in rhyming verse called "The Two Cocks," first published in 1678 by the French writer and political satirist Jean de la Fontaine. The situation in La Fontaine's version is similar, though not identical, to that of the film: two cocks in a barnyard live in peace until they begin to fight over a seductive hen; the battered cock who loses the fight drags himself away, while the victor jumps to a roof and crows with exultation. His prideful cry, though, attracts a hawk, who kills him at a stroke, after which the loser creeps out and takes over the "harem" of the hens. Even though La Fontaine's fable alludes directly to the fight over Helen that precipitated the Trojan War—which Homer chronicled in *The Iliad*, whose epic style La Fontaine spoofs—the French writer was also clearly basing his fable on a famous one by Aesop. In that

22 CARRIOCA PULLET AND CHAMP

SC-22

22A PULLET AND CHAMP UP TO
CAMERA SHAKE DOWN

SC-22A

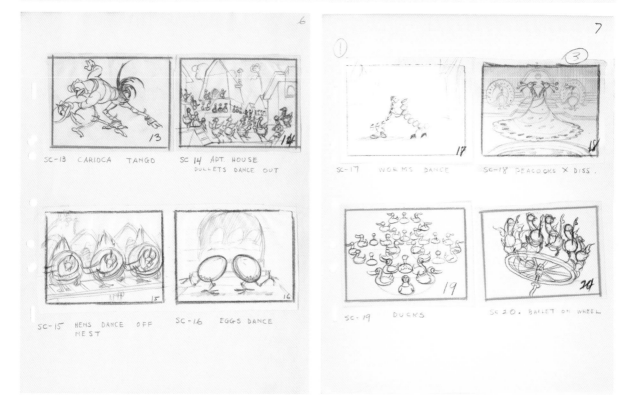

6

SC-13 CARIOCA TANGO

SC 14 APT. HOUSE
PULLETS DANCE OUT

SC-15 HENS DANCE OFF
NEST

SC-16 EGGS DANCE

7

SC-17 WORMS DANCE

SC-18 PEACOCKS X DISS.

SC-19 DUCKS

SC 20. BALLET ON WHEEL

THIS PAGE: *Story sketches for the 1935 Silly Symphony* Cock o' the Walk, *including the carioca tango, and the dances of the pullets, hens, eggs, worms, peacocks, and ducks.* OPPOSITE: *Clean-up animation drawings of the ducks' water ballet for* Cock o' the Walk.

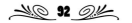

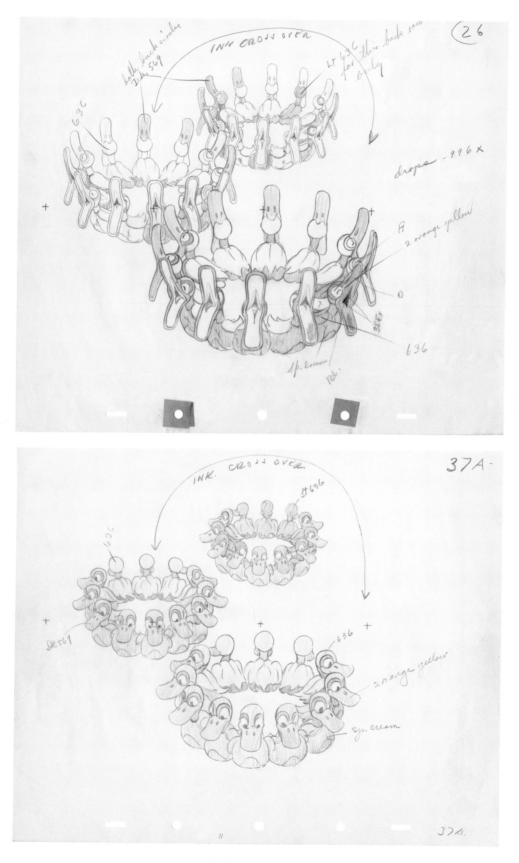

Prunella Pullet offers her seductive Champ a worm as they seem just about to join up to dance. This scene compresses several from the actual film. Prunella and the Champ do dance at this moment; however, the worms in the picture are animated, with personalities. In one passage, a boy worm (with a necktie) and a girl worm (wearing tiny high heels) dance a bit of the carioca: they represent Prunella and her true love, Hick. In another passage, a newly hatched girl chick aggressively pursues a boy worm (again wearing a necktie) and is knocked out by him: they represent in miniature both the Champ and Prunella and the Champ and Hick, who finally knocks out his rival.

laconic ancient version, the least romantic of all, no female character is singled out. Two cocks simply battle for sovereignty of the barnyard; the one who loses hides in a hole, while winner celebrates his victory, thus attracting the attention of an eagle, who swoops down and carries him off. Then, (according to Samuel Croxall's rather charming version of 1728) "the Cock that had been beaten, perceiving this, soon quitted his Hole, and shaking off all Remembrance of his Disgrace, gallanted the Hens with all the Intrepidity imaginable."

How very different in emphasis from both of these is Disney's *Cock o' the Walk*. Here, in place of a predatory hawk or eagle, it is the exposure of the crowing victor's own guilty secret about a wife and children back home that does him in. And the "young pullet" (named Prunella) at the center of the story *chooses* one partner over another at every point: she is not treated as property but, rather, is allowed to follow her heart, even when it leads her to the "wrong" fellow.

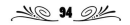

This portrayal of feminine initiative is quite absent in La Fontaine's fable, and in Aesop no female even emerges as a character.

Moreover, Prunella represents a departure from the way women are characterized in the 1930s Warner Bros. musicals choreographed by Busby Berkeley, to which the big dance in the Disney cartoon refers. Berkeley's iconic production numbers—featuring scores of identically costumed and coiffed beauties geometrically arranged along rotating ziggurats, or spread-eagled in eye-popping kaleidoscopic designs—are objects of affectionate satire in

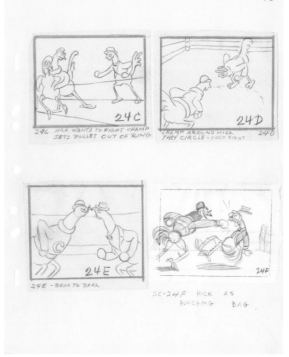

The dance floor is converted to a boxing ring as Hick and the Champ face off for their momentous confrontation in Cock o' the Walk.

the cartoon, by way of an elaborate barnyard version of those spectacles, complete with fantailed peacocks. And yet, although *Cock o' the Walk* borrows aspects of Busby Berkeley's cinematic dance designs, the motivating sensibility for the animation comes from quite another source. For all its elaborate frivolity and visual charm, Berkeley's dance imagery can be quite dark and bitter, in the manner of Bertolt Brecht and Kurt Weill or of 1930s Parisian Surrealism. (If, for instance, you turn off the sound track when you watch what most dance critics would say is Berkeley's dance masterpiece—"The Lullaby of Broadway" number in *Gold Diggers of 1935*—you'll see a nightmare hallucination of New York, death-ridden and scary. When you watch with the sound on, the number—which incidentally contains more real dancing, by a cabaret-ballroom couple and a corps de ballet of ballroom-tap dancers, than any other Berkeley picture for Warner's—is sweetened by its melody and lyrics.)

For tone and, in many places, particular choreographic figures, the dominant Hollywood references in *Cock o' the Walk* are certainly the sunnier and much dancier Fred Astaire–Ginger Rogers films for RKO. The most pervasive Astaire–Rogers elements in the cartoon derive from the 1933 *Flying Down to Rio*, the team's film debut. *Cock o' the Walk* borrowed not only Vincent Youmans's song "The Carioca" but also the dance's odd forehead-to-forehead partnering stance, some of the steps that Fred and Ginger performed, and others performed by *Rio*'s separate Caucasian and Creole corps de ballet (the ensemble numbers were choreographed by David Gould). There are even variations on the *tableaux vivants* arranged around

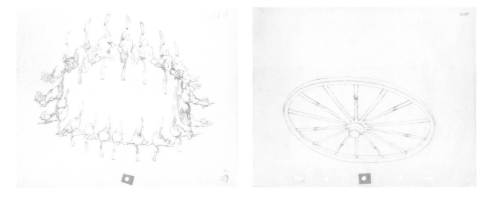

Animation drawings for the pullets' ballet in Cock o' the Walk. LEFT: *A roundel of pullets in* arabesque penchée. RIGHT: *The wheel on which the pullets perch. The inked and colored drawings will be layered together in the completed animation.*

a miniature wedding-cake platform in *Rio*'s carioca—that movie's underpowered attempt to compete with Busby Berkeley.

Carioca means "native or resident of Rio de Janeiro" in Brazilian Portuguese; the social dance of the same name is a variant of the samba, while choreographed versions of it may include steps borrowed from other Latin dances, such as the maxixe, with rhythm tap mixed in too. *Cock o' the Walk*'s carioca for the champ and Prunella also contains a move that evokes one Astaire and Rogers made famous in their "Pick Yourself Up" number in *Swing Time*, in which the partners incorporate a bit of the set in the course of a flying, swinging lift. Rogers and Astaire leap together over a low white fence and back again; Prunella springs off a small stool positioned near the low white ropes of the "fight ring." Yet *Swing Time* wasn't released until 1936: could it possibly be that Astaire and Rogers were inspired by an invention of the Disney animators? Since RKO courted Disney for several years prior to taking over the distribution of Disney's films in 1936, there may well have been more contact between performers and crews of the two studios than historians today commonly realize.

In 1935, the year of *Cock o' the Walk*'s release, Astaire and Rogers co-starred in two hit film musicals: *Roberta* (set among White Russian émigrés in Paris) and—probably their most famous film—*Top Hat* (which earned the second largest gross worldwide of any Hollywood film that year). In fact, the story of *Top Hat*, which revolves around Ginger's mistakenly thinking that Fred is married, when, in fact, he's single, could well have provided a kind of reverse inspiration for the explosive conclusion to the champ's romance with Prunella, with the revelation that he's a married rooster. And do the cartoon choreography's art deco backbends for Prunella in her dances with the champ and another cock named Hick reflect something of the melting, Russian-style backbend for Rogers in the "Smoke Gets in Your Eyes" adagio with Astaire in *Roberta*? The production schedules of the various films leave open the possibility of influence. The Disney cartoon initiated its story development in January of 1935; the animation didn't

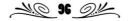

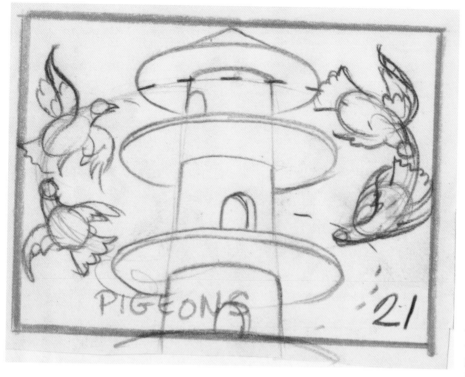

Another homage to Busby Berkeley. In the film, the pigeons shown circling the three-tiered coop here assemble themselves into a circle of courting males who puff out their chests in front and their tails behind to form hearts as the females fly in a circle overhead.

begin until May and wasn't complete until October. *Roberta* was given its world première on March 8, 1935. *Top Hat* wasn't released until September of 1935; however, Astaire would have been working out the dances with his frequent collaborator, choreographer Hermes Pan, and then teaching them to Rogers on the RKO lot much earlier. We may never know, exactly; what matters is to realize how well versed the Disney animators were in the Hollywood dance culture of their era and how skilled they already were in depicting such a variety of dance styles.

The marvelous animation (by Bill Tytla) for the Champ and Prunella in the carioca adheres to Astaire's requirements that dancers always be filmed full-figure and that a dance be shot from beginning to end with few, if any, cuts, to maintain the choreography intact. Meanwhile, in the spirit of Berkeley, the "camera angles" through which we perceive the action shift fluidly—a feat accomplished entirely through drawing.

THE ROAD TO *FANTASIA* ● The Silly Symphonies constitute in every way an extraordinary body of work, and have been recognized as such ever since the 1930s. Merritt and Kaufman note the popular and critical success the series enjoyed:

> Silly Symphonies won the Academy Award for cartoon shorts for every year the Awards were offered in the 1930s [seven in total], with as many as three Silly Symphonies nominated each year....Symphonies and Mickey Mouse shorts were the only American cartoons honored in international film festivals during the 1930s. Mickey Mouse cartoons, it should be added, although always the bread and butter that paid for the Symphonies, never won an Oscar.

Imitation being the sincerest form of flattery, the Silly Symphonies also provoked a host of imitators, who could not resist emulating the series's irresistible title, including Warner Bros.' Looney Tunes and Merrie Melodies, and MGM's Happy Harmonies and Color Rhapsodies.

For Walt Disney himself, I think, the Silly Symphonies, despite their numerous achievements, were more a means to an end than an end in themselves, and that end was feature animation. In this sense, all Silly Symphonies lead to *Fantasia*. Disney music historian Ross Care, whose 1970s essay "Cinesymphony: Music and Animation at the Disney Studio 1928–42" is perhaps the single most influential statement on the subject, chronicles the Symphonies according to the various musical-theater genres they showcase and upon which they draw: operetta, vaudeville, bandstand anthologies of concert music, jazz dance—and, again and again, ballet. In my view, *Fantasia* should really be considered the ultimate, summarizing Symphony, the culmination of a decade's investigations that broadened and deepened the power of moving drawings to create the illusion of life—and the illusion of dancing—and the ultimate proof of the remarkable seriousness that produced all that glorious silliness.

OPPOSITE PAGE: *An inspirational sketch of Mickey Mouse axing a relentlessly advancing broom in* "The Sorcerer's Apprentice" *sequence of* Fantasia. *In the finished film, this event occurs entirely in noirish silhouette. Courtesy the Cowan Collection (Jenny and Robert Cowan).* ABOVE: *A publicity image of the milkweed ballet in* Fantasia's "Nutcracker Suite." *This image, as such, doesn't occur in the film; however, it conveys the mood of the milkweed sequence.* LEFT: *George Balanchine, Igor Stravinsky, Disney animator T. Hee, and Walt Disney examine animators' models of the characters in* Fantasia's "Dance of the Hours" *during a 1939 visit that Balanchine and Stravinsky made to the studio. T. Hee was the director of the* "Dance of the Hours" *sequence.*

The English word *cartoon*, meaning an illustration associated with the comics pages of newspapers, dates from the 1880s; it referred especially to drawn caricatures with a political dimension. However, according to the Oxford English Dictionary, the first documented appearance of the word in English is much older: 1671, the year in which the British diarist John Evelyn, a London contemporary of one of the greatest diarists of them all, Samuel Pepys, met the master woodcarver Grinling Gibbons and noted, "I perceived him [Gibbons] carving that large cartoon, or crucifix, of Tintoretto." Evelyn was using *cartoon* here in the sense that art historians and some artists still use it too: to mean a design, usually drawn (though, in Gibbons's case, carved), that provides a kind of blueprint made to underlie and therefore guide the creation of an image in another medium—oil painting, tapestry, mosaic, mural, woodcarving. In this sense, a "cartoon" is not the finished product but an intermediate stage on the way to something else. This may help to explain why the later usage of *cartoon* to mean a newspaper illustration and, after that, an animated film, carries within it a patronizing undertone, even though some cartoons—such as those produced by the Disney studio in the 1930s—were at least as intensively worked and as finely finished as some of the murals and mosaics being simultaneously created in public spaces across the United States under the auspices of the Works Progress Administration.

Mickey Mouse inadvertently demonstrates an attitude allongée position in the course of showing off his prowess at speed skating in the 1935 short On Ice.

Nevertheless, the idea that a cartoon refers outward from itself—either to another, more finished work or to an original target of satire or caricature—is embedded in the word. Furthermore, at the Disney studio, that idea of a reference you don't actually see was made quite literal in several ways. As Frank Thomas and Ollie Johnston explain in *The Illusion of Life*, their authoritative history of Disney animation, the pursuit of persuasive representation of movement and physicality by Disney artists took several forms. The animators sketched their own faces as they adopted expressions associated with specific emotions. They sketched one another performing movement they needed for their characters (as in the photograph of animators dancing on this page). They sketched other live models—human, animal, vegetable, or mineral—in the studio. (Once formal classes in life drawing were inaugurated with Don Graham and other teachers, ballet dancers frequently served as models for the artists.). They made models of characters in a given pose, and used the models to develop other poses and attitudes. They analyzed and sketched sequences of live-action films, including the dancelike turns of such stars as Charlie Chaplin. And they made selective use of a machine called a rotoscope, a device whose function for the Disney animators has sometimes been misunderstood. Invented by Max Fleischer—the artist, animator, founder of the animation studio that bore his name, and a self-taught prodigy of drawing and a genius of mechanical invention—the rotoscope, developed in 1915 and patented in 1917, was a kind of light table that permitted the animators to trace individual frames of a live-action film projected onto glass. Eventually, the rotoscope machine itself was abandoned in favor of photostats (paper copies) of individual frames of film, which the animators could affix like animation paper to pegs on their desks and riffle through like flip books to check their own efforts at animating movement in people, animals, and lively, so-called inanimate objects.

In *The Illusion of Life*, Thomas and Johnston explain the uses and limitations of these cinematic and photographic references. Always, the ultimate goal is Walt Disney's: to arrange what are essentially abstract lines and colors so that they connect with an audience emotionally:

ABOVE: *Story sketch—including action lines to signify energetic motion—of Daisy Duck in a Charleston step and Donald Duck struttin' and Truckin'.*

Although Donald Duck's stardom at Disney was long established by the time the studio released *Mr. Duck Steps Out* in June 1940, it was lonely up there at top. In this picture—Daisy Duck's formal debut film (the character had first appeared as Donna Duck in the 1937 short *Don Donald*)—Donald gained a permanent love interest, and he got the girl by *dancing*. Donald dances the jitterbug, to be precise, with elements of other popular dances of the era mixed in. One of them was a step known as "Truckin'," in which, according to the excellent Web site on the history of swing dance founded by competition dancer and teacher Sonny Watson, "the main feature . . . is the shoulders, which rise and fall as the dancers move towards each other while the forefinger points up and wiggles back and forth, like a windshield wiper." Watson describes the result as "the strutting walk done when one is happy and joyful"—a walk performed "slightly pigeon-toed" in a shuffling rhythm; and he explains that some dance historians trace it back to the performances of the white minstrel Thomas Dartmouth (T. D.) "Daddy" Rice (most famous for his

character Jump Jim Crow, based on the 1828 song of the same name) in Louisville, Kentucky, during the 1830s.

Truckin' only took off for the general public, however, in the late 1920s in Harlem, where it was associated with entertainer Dewey "Pigmeat" Markham, a headliner at the Apollo Theater. By the mid-1930s, the dance had reached London, Duke Ellington and his band had recorded at least three "Truckin'" tunes, and the motif had been featured in many films and cabaret shows (including shows at Harlem's Cotton Club and at Radio City Music Hall). And Truckin' is just one element in the dance that Donald and Daisy perform—with intermittent interruptions by Donald's three increasingly mischievous nephews—in Daisy's living room. Every step and posture they do has a name and a history.

Any dance aficionado who looks at the cartoon will know that the dancing of the cartoon characters had to be choreographed, because the steps are rendered in such detail and the rhythmic continuity is so beautifully sustained. Yet it turns out that the story of the dancers

behind the ducks shared a drama beyond the dance's creation, a story that began early in 1923, when Walt Disney was still living in his native Kansas City, Missouri, striving to break into the cartoon industry and dreaming of going to Hollywood.

Enraptured by Max Fleischer's Out of the Inkwell series of film shorts, which introduced cartoon characters into a live-action world, Walt Disney made a film, with the help of a group of other artists, called *Alice's Wonderland*, based on his childhood fascination with Lewis Carroll's books, in which a real child actress was introduced into a cartoon world. It wasn't Walt Disney's first effort at animation, but it was his most ambitious to date. The actress who personified the title character was four years old. Her name was Virginia Davis, and she was already a professional: as historians J. B. Kaufman and Russell Merritt explain, Walt Disney had discovered her in a Kansas City Film Ad Company advertisement for Warneker's Bread. Later the same year, an impoverished young Walt Disney traveled to California with *Alice's Wonderland* wrapped up in a tin, and he found a distributor for the film, as well backing to make a series based on Alice. Disney wrote to Virginia Davis's mother back in Kansas City and offered her daughter a contract, which they accepted, and they moved out to California to join Disney (Mr. Davis followed later) in his pursuit of his dreams. Eventually, other children were added to some of the Alice pictures, and several other young actresses replaced the lovely Miss Davis—and, as time went on, she ventured beyond his radar range altogether.

Davis re-emerged in the late 1930s, grown, still very lovely, and an applicant for a job at the Disney studio in the all-women ink-and-paint department, and she landed the position. A year or two later, when (as a company press release puts it in the zippy lingo of the era) "a call went out for studio jitterbugs to do some rug-cutting for artists working on 'Mr. Duck Steps Out,' a short production in which Donald Duck and his girl friend, Daisy, are shown as super hep-cats," Davis was chosen to go before the cameras as a live-action reference model with, as her partner, Garland Ladd, described in the release as "number 1 jitterbug of the Disney traffic department." The cartoon heart that appears on the title card of the short, then, expresses Disney's personal affection for the human dancer hidden behind Daisy as well as Donald's public affection for Daisy. (Between the mid-1920s and the mid-1940s Davis also appeared, often as a dancer, in nearly a dozen live-action features for other studios, including King Vidor's 1931 *Street Scene*, Gregory Ratoff's 1942 *Footlight Serenade*, and George Sidney's 1946 *The Harvey Girls*.)

There is a fair amount of dancing, especially for the animated figures, in Walt Disney's Alice Comedies. In the main, the movement is set to jigs and reels and consists of rather basic stamps and hops, but, as with the jitterbug in *Mr. Duck Steps Out*, the inspiration and mood are joyful. (For the 2005 DVD release of some of the Alice films, which were originally silent, Alexander Rannie created original scores for a an ensemble that replicated a typical small-town silent-movie–theater orchestra, based on extensive study of period music for cartoons in Germany and the U.S.) The music for *Mr. Duck Steps Out* was composed by Charles Wolcott, who worked for Disney and then MGM from 1937 to 1958.

During the later 1940s and the 1950s, jitterbugs figured in other Disney animated pictures, most notably in the "All the Cats Join In" section of the 1946 anthology *Make Mine Music*, in which the dancers are human rather than animals. However, the less well-known *Mr. Duck Steps Out* is the most charming example I have seen of that particular dance in the Disney catalogue.

ABOVE: *Virginia Davis and Garland Ladd, the live-action reference models for the 1940 Donald Duck short* Mr. Duck Steps Out, *trip the light fantastic in a posed publicity shot. Both worked at the Disney studio, and Davis, as a small child, had also starred in Walt Disney's earliest Alice Comedies.* RIGHT: *Story sketch showing Donald and Daisy truckin' in tandem for* Mr. Duck Steps Out.

Whenever we stayed too close to the photostats, or directly copied even a tiny piece of human action, the results looked very strange. The moves appeared real enough, but the figure lost the illusion of life. There was a certain authority in the movement and a presence that came out of the whole action, but it was impossible to become emotionally involved with this eerie, shadowy creature who was never a real inhabitant of our fantasy world.

Not until we realized that photographs must be redrawn in animatable shapes (our proven tools of communicating) were we able to transfer this knowledge to cartoon animation. It was not the photographed action of an actor's swelling cheek that mattered, it was the animated cheek in our drawings that had to communicate. Our job was to make the cartoon figure go through the same movements as the live actor, with the same timing and the same staging, but, because animatable shapes called for a difference in proportions, the figure and its model could not do things in exactly the same way. The actor's movements had to be reinterpreted in the world of our designs and shapes and forms.

Other animation studios used live-action films in conjunction with the rotoscope as well; however, at Disney—inspired by the boss's obsession for excellence and supported by the resources and manpower necessary to realize it—the tracings these rotoscoped films helped to produce were not ends in themselves. Rather, long before digital video and computer animation, the rotoscope images served the artists as vehicles for what we would now call "motion capture": they showed the continuity of muscular exertion or minute physical changes within the figure during an action, thereby permitting the animators to exaggerate details in line with their own conceptions of the characters and story without losing the truth of the action's energy and motivation. Furthermore, as the animators grew increasingly sophisticated at planning camera angles for specific scenes in the live-action films, according to what they wanted to accomplish in their art, the photostats and rotoscoped images served as visual references for changes in dimension and proportion as figures moved closer to and farther from the camera lens (which is the stand-in for the viewer's eye). Even so, as Thomas and Johnston explain, for the true realization of the "illusion of life," the camera alone is not sufficient:

No one knows for sure why a pencil tracing of a live-action figure should look so stiff and unnatural on the screen, unless there simply is no reality in a copy. The animators had learned this in art classes, but, somehow, studying film of a moving model made them think that live action was different. The camera certainly records what is there, but it records *everything* that is there, with an impartial lack of emphasis. On the other hand, an artist shows what he sees is there, especially

that which might not be perceived by others. His drawings can be closer to the true realism of an object because he can be selective and personal in what he chooses to show. From the photostats, the animator chooses only those actions that relate to the point of his particular scene; then he strengthens those until they become the dominant action, with everything else either eliminated or subordinated. What appears on the screen is a simple, strong, direct statement that has clarity and vitality. The spirit and life have been gained by adapting the human form to an artist's own designs, the shapes and forms that he uses in reaching an audience. This is no more than what artists always have done.

When the Disney animators had grown so experienced and so deeply knowledgeable that they were aching to improve on reality in the service of art, the use of photostated frames from a live-reference film, rather than the film itself, made them feel free:

> Animators always had the feeling they were nailed to the floor when their whole sequences were shot ahead of time in live action. Everyone's imagination as to how a scene might be staged was limited by the placement of the camera, for once a scene had been shot it was very hard to switch to a whole new point of view—even though in animation it is quite easy to hang the camera from a star, or a nearby cloud, or let it drift with the breeze wherever it is needed.

Where the live-action references could be of special usefulness to an animator, however, was for scenes involving dance. From the 1930s on, many dancers—famous and not—as well as living flora

ABOVE: *Animators draw dancer Helene Stanley, the live-action reference model for Aurora, on a mockup set for the 1959 feature* Sleeping Beauty. OPPOSITE: *In this cel setup, barefoot Aurora, on high 7/8 pointe, dances with her forest friends as they inhabit Prince Phillip's hat, cape, and boots.*

and fauna, lent their physicality to the Disney enterprise, as did knowledgeable nondancers who obligingly put themselves through the paces. When you see the title character of Disney's 1958 *Sleeping Beauty* walk barefoot through a forest, you are seeing a trace of the live-action reference ballet dancer and frequent Disney art-class model Helene Stanley, who provided that gait and certain physical traits of the character, such as her tiny waist and slender ankles.

When you see the vaudevillian crows in *Dumbo*, you are glimpsing the choreography and improvisations of the irresistibly charming Jackson Brothers, an African American dance duo, whose bravura tapping and amusing use of props kept them working steadily in theaters and cabaret on the West Coast during much of the twentieth century. (See sidebar page 141.)

When you watch the thistle Cossacks performing a deep-knee Russian *kazatchka* in the "Russian Dance" segment of *Fantasia*, you are privy to the afterlives in excelsis of humble weeds that the unsung Disney artists Sylvia Moberly-Holland (in charge of the story department for "The Nutcracker Suite"), Bianca Majolie, and Ethel Kulsar discovered trembling in vacant lots near the studio and wittily transformed, through drawing, into vigorous dancers. British Disney historian Robin Allan

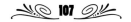

An inspirational watercolor of an Orchid Girl being partnered by a Cossack thistle in Fantasia's *"Nutcracker Suite" section. Although this is technically a character (that is, theatrical folk) dance, the lady is on pointe, thanks to her tapering stems; a* kokoshnik, *or traditional Russian headdress, has been wittily suggested by the petal that serves her as a head.*

believes, as he writes in *Walt Disney and Europe*, that the presence of these women contributed to the feminine element in "The Nutcracker Suite" that is "absent from the rest of the film. Power imagery (podia, rocks, mountains, trees) is lacking, and camera movement is predominantly lateral and horizontal, not vertical. The animation is circular, oval, elliptical."

When you see the sultry ballerina carp, sinuously veiling herself with her own transparent fins, in the underwater "Arab Dance" section of "The Nutcracker Suite" in *Fantasia* (a title suggested by the picture's on-camera conductor, Leopold Stokowski, in place of the working title, *The Concert Feature*), you are seeing a fish's motion overlaid with the ghostly undulations of Middle Eastern dancer "Princess Omar," as well as the choreography of dancer Joyce Coles—who, in fact, may have been the princess as well, as is suggested by an in-house "Concert Feature" memo

of December 2, 1938. (In this case, the double or triple vision, characteristic of the very best Disney animation, was caught for posterity by animators Don Lusk and Sandy Strothers.)

When you see Ben Ali Gator partner Hyacinth Hippo in the "Dance of the Hours" in *Fantasia*, you aren't only witnessing the influence of earlier animal satirists, such as Heinrich Kley and T. S. Sullivan, on Walt Disney and some of his staff (such as James Bodrero, a concept artist in Disney's Character Model Department, and animator John Lounsbery, both of whom worked on the alligators), but also the muscularity and schooling of a brilliant teenaged dancer named Louis Hightower, fused with the dancing of the de Basil Original Ballet Russe dancer David Lichine.

Thomas and Johnston discuss the challenge to animator Les Clark as he worked on the "entertainment" scene in the 1937 *Snow White and the Seven Dwarfs*,

ABOVE: *Ballerina fish in the "Arab Dance" in* Fantasia's *"Nutcracker Suite." The use of her undulating fin as a veil was based on live-action reference film of a Middle Eastern dance.* BELOW: *Model sheet for flower dancers in* Fantasia's *"Nutcracker Suite."*

FLOWER BALLET SKETCHES
FANTASIA
• F-128 •

in which the Dwarfs lift the spirits of the heroine with music played on fantasy instruments and a combination of vaudevillian hoofing, variations on the one-step, and square dancing. At one point, Snow White is simultaneously partnered by Sneezy and Dopey, when Sneezy hoists Dopey onto his shoulders and covers them both with his oversized coat, thereby converting the twosome into a single figure tall enough to look Snow White in the eye and easily take her hand. In the course of their discussion of this scene, Thomas and Johnston describe how the animators reproduced the visual effect of watching figures move "near" or "back away," changing the Dwarfs' height and orientation in space so as to replicate the perceptions that viewers would have of them if they were actually in the room:

> Les Clark was given the scene to animate of the three dwarfs dancing with Snow White—the only long shot that showed the dimension of the dwarfs' room and the scale of the characters through their movement. Animating the decrease in the girl's size as she moved away from the camera was controlled by working from the live action film, but the matching perspectives of the dwarfs that Les animated from imagination made the scene amazingly convincing and added credence to the whole sequence.

Finally, Thomas and Johnston go on to link the animators' concern with the presentation of dancing to their presentation of choreography:

Dancers whose art contributed to the dancing of Hyacinth Hippo and Ben Ali Gator, stars of Fantasia's *"Dance of the Hours."* ABOVE: *Teenagers Louis Hightower and Marjorie Belcher (later Marge Champion), photographed for a spread on her in* LIFE *magazine. Champion's choreography is showcased in the finished film, and Hightower's physique and personal style of movement are clearly demonstrated in the Ben Ali Gator character.* BELOW: *De Basil's Original Ballet Russe stars David Lichine and Tatiana Riabouchinska in a publicity photograph. This pair also were filmed for the "Two Silhouettes" section of the 1946 anthology,* Make Mine Music.

Any dancing scenes in a story should be shot early and planned throughout the musical number, rather than handed out piecemeal when an animator needs them. Obviously the choreography will be richer if a dancer plans it all, instead of leaving it up to the unresolved fantasies of some storyman. In the scene Les had, there was a special problem with Snow White's hand positions. Just how high can a dwarf reach up comfortably to dance with a young girl? The height of each dwarf had to be planned, not in relation to the girl doing the live action but to her cartoon proportions, derived from the photostats of her dancing. For the scene to be effective, it was important that the dwarfs should not strain or be awkward as they reached to take her hand. Fortunately, with Ham Luske shooting the live action, all such details were carefully covered.

But Snow White's body and movement were not entirely products of artistic imagination—and neither were the movements of the Dwarfs or the prince, who was embodied for the Disney animators in reference films by Louis Hightower, the same young dancer who would go on to serve as a model for Ben Ali Gator. (Hightower enjoyed a promising stage career afterward, which was cut short when he joined the service and then was killed in Sicily during World War II.) For the

TOP: *In the Dwarfs' entertainment scene from the finished* Snow White, *Dopey stands on the shoulders of Sneezy to dance with the heroine—a figure for whom tall Disney composer Oliver Wallace stood in to dance with Marjorie Belcher (Marge Champion) in the live-action reference film.* ABOVE: *A frame of Champion and Wallace in a maneuver from the reference film.*

An inspirational watercolor, probably by artist Lee Blair, of Ben Ali Gator throwing off his cape with a flamenco-like flourish as he spots the delicious Hyacinth Hippo in Fantasia's *"Dance of the Hours." Courtesy the Cowan Collection (Jenny and Robert Cowan).*

heroine of *Snow White and The Seven Dwarfs*, live-action reference films exist in the Disney archives, and they feature the young dancer Marjorie Belcher, who went on to become famous as Marge Champion, one half of a celebrated dance partnership with Gower Champion, whom she met when they were both in junior high school and to whom she was married from 1947 to 1973. Long before that, though, in 1934, when she was barely fourteen, Marjorie Belcher was working for Disney. She had grown up in the Los Angeles dance studio of her distinguished father, Ernest Belcher, ballet teacher to the stars (Gower Champion, Shirley Temple, Maria Tallchief, Carmelita Maracci, Mary Pickford, and John Barrymore, among them), as well as to many other professional dancers—(including Louis Hightower) and choreographer for such movies as Al Jolson's *The Jazz Singer* and Lon Chaney's *Phantom of the Opera*. Champion, a precociously gifted dancer herself, began studying ballet with her father when she was five and teaching ballet for him from the age of twelve. Gower Champion's biographer, John Anthony Gilvey, relates how she got to Disney:

> From age eight, Marge spent nearly all her afternoons at her father's school learning ballet, tap, Spanish dancing, and acrobatics. Soon she was conducting

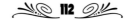

evening classes for working women and appearing as a dancer in the Los Angeles Civic Opera productions of *Blossom Time* and *The Student Prince*. This led to her first break on the legitimate stage, performing opposite her handsome partner, Louis Hightower, in *Tonight at 8:30*. One evening a talent scout saw the five-foot-two, 102-pound thirteen-year-old and was taken with her flawless performance, piquant quality, and lovely face. His endorsement led Walt Disney to sign her and Louis as the models for Snow White and Prince Charming. . . .

At Disney, Champion worked as a live-action dance reference for cartoon characters who have since become immortal, devising spontaneous movement for herself or directing others in her own choreography at the request of various animating directors, according to what the animators needed to analyze. Much of this film was preserved, and excerpts can be found on DVDs of *Snow White* and *Fantasia*, in which Champion contributed her dancing, by way of reference films, to the inverted white blossom that slides over the waterfall during "Dance of the Reed Flutes" in "The Nutcracker Suite" and to both the ostriches and Hyacinth Hippo in "Dance of the Hours." Her choreography—with fans and other props—for a corps de ballet of female students from the Belcher studio was a major reference for the dancing of the ostriches (which, from the start, Champion called "the storks"

A Lee Blair story sketch of Hyacinth Hippo being partnered enthusiastically in arabesque on pointe by Ben Ali Gator in "Dance of the Hours." Lee Blair was married to Disney inspirational artist Mary Blair. Courtesy the Cowan Collection (Jenny and Robert Cowan).

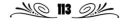

because of their outsized, elongated toe shoes), the hippopotamuses, the elephants, and the pas de deux for Hyacinth and Ben Ali Gator.

Champion's role as a live-action reference model for the "Dance of the Reed Flutes" in "The Nutcracker Suite" is put in context by *Fantasia* historian John Culhane, who, in the following passage, describes Walt Disney's overall concept, articulated in a story meeting; the moment in the finished animation; the live dancers' contribution; and the process of turning flowers into dancers—an idea that had been kicking around the studio for years before *Fantasia* was conceived in the form of a projected Silly Symphony known as *Ballet des Fleurs* ("Flower Ballet"), possibly in keeping with Walt Disney's affection for the ballet pastels of Frenchman Edgar Degas:

> In the Disney version of "Dance of the Reed Flutes," inverted blossoms wafted by a breeze suggest ballerinas with gauzy bell-shaped skirts. That was the way Walt saw them when he looked at some flower sketches.
>
> "Those little flowers," he said, "I see no reason why they can't dance right on the water. If you throw a flower blossom on the water it floats; they could skim right on the water; it would make a beautiful setup. . . . When those little blossoms land on the water it's almost like the wind is blowing them around; just like the little things are dancing, but really the wind is blowing them. Then in the end—that boom—they all go over something and disappear."
>
> As it reached the screen, a white flower landed on a stream in a pattern of swirling movement that is one of the loveliest in *Fantasia*. It is carried ahead of the multicolored flowers, like a solo dancer accompanied by a colorful chorus. Cy Young, an effects animator with a feeling for the abstract, did this scene, and he also whirled the blossoms toward the camera and—boom—over a waterfall, which turned out to be the 'something they all go over and disappear.
>
> Considerable live-action film was shot for this dance, performed by two professional dancers, Joyce Coles and Marjorie Belcher. Miss Belcher had already modeled for Snow White and for the Blue Fairy in *Pinocchio*. For this dance she and Miss Coles were costumed in long tulle ballet skirts that resembled the shape of the blossoms that were to skim across the water. The difference between that live action and the animation that resulted is the difference between dancing on a stage and dancing on water.

This passage provides an excellent example of the way an idea in an animated Disney picture—usually Walt Disney's idea—was realized by a team of individuals who brought a variety of gifts and skills into a common focus. However, an important team member unmentioned here was the Hungarian-born artist and photographer Jules Engel (1909–2003), who worked on *Fantasia* as an uncredited consultant for choreography. Engel was not a dancer. He had a gift for abstract design, however;

and, upon seeing a performance of *Swan Lake* when he was still in high school, he developed a career-long passion for dance and spoke of it as a major influence on him as an artist. (In an essay entitled "Reflections: Graphic Choreography," he names Martha Graham, Merce Cunningham, and George Balanchine as the choreographers who inspired ideas in him concerning rhythm in his own art.) It was Engel's pastels on black paper that inspired the animators of the "Russian Dance" to use glamorous black for the background. And when you see the moment in the "Dance of the Hours" when the huge feet in pointe shoes—framing the scene like the sides of a theater's proscenium arch—suddenly burst into a classical *échappé* (a step in which the heels are quickly brought flat on the floor in ballet's crossed fifth position and then spring apart to an open position on full pointe), you are seeing the imagination of Jules Engel, who, nondancer though he was, knew enough about ballet technique that he would occasionally jump up and demonstrate it for his colleagues. Disney historian Robin Allan quotes from a February 1976 interview that Engel gave to *Millimetre* magazine in which Engel, speaking of how he would churn out "up to 50 pictures for a one minute movement" to demonstrate his ideas for the various sections of *Fantasia*, declares: "Miraculously, many of my original conceptions—for example, the pure black backgrounds on the low-angle perspectives on the twirling Russian flowers—and the choreography on the Chinese and Russian Dance [sic] actually survived into the finished product." Engel adds that his own fluid, restless way of making marks on paper—and the styles of some of his colleagues as well— were strongly influenced by the gestural drawing of the nineteenth-century French satirical caricaturist Honoré Daumier. "Although his drawings didn't move, you can *see* movement," Engel explained.

This is hardly to say, though, that Engel was *entirely* responsible for the choreography in these sections, or even that he contributed more to them than some self-contained moments or effects. Before a single cel is animated, thousands of decisions have to be made about the concept of a sequence, the color palette and atmosphere, the evolution of the action, the construction and relationship of the characters, and many other elements. Take, for instance, the beloved "Chinese Dance" in "The Nutcracker Suite." Although the animation of the dance is attributed to Art Babbitt, one of Disney's top animators, well before Babbitt addressed his pencils a tremendous amount of work had been done on the dance by many others. Set to the Tchaikovsky music known to dancers as "Tea" from the second act of the composer's full-length 1892 ballet *The Nutcracker*, the Disney "Chinese Dance" is

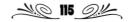

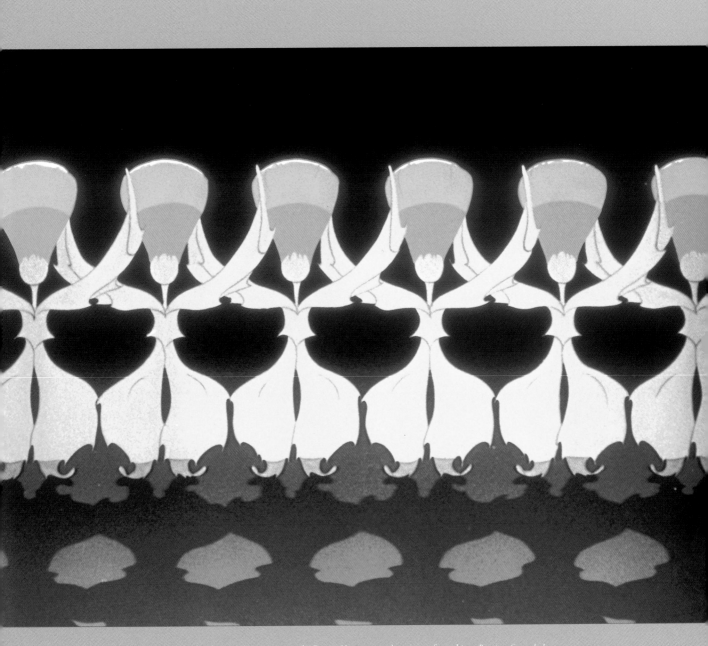

Thistles, discovered growing near the Disney Hyperion studio, as transformed into Russian Cossack dancers in Fantasia's "Nutcracker Suite." Note the black background, an idea attributed to artist Jules Engel.

performed by a corps of tall mushrooms and one little soloist mushroom, identified in the *Fantasia* program as "Hop Low and the Mushroom Dancers." Among the myriad interpretations of *The Nutcracker*, this vision of "Tea" remains both original and unique. (In traditional ballet productions, the number is danced by a soloist or a small group of dancers dressed in Chinese-style embroidered jackets and sometimes sporting pigtails.) In this instance of Disney choreography, the dance and the dancers were entirely the product of nondancing artists and storymen—as a dance fan might guess, since the round bodies of the dancing mushrooms cannot twist and bend articulately the way creatures with bones and joints do. It was Walt Disney himself who suggested that the "Chinese Dance" be cast entirely with mushrooms; in an earlier scenario, the mushrooms had been mere lamplighting supernumeraries, while vaguely Asian lizards danced for a frog mandarin.

Hop Low, the continually out-of-step star of the number, was indelibly brought to life by Babbitt, a brilliant specialist in animating dancelike motion (and, for less than a year, Marjorie Belcher's husband). In Culhane's history of the film, *Walt Disney's Fantasia,* researched and written while Disney and his colleagues were still alive, Culhane asked Babbitt how Hop Low's dance was developed. "'He developed in many ways,' said Babbitt," who continued:

> For instance, the anticipation for his steps at the beginning of the dance is almost a direct swipe—although you may never have recognized it—from these three zanys who keep slapping each other all around—the Three Stooges. One of the Three Stooges always did a funny little action where the knees overlap. When he would get angry he would do this little furious step, with his knees crossing, one over the other. And instead of just an ordinary anticipation, I used this, because the music called for a trill. So during the trill, he did this little anticipatory act.
>
> Also, the music dictated certain things. I don't know a hell of a lot about music, but there is a phrase that is stated once: there's a statement. Then I think it's repeated, the same phrase. Then there's an answer, I don't remember if it's repeated once or twice. And then they come back to the original line of music. So that gave me the architecture.

Babbitt's studiously colloquial language belies his highly focused, almost scholarly attention to Tchaikovsky's music. As Culhane writes:

> To work out the choreography, Babbitt drew with a music score pinned to his desk, so that he could relate the action not only to the melodic line, but also the counterpoint—"those nasty little notes underneath." For instance, in the "Chinese Dance," Babbitt explains, "there's a bass underneath. So something has to be related to that, too. So, as I played the music over and over again, and studied the sheet,

I began to 'see' what is happening. I can actually *see* it. When you have 'Buh-buh-buh-buh,' that's the little guy coming forward; and then it repeats, and he goes backward."

Al Zinnen, the layout man, "planned the overall *ideal* composition," said Babbitt, "but you can't stick with that, because your characters are moving around constantly, and what might be a composition for one bit of action doesn't necessarily fit a succeeding bit of action. And your camera is not nailed down. In effect, you are the camera.

"The only choreographic suggestion I ever got came from Walt Disney himself. I had animated the little mushroom taking his bow on the last note of music. Walt suggested he take the bow after. Both ways would have worked, depending on one's translation of the little guy's character."

One of the most remarkable things about the way the Disney Studio worked in the early days was its relative absence of bureaucratic hierarchy. Walt and his leading animators respected good ideas, and welcomed them from any quarter. As Babbitt notes, an animator could improve upon—in effect contradicting—a supervising layout artist. Even a hired reference-footage dancer could exert a decisive influence on the final animation. Marge Champion avers that it was her idea for the animators and directors working on "Dance of the Hours" to consider using the "Water Nymph Ballet" that George Balanchine devised for Vera Zorina, William Dollar, and members of the American Ballet in the 1938 movie *The Goldwyn Follies* as a model for the set and some of the action in the sequence. In the "Water Nymph Ballet," Balanchine indulges himself in a quasi-mystical glorification of his star dancer (Balanchine was deeply in love with Zorina at the time and married her soon after) as a goddess who emerges from a pool like a statue by Brancusi, and then comes to flesh-and-blood life as a ballerina. The setting is a columned rotunda with a giant white statue of a rearing horse; the locale seems to be Mount Olympus by way of Rodeo Drive. The number teeters perilously on the edge of unintentional humor, even camp, but never tips over: the whole sequence is imbued with a touching seriousness that makes it look like a vision. And that seriousness was translated to "Dance of the Hours," along with Balanchine's set elements, even as the *Follies*' human dancers were replaced by ostriches, hippos, elephants, and alligators. The choice of tone came from the top, from Disney himself, who told his team during a story meeting:

"Let's take these animals, screwy as they are," he said at the story conference, "and stage this all as legitimate, and done as a perfect ballet. . . . Later, then, let the slips come, rather than in the beginning."

[Story director] Joe Grant got his point. "Don't be blinded by gags."

"The whole incongruity of the thing," said Walt, "is the elephants and hippos doing what graceful people do. Of course, they can use natural props like their trunks."

Ultimately, of course, it was Disney's artists who were responsible for fulfilling the boss's brief, and translating the seriousness of Balanchine's vision to the animated realm. Some of the artists were self-confessed balletomanes, and all were intent on doing their best to suggest classical art through a modern prism. Culhane credits the head of layout, Kendall O'Connor, who worked with two main background painters under T. Hee's direction, with the classical setting for the ballet, the oddly impersonal—almost de Chirico–like—Greek Revival structure, a luxe aerie that seems to be perched on a mountain peak, its semicircular stone colonnade and pool commanding a sky vacant of everything but blushes of color to indicate the setting sun. (Robin Allan quotes Jack Caldwell, the Disney storyman on "Dance of the Hours," who apparently may also have appeared in some of the reference footage, to the effect that the designs for the background were inspired by the theories and stage designs of Gordon Craig and Robert Edmond Jones.)

In the course of the "Dance of the Hours" ballet, the animators make use of those columns for some wonderful gags. And the subtle yet steadily deepening tones of the sky help to focus the audience's attention on the dancing animals as well as remind us that this is, in fact, a ballet about the passage of time in a day: the music, from the third act of Amilcare Ponchielli's 1876 opera *La Gioconda*, originally accompanied a choreographic pageant featuring ballerina Virginia Zucchi and a quartet of sylphs (woodland sprites) who danced in a beam of electric light in the celebrated staging of choreographer Luigi Manzotti. Allan relates how, with the help of a scale model of the set and models of the characters, "Bob Jones, who worked in the Character Model Department under Joe Grant and with [Disney inspirational artist] Albert Hurter, designed a special lighting rig that matched the passing of the daylight hours. He calibrated the sun by light on a tracer which gave meticulous detailing of the shadows cast throughout the day." In conceiving the dance's structure, the animating team further devised a principal geometry for each section: awakening ballerina ostriches greet the dawn with their vertical necks and horizontal pointe shoes; sultry ballerina hippopotamuses usher in midday with elliptical figures and circular movements; giddy ballerina elephants greet the sunset with sinuous trunks and bubbles; and romantically caped, toothy alligators lust in vigorous zigzags after all of the

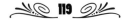

female dancers into the velvety night. As T. Hee, co-director of "Dance of the Hours," explained to Culhane:

> Ballet, of course, is an abstraction, in the way of movement, of story telling. . . 'Dance of the Hours' tried to tell the story of morning, noon, and night—and night is a time of revelry, when everything breaks down. If you just take it a little bit further, it becomes a satire. Chaplin often said that he walked a tightrope with comedy on one side and tragedy on the other; if he tipped to one side, it would be tragedy; if he tipped to the other side, it would be comedy. This was the kind of thing I was thinking of when we were doing this: that this would be comedy, because we could lean it just a little to the comedy side.

Dance critics and historians—among them Alastair Macaulay, who has written on the subject—recognized the resemblances between Balanchine's and Disney's versions of the dance decades ago, as did some leading historians of animation, such as Robin Allan in *Walt Disney and Europe*, his richly speculative study concerning artistic influences on the Disney animated features, from *Snow White* to *The Jungle Book*, that were made during Walt Disney's lifetime. No one has yet suggested, though, at least in print, that Balanchine had any direct involvement in "Dance of the Hours," although I wonder. There is a photograph in the Disney archives that shows a group including Walt Disney, Igor Stravinsky, Balanchine, and T. Hee looking at what seem to be preparatory materials for the "Hours" ballet, which is clearly storyboarded behind them. The picture must have been taken when Stravinsky and Balanchine visited the studio in December 1939, and "Dance of the Hours" was in production: it is at least possible that Balanchine may have made a comment or answered a question in a way that affected the animated ballet. And while it is true that the program's name for the leading ballerina elephant—Elephanchine—may simply have been a joke derived from the names of several prominent Russian dancers at the time, there is also a chance that it indicates actual participation by one of them. And is it also mere coincidence that in 1942 Balanchine was hired to choreograph a ballet for Ringling Brothers and Barnum and Bailey Circus for elephants and their showgirl riders, set to a commissioned score by Stravinsky called "Circus Polka"? (My speculation is not idle. A privately published 2004 memoir of life with Disney animator Bill Tytla by his wife, Adrienne, has a chapter devoted to the couple's encounters with Balanchine. It notes, for example, that when Balanchine and Stravinsky visited the Disney studio in 1939, they spoke for a time, apparently in Russian, with Tytla, a New Yorker whose parents were Ukrainian. "During their animated conversation, they jointly rejoiced in memories

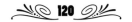

In December 1939, Igor Stravinsky and George Balanchine visited the Disney studio. In this photograph, the group seems to be amused by what they see on the movieola—in all likelihood something associated with "Dance of the Hours," which is storyboarded behind them. From left to right: Alexis Kall (friend and intermittent agent for Stravinsky), Stravinsky, Gregory Golubeff (translator and assistant to Kall), Balanchine, Walt Disney, and "Dance of the Hours" director, T. Hee.

A staged publicity photo of star Vera Zorina and members of the American Ballet who performed in George Balanchine's "Water Nymph Ballet" for The Goldwyn Follies (1938). This sequence, including the neoclassical set and lotus pool, served as a key inspiration for the choreography and set of Fantasia's "Dance of the Hours."

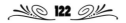

LEFT: *A frame of Vera Zorina's aquatic entrance, envisioned by choreographer George Balanchine, for the "Water Nymph Ballet." The cinematographer on* The Goldwyn Follies *was the remarkable Gregg Toland, whom Balanchine greatly admired.* BELOW: *Choreographic plan for the pas de deux of Hyacinth Hippo and Ben Ali Gator in "Dance of the Hours."*

and feelings that were profound parts of their pasts," Mrs. Tytla writes. "They not only enjoyed each other's company, there was great mutual respect between them as artists." She also recounts how, when Balanchine and Stravinsky reached the Model Department, Walt Disney "showed them the ostrich Prima Ballerina appearing in the "Dance of the Hours" ostrich ballet. 'This is Mademoiselle Upanova,' said Walt, with a grin. They didn't get it. 'Up an ova.' Walt tried again, laughing. They were polite, but hadn't the foggiest. Then they had their smiling pictures taken. Walt gave up on the gag. It was no use.")

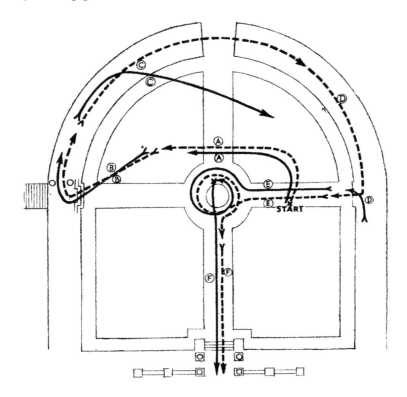

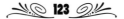

FOR SEVERAL YEARS when Marge Champion (born Marjorie Belcher) was a teenager, she served as a live-action reference model for the animators at the Walt Disney studios, which made many 16 mm films of her dancing and choreography (or as Champion modestly insists, improvisation and dance direction), performed on what she describes as "a small, not very well-equipped soundstage." What follows is an edited transcript of an oral-history interview with Champion concerning her work for Disney, from about 1934 to 1940.

I conducted this interview at the New York Public Library for the Performing Arts at Lincoln Center on July 28, 2005. The tapes and a full transcript of the entire interview, with Marge Champion's amendments, are available at the library. I have condensed the interview for this book, edited it for clarity, and included a few notes in brackets.

The interview opened with Champion displaying two photographs of herself wearing a costume for Snow White—one of the Disney characters for which Champion served as a live-action reference model.

MARGE CHAMPION (MC): I went to work for Walt Disney in September of the year that I was fourteen, so that would have been 1934.

MINDY ALOFF (MA): So you were already working for three years before *Snow White and the Seven Dwarfs* was released in 1937?

MC: It was about two years, because by the time it was released I had also worked on *Fantasia* for the hippo. And Blue Fairy. That was not as large a part and didn't take as much preparation or anything like that, but I did do the Blue Fairy in *Pinocchio* whenever they needed.

MA: Would you discuss your audition for Disney?

OPPOSITE: *Marjorie Belcher (Marge Champion), the sole live-action reference model for Snow White, wearing a glamorous version of the heroine's dress, which was not used for the film. Photos courtesy Marge Champion.*

LEFT: *Pinocchio's* Blue Fairy, *in the flesh and on the page: Champion holds a drawing based on her modeling and movement for the beneficent character. The studio's caption for this picture was: "Marge's beauty was the inspiration for* Pinocchio's *gorgeous Blue Fairy, for which she also was the live model."* ABOVE: *A moment from the finished film for the Blue Fairy and the title character, his nose now quite extended owing to his untruthfulness.*

 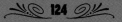

MC: I was still thirteen when I auditioned, and I wasn't yet quite at Hollywood High School. The audition, as I remember, came somewhere in February or March of that year, when I did turn fourteen. I was chosen out of my father's class by—I don't remember who it was—a talent scout for Disney to find the girl that would eventually be the live-action model for Snow White. They already had the voice, who was Adriana Caselotti, and all that had been prerecorded. When I finally got the job, I worked to her playback whenever there was a singing part to do.

However, they chose three young women from my father's school to go over to the Hyperion Studio and audition. I didn't hear from them until it was September of that year, when I had been enrolled in Hollywood High School. I remember very clearly my teacher, who was a man named Arthur Kachel at Hollywood High School, a much-beloved drama teacher. I had told him that I had this audition coming up and that I had to do something called an improvisation, and I didn't even know what that was.

So he had me get up in front of the class, and he gave me my first improv, which was really embarrassing. I had to flit around picking daisies and doing all sorts of things. There were a couple of football players in that class, and I really felt kind of uncomfortable doing it, but I did it anyway. I think he really helped me an enormous amount in getting over my schoolgirl inhibitions about just doing something. From him, it was an oral request, but when I got to the studio, they showed me storyboards, and that's when I would see what they had in mind, unless it was something that had been prerecorded by Caselotti.

MA: Storyboards?

MC: Storyboards are a mock-up of what each animator needs to expect from a script. Ham Luske was the director, at least of the sections I did. He was a very well-known animator. The animators would be assigned to certain segments [of a feature-length animated film], and so they would be on the set when they did the [live-action] filming, because they had something very definite in mind. What they had done was to make little pencil drawings,

what they called storyboards, in this case, quick drawings of what they expected. Oh, let's say the section where I was running through the forest, or the section where I was dancing with two of the Dwarfs, one on top of the other because they were so short and one of them jumped on top of the shoulders of the other one. Now, this turned out to be one of the taller animators. [*Actually it was Disney composer Oliver Wallace, who stood in as the two Dwarfs to dance with Champion in the live-action film*].

MA: So the animators had already figured out . . . ?

MC: Plot points—how to get from A to B to C to D. Now, in the case of when they were doing the Dwarfs or when they were doing the animals, they were getting the personalities and the movement by looking in mirrors that were beside their animating equipment. They would have a mirror, and they would get it out of their own personalities. I remember them telling me at the time that they had one Japanese animator [Tyrus Wong] who was assigned to several sections of Mickey Mouse cartoons, and they could tell when he had done it because, at that point, Mickey looked a little bit Asian or Japanese. The animators were so adept at identifying that they didn't even have to be told which of the animators had done that particular section.

Now, the reason they needed me—and, also, Billy Gilbert for Sneezy, who was a very well-known comic at the time—was because, they said, they couldn't get, let's say, the afterflow of my gown when we were doing turns and flitting around; they couldn't get that out of their own personalities, their own imaginations. They had to have some guideline. So all the film that was done on me was enlarged and processed by what they called rotoscoping. Rotoscoping, actually, was tracing. They felt that the audiences would not understand the process, which was a guide for their action: they didn't necessarily have to use every frame of what I did. But the words *rotoscoping* or *tracing*—they were forbidden. So I was sworn to secrecy about all that I did.

MA: Oh, no one knew about the rotoscoping?

MC: No. I didn't even know about it until many years later, at an opening of a cartoon museum in San Francisco, when they were featuring *Snow White* and they had gathered together at this cartoon museum all the animators who were still with us, and also the women who did some of the backgrounds—because, in those days, there were no women animators, only men. But women did do the inking and the backgrounds. Diane Disney was there, too, [one of Walt and Lillian Disney's daughters]. While they were getting set up to take sort of a class picture of all these people gathered at the museum, one of the men next to me said, "I'm sure glad to meet you after all these years. I certainly traced you enough times."

I said, "What?"

He said, "Yeah, rotoscoping." He took me over to the table, where he explained what rotoscoping was and all of that, and that he had been one of those who, with the blown-up films, had traced them.

But there was even a little more to it, because when my friends went to the studio, Snow White—the way she was shown to me on drawings—had really round, Betty Boop–kind of eyes with eyelashes, and she had a tiny little waist like Betty Boop. Well, by the time [the Disney staff] got around to actually showing some of the [fully animated] footage, her eyes had become almond-shaped, like mine were, and her waistline had been released a little bit, because she was supposedly just about my age.

MA: Please describe your first day on the job.

MC: They had made me a mock-up, as you see in that photograph, of the Snow White costume. In cartoon language, the head is always larger than it is on the body of a human being, at least the way they were animating in those days. So, in order for them to see, I guess, the proportions, they had taken a football helmet and punched holes in the top and had painted Snow White's hairline around it.

I was under very strong lights. Now, with this football helmet on to make my head bigger, I was doing whatever they showed me on their storyboards. Well, these are the days before air-conditioning. I nearly fainted under the lights, and I was not prone to fainting; I was a very sturdy young woman. But all I can tell you is, it was a most uncomfortable day, and it hampered my movements tremendously, because the football helmet was heavy, and I was sweating like mad underneath it.

I don't remember how many times we used that helmet, but it suddenly dawned on them that they were not getting the best out of me, especially when I was dancing around with the animators, who couldn't dance anyway, because they were imitating the Dwarfs. So they did eliminate the football helmet, and, as you see in that picture, it is my own hair, which was kind of ash blond. They didn't even darken it. That was just a picture that they took of me like they do on regular movies. They were called wardrobe shots. You usually had front, side, back snapshots of anything you wore on screen in those days, so that they would know exactly—if they had to come back a month later and match it, they would have a record of what you wore and what your makeup was like, and all of that.

A publicity or wardrobe shot of Champion in a version of Snow White's dress that is similar to the character's final animated costume. Here, the boldly outlined seams and details would have been included for legibility in the course of rotoscoping. Courtesy Marge Champion.

MA: What time did you begin working each day?

MC We'd start working about nine o'clock a.m. and finish about five or six p.m. I guess there was a half an hour for a sandwich. They had a theater at that studio where the animators would gather with their brown-bag lunches every so often, and they would show movies of what everybody was doing, or they sometimes had demonstrations of, if you can believe it, hypnosis.

MA: What?

MC: One of the animators, Art Babbitt, was a very good hypnotist, and he would put people out during lunch hour and give them a post-hypnotic suggestion that was a kind of joke. He put out one of the boys [who did errands around the lot], and he gave him a post-hypnotic suggestion that he would go into every animator's cubbyhole and say, "Have you found the stipple dots?" Well, of course, the stipple-dotting is a process. There is no such thing as a stipple dot. Or he would say, "Have you seen the oranges?"

Of course, the animator would look at this kid as if he'd lost his mind, and say, "Don't bother me," and go on. And the kid would not understand why he had had this post-hypnotic suggestion; well, he didn't know, because he was out. It was amazing how many people would kind of go out. It was just for fun and games, but Babbitt would hypnotize people at lunchtime. Once in a while, somebody asked him to do it therapeutically.

MA: You were briefly married to Art Babbitt?

MC: Yes. A month before I was eighteen, I was briefly married to Art Babbitt. You know, in those days, nice girls did not go and live with their boyfriends before they had a ring on their finger. Art was a very nice and funny guy, and I guess I was just at that point in my growth and my maturation that I thought I was madly in love with him for a while. We were married a little less than a year.

MA: He worked on dance sequences in the early animated films?

MC: Oh, he did. He had a great love for dance sequences. There is a documentary made in Great Britain called *Animating Art*, which was really all about Art Babbitt, and from that documentary I was able to get some film, because he also had a sixteen-millimeter camera; and he would come into the studio and shoot me doing a lot of things, long before the days of DVDs made it all right for the Disney studio to show me doing the dances or whatever I was doing on the film. So I was able to get copies of that [Babbitt's documentary]. He had a great affection for dancers. He was not only married to me, but in his later days, he was married to a great friend and co-worker of mine, named Barbara Perry. They remained married until his death.

MA: I was reading something wonderful about his work on *Fantasia*—the dance of the mushrooms, the "Chinese Dance."

MC: Well, he did all of the dance of the mushrooms. He was very drawn to all of that, and that dance of the mushrooms is a wonder and a classic, because you realize that every single mushroom was running around at a different pace or a different timing, like the Dwarfs did. Whenever they did a sequence where there were seven Dwarfs on-screen and Snow White, every single frame had to be just a tiny bit different than the one before; and all of them were doing something different. I mean, the full animation of those days was absolutely awe-inspiring.

MA: Did he have models for his mushrooms?

MC: I don't remember that he did. Also, at home he had an animation table duplicating his studio setup, because it was not enough for them to draw from nine till six, or whenever they got through. They very often had to take work home at night in order just to meet any kind of a deadline. He worked—after dinner he would work sometimes two or three hours at that animation desk, with the light coming up into his eyes, because the light was underneath the drawings, and the mirror that they used to make faces at themselves usually was on the left, if they were right-handed, or on the right, if they were left-handed. He worked sometimes until ten or eleven at night. Didn't make for a great—for a newly eighteen-year-old young wife—a great social life. You know, Art Babbitt was famous for having also led the [1941] strike against Disney. That was after he came back from World War II. Then, of course, he was fired and reinstated by the National Labor Board. But he didn't stay there long after that, because it was just too uncomfortable.

I became good friends with his good friends [Disney animator] Bill Tytla and his wife, Adrienne. The work was just staggering that all of them put in, on a weekend—and that was a six-day week. In those days, even at the regular [movie] studios, we worked six days a week. Even when Gower and I were at MGM, those were six-day weeks. *[Gower Champion, Marge Champion's second husband, was a leading dancer and choreographer of film and stage musicals active from the late 1930s until his death in 1980.]* You had only Sunday off, and very few stores in those days were open on Sunday, so that you could do your shopping or whatever. You just had to rest on Sunday.

MA: You said you made ten dollars a day; did I hear you right?

MC: About two days a month. That was twenty dollars a month. I could do enough in a day to keep the animators busy for at least two weeks.

MA: Since you didn't know about the rotoscope, what did you think was the process? What did you think they were doing with the film?

MC: They told me that it was a guide for their action, just to see how the skirt would move after you made a turn, or something like that. Now, when I finally saw the finished product, I realized—if you see the film, and you then saw what I did as a young person on the film, you would know

that every single movement was mine; and some of that movement, without the animators' even thinking about it, came into the film when it was not, perhaps, on the storyboards.

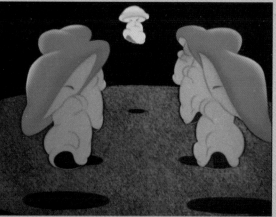

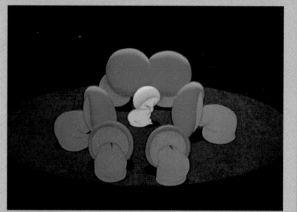

Art Babbitt, a top Disney animator, worked on the mushroom dancers of Fantasia's "Chinese Dance" while he and Champion were married. He created the personality of the little mushroom, Hop Low.

NOTE: – SEE INSTRUMENT MODEL SHEET FOR DETAILS ON SL. FISHORN – DOCS SWANNETTE – BASH CONCERTINA – NOTE ALSO FORE SHORTENING ON SL. FISHORN.

Because they would say very often, "Well, now run through the forest the way you would see it." They had a clothesline lined up, and they had a bunch of ropes hanging from the clothesline, and that was the trees, what I had to push aside. But my acting—*that* just came out of instinct, because I was not a trained actress. All of that gave them much more than a guide for their actions. Some of it was traced. Not all of it.

By the time I got through with the hippopotamus in *Fantasia*, I really had thought up a couple of things for them that I thought would be amusing, and they were incorporated into the script.

MA: Who did the choreography for *Snow White*?

MC: I did. I mean, I was used to flinging myself around by then. I thought they were all fun, and also they had a choice of things to decide upon. [*Here Champion explains that after she had demonstrated what she understood the animators wanted by copying the action in the storyboards as exactly as she could, they often consulted her about what else she thought the character might do to elaborate or extend the action.*] I'd say,

"Well, I think I would do so and so and so." I didn't know what I was doing. But I also had no fear by then, because they were not going to laugh at me, unless I did something so amusing that they wanted to put it into the film.

MA: Who did the choreography for the Dwarfs' entertainment of Snow White?

MC: That's not really choreography. That's what I call dance direction. I was not a trained choreographer, nor did I have a language, a choreographic language, that was anything spectacular. We were just dancing around, having some fun. They could get [*that is, the animators could draw*], let's say, the lines of what I was doing, because I had a freedom about dancing. From the time I was five or six, I had a freedom, which is what they wanted.

I have one set of films where Ham Luske is backing up, practically on his hands and knees, when I'm shooing the Dwarfs away, and he was imitating this backing up by being on his heels with his knees bent, so that he would be the right size for them to see my action when I'm shooing them out the door.

MA: Just a point of information: you have archives of most of this on sixteen millimeter?

MC: No, I have some of it, and I only have some that Art Babbitt had from his own camera. On the DVD of *Snow White* there is a section where you can go to "the making of *Snow White*," where they show me dancing with the Dwarfs. But I have not seen everything that is available. I know that they have kept all of it, or at least most of it.

If we want to go to *Fantasia*, I was older by then, and I did contribute one idea to the animators which is still in the film.

MA: Which one is that?

MC: I had been to see *The Goldwyn Follies* [of 1938]. Vera Zorina, the great European dancer, had done a ballet where she came up out of a pool. She was on some sort of an elevator that brought her up, and then she made a little flip with her hand that was over her head and batted her eyelashes. Well, the next time I was at the studio, I told them about this, and I said, "The hippo has just got to do that." I had a little tutu for modeling for the hippo, which I had had for one of my father's recitals, and so I wore it, and I have film of me actually doing that. I wasn't in a pool, but I was down on my knees, right to my toes, and I rose very slowly up out of this imaginary pool and flipped my hand, and they actually used that for the beginning of the hippo ballerina dance.

MA: Then Hyacinth Hippo puts her arms behind her, like a vamp.

MC: Yes. Yes. So I have a feeling that they didn't all rush to see *Goldwyn Follies*.

[For "Dance of the Hours" in *Fantasia*] I had eleven girls [to make choreography for], and I made the twelfth one; I have that on film. Eleven people to work with for one of the sequences where the elephants are tossing balloons. They were from my father's dancing school. I have some of that [on film], again, thanks to Art Babbitt.

MA: When did you begin to work on *Fantasia*?

MC: I think it probably was early in '37. December 21st was the opening night of *Snow White*, at the Carthay Circle Theatre; it's in Los Angeles. That was during the days that I was not supposed to have any publicity.

MA: Why not?

MC: Well, because the audience would misunderstand, or they would think that I—I don't know. The Disney studio did

OPPOSITE: *A rough layout drawing for the scene of the Dwarfs' entertainment in* Snow White. ABOVE: *Production drawings for* Snow White *made prior to the film's actual animation.*

not want it. Adriana Caselotti got all the publicity, because it was okay for the voice to get publicity. I got none, until an editor from *LIFE* magazine, named Alexander King, was sent [to cover the *Snow White* première]. At the time *LIFE* had no bureau out in the West Coast. King had been an artist; he was kind of a Renaissance man. He had been a writer. He was on the magazine, which, at that time, was the top-selling magazine.

On his way out on the train, he thought of several ideas that might be of interest for them to print, and one of them was that there must have been a model for Snow White. He went to the studio and said something, and he had to sign an agreement that they would have to see the text before it was printed. But he did get permission to photograph me and Louis Hightower, who played the prince, who was also a student at my father's school. And those pictures did appear in *LIFE* magazine.

That's when the Disney studio started loosening a little bit, as long as it [King's report] said I was only a guide. As long as it never mentioned the rotoscoping, I was able to have some [press coverage]. But it's only in recent years that people have known how many people they had hired to give them movement ideas. For whatever reason, they just wanted everybody to think that the animators just [did it all themselves]. Like the birdies: I mean, obviously, they would study birds and how they moved, and maybe even have photographs, so that they got the correct swooshing around or whatever. But, for some reason, and I think that was Walt's decision, they did not want people to think that there were any [human] models.

[*The next part of the interview concerns the ostrich ballerinas in Fantasia's "Dance of the Hours." Champion refered to them as "storks"; I've replaced her references to "storks" with "ostriches," which is what she meant.*]

MA: When you started working on "Dance of the Hours" in *Fantasia*, did the Disney animators already know that they were going to have hippos, elephants, and alligators?

MC: And ostriches. Don't forget the ostriches. I did quite a bit

with the ostriches. I had two big fans, and the animators wanted me to do that [improvise the dance] with a bathing suit on, which I did. In fact, I did quite a bit of even the hippo's movement in a bathing suit, because they wanted to get the body line—but particularly the ostriches. I don't remember whether it was my idea or their idea to get these big feather fans so that I could flap, as though I could flap my wings around and do things for them to give the feeling of this—she was like a ballerina. She finally ended up in a big split, as I remember. She was lowered down from somewhere in the heavens, and she did a big split. Of course, I was always kidding around with them in those days, and very free, so I might even have done that.

MA: They were all on pointe, the ostriches.

MC: They were on pointe. I did quite a bit on pointe for them. I was not a great pointe dancer, but I did do quite a bit for them.

MA: That's real choreography, where Mademoiselle Upanova's in the center, and the others are around her.

MC: Yes, she's in fifth position, and she does *pas de chat* ["cat step": a small leap on two feet, with both knees momentarily pulled up high in the air]. I did all of that, but, you know, to me they were just classroom steps that I put together. I never think of them as choreography. Choreography is something that Mr. Balanchine does. Dance direction is something that my father did, like the "Merry Widow Waltz" for Mae Murray and John Gilbert. My father, Ernest Belcher, did a lot for even Charlie Chaplin. He worked for Charlie Chaplin, some of his movement. But nobody ever took choreographic title from that. It's always seemed to me that there should be two delineations. One is choreography, which Martha Graham did; she even invented a language of dance. Jack Cole [with whom Marge and Gower Champion worked in Hollywood films] invented another language out of three or four different dance languages.... [Choreography is] taking a piece of music and creating almost a language for how it should be interpreted.

MA: Did you see Walt Disney, himself?

MC: Oh, sure.

MA: Could you speak a little bit about your interaction with him and your feelings about him?

MC: Yes. I was young, so I was told to call him "Uncle Walt," because the animators, they all called him "Walt." That was part of the camaraderie of the studio. The animators were very young in those days. There was hardly one of them that was thirty.

Uncle Walt. He was very protective. He had two daughters that had studied in my dad's school. He was not a social friend or a close, intimate friend of my father, but they knew each other. He was very supportive. I don't know how much of the work I did he saw, because he wasn't on the soundstage very often. It was usually the director and a couple of animators and a lot of scenery very crudely put together. The backgrounds were not complicated. We didn't have any trees; they just never worried about that, because they were going to draw those in.

But he was always very cordial whenever I saw him at the studio, and, "How are you doing?," and blah, blah, blah. After I was married to Art, I would hear him

Watercolor inspirational art for "Dance of the Hours."
For the ultimate inspiration, see page 123.

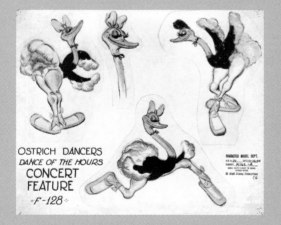

An early model sheet of the ostrich ballerinas in Fantasia's *"Dance of the Hours"—so early that the film was still being called "The Concert Feature." The ostrich in the upper left corner is in a position between ballet's first and third; the one in the upper right corner is almost in a fourth position; the leaping ostrich executes an avian* grand jeté.

grumbling about how badly he felt the animators were being treated and [how little] they were being paid—and that was not fair, because, by that time, the Disney company had had a big success with *Snow White*. It was not fair that the people who had worked so hard didn't, in some ways, share in it. Of course, the prices then were so different. I remember he [Babbitt] had a Latina woman who lived in, and I think she got ten dollars a week, which was the pay at that time. In those days, twenty-five thousand dollars was a CEO's salary.

MA: And the directors?

MC: I would have to go down the list with you about the directors, but they were all young, really fun and fun-loving people. Most of them had eye problems from looking into those lights all the time. They were breaking ground. They were doing something that had never been done before: full-length animated cartoons. They didn't get any royalties. But, then, at that point the studio wasn't making that much money, either. We were delayed because—as I remember, hearing some of them talk—about the fact that the Disney studio had to raise another million and a-half or something to finally finish *Snow White*. It was touch-and-go.

MA: Could we go back to *Fantasia* for a moment? I was particularly struck that, in "Dance of the Hours," it's not only Zorina's part that was modeled by real dancers for the Disney version.

MC: I actually did the choreography for that, if you want to call it [that]. I did quite a bit of it. I'd have to look at it again to know. They used a lot of things that I did with the twelve girls—actually eleven girls. We borrowed my father's costumes for that so they would have on kind of Grecian costumes. And we did much more than they ever used. You know, they had plenty of stuff to throw out. We did a whole thing for the "Dance of the Hours."

MA: A whole ballet, essentially.

MC: A whole piece, yes.

MA: And Louis Hightower?

MC: He was the alligator in that. And he was also the prince in *Snow White*. Because they ran out of money, they never did get the technology to ground the prince [that is, to give the animated figure the illusion of weightedness, of gravity]. When he walks across the screen, he kind of flies a little. They knew that they would have to delay the release of it another six months or so and go back over all of his drawings. They had the technology, but they couldn't afford to use it.

They cut an awful lot of the stuff that we did because they couldn't ground him; and so he looked a little effeminate. And Louis was not effeminate at all. He was a really extremely heavy-duty dancer and very muscular, and he actually was killed in Italy in World War II. Louis and his brother, Bernie [also a dancer], and his sister: they were not part of the Hightower family.

MA: You mean Rosella Hightower, the ballerina?

MC: They were not part of that family. They had come to Los Angeles from Florida, and their mother put them in the dancing school. Bernie was not nearly the dancer that Louis was, but he eventually married [the Hollywood star] Vera-Ellen. He and Louis were in a [1939] show called *Very Warm for May* [a collaboration between Jerome Kern and Oscar Hammerstein II; although it was a flop, one of the songs, "All the Things You Are," has become a standard]. Louis left *Very Warm for May* so that he could come and dance with me [in another show, The Little Dog Laughed, which folded before it got to Broadway]. We were the principal dancers, next to Paul Draper. It was not too long after that, because that was in the early forties, that Louis enlisted, and he was killed in Sicily.

MA: Did you graduate from Hollywood High?

MC: Yes, and that's the end of my formal education. [Champion, who graduated high school at sixteen, then enrolled at UCLA.] But UCLA was a new facility, and I was being rushed for a sorority and stuff; and my father said to me, "You can either dance or you can go to college. You are of an age when, if you're not hired as a dancer now, it's just not going to happen for you." Because there were no programs in universities at that time so that you could do both. So my only consolation is that I have four honorary degrees from different colleges.

ABOVE: *Marge Champion and incarnations of Snow White and Mickey Mouse at the ceremonies of the 2007 Disney Legends awards, when Champion was inducted into the Disney hall of fame.* OPPOSITE: *Champion (then working professionally under the name Marjorie Bell) on the Disney float in the Rose Bowl Parade, January 1, 1938. Photos courtesy Marge Champion.*

As the surviving live-action reference films for *Snow White* record, the living dancer who gave her motion to the animated heroine—and even to a Dwarf or two—was petite and nimble, with agile legs and strong feet: this is the teenage Marjorie Belcher—Marge Champion—improvising dances and bits of physical comedy before the camera. Sometimes she's taking Harpo Marx–like strides while wearing layers of ragtag coats, not much different from the one that *Snow White*'s Dopey wears, and sometimes she demonstrates restrained and aristocratic social-dance phrases while wearing versions of the dress finally given to Snow White herself. In one reference scene, in the formal manner of the animated Snow White's minuet moment with Sneezy/Dopey, Belcher takes the hand of, and politely cuts the rug with, a large, genial fellow, who turns out to be Disney composer Oliver Wallace. When, in the finished film, you see the fluency of Snow White's upper-body movement in the course of a dance, the contrapposto of her neck and shoulders as they gracefully oppose her moving weight, her light step, her winning way of opening her face so that we always observe it from a slight angle, the smile that causes her eyes to squint slightly with pleasure, her look of intelligent innocence—when you see all these qualities of Snow White's dancing, you are witnessing Champion, dancing in those black-and-white films made on the small Disney soundstage in the mid-1930s. (The construction of Snow White's facial features had other sources, as discussed on page 56.)

These dance qualities demonstrated by Champion (and by Louis Hightower) in the Disney live-action reference films reveal the fine training they enjoyed from Champion's father. In her exemplary essay on the life and art of the British-born Ernst Belcher, dance historian Naima Prevots quotes another one of Belcher's students, June Roper, who called him "an expert purveyor of the Cecchetti ballet method, approaching dancing as a scientist." The Cecchetti method—which is the basis of the Royal Academy of Dancing (RAD) syllabus and until very recently the foundation of training at the school of the Royal Ballet in London, and which is essential to the work of choreographers Frederick Ashton and Antony Tudor, the two greatest British dance-makers of the last century—was developed by the virtuoso dancer, mime, and teacher Enrico Cecchetti (1850–1928) during his years with the Imperial Ballet in St. Petersburg from 1887 to 1902 and again from 1905 to 1909. (One of his students was Anna Pavlova; from 1907 to 1909 he coached her exclusively.) Cecchetti's approach stresses great strength in the feet, precision of small beaten steps, centering of the spine in multiple pirouettes, and precisely faceted positions for the head, shoulders,

torso, and arms. From the 1950s to today, when Disney animators have called on ballet dancers for live-action reference, the dancers all seem to have been trained in other techniques, which may help to explain the absence in the other animated characters of the particularly open and faceted, forcefully but gracefully three-dimensional look of the dancing body that characterizes Snow White.

As the years and films go on, there is simply less shading in the dancers' bodies, particularly in the relationships between head and shoulders—what classical ballet calls *épaulement*. If you look at Hyacinth Hippo in *Fantasia*'s "Dance of the Hours," and then compare her cameo appearance in street clothes in the 1988 *Who Framed Roger Rabbit* (an enchanting collaboration between the Disney company and Steven Spielberg's Amblin Entertainment), you will find that Hyacinth has been transformed from a dancer into an actress, still seductive and charming but more animated in her face than in her body. And if you then compare both of those Hyacinths with the *Fantasia* hippos of the figure-skating spectacle in the 2004 Disney Christmas short "Belles on Ice" from *Mickey's Twice Upon a Christmas*, you'll find not only that there's no faceting of the body whatsoever—no strong feeling of the body projecting into three dimensions, since the physical orientation of the figures is so flat and frontal—but that Hyacinth and her sisters have been put on such stringent diets that they're almost unrecognizable. (On the other hand, the stars of the show—Minnie Mouse and Daisy Duck, who seem to be reproducing the 1998 Olympic rivalry between Michelle Kwan and Tara Lipinski—lucked into having none other than Kwan herself as their beautiful and exacting live-action reference model, as you discover in a bonus film interview with Kwan on the DVD.)

"It is not difficult to parody the classic dance. Frequently the form itself in performance is so preposterous, affected and brittle that it becomes a parody of itself." That's Lincoln Kirstein, champion of George Balanchine and the man who sought to establish an American school of ballet, writing in 1940. He continues, referring to "Dance of the Hours" (though he gets Hyacinth Hippo's name wrong): "Disney does not stoop to mere irreverence. His ballet dancers, whether hippos, alligators, elephants or ostriches, have spent their long hours at the *barre*. The *pas de deux* of the alligator and Susan the hipperina is as satisfying as the Bluebird with Markova and Eglevsky, in a different tone, to be sure, but just as satisfying."

After studying how the Disney animated films were made at the time Kirstein wrote, I find that, although I agree with him wholeheartedly about the quality of the pas de deux in "Dance of the Hours," I must take issue with him regarding his

Batty ballet

Hit of Walt Disney's new feature production, "Fantasia," is Mlle. Upanova (pronounce it slowly and you'll get the gag), the ostrich ballerina with feet like gunboats who performs "The Dance of the Hours." In animating this hilarious character, Walt used human ballerinas as action models. The grace of these ladies was transformed with wicked skill to Mlle. Upanova. "Fantasia," released by RKO Raio, is unlike any motion picture ever made.

assertion about parody: while it is easy to parody ballet, or any classical art form, cheaply, it is quite difficult to parody ballet *well*, onstage or in animation, in a way that makes the jokes work for general audiences—difficult, labor-intensive, and frustrating, with lots of false starts and promising ideas for gags that prove unfunny before live audiences, even though they may seem hilarious in the studio.

The heart of the difficulty seems to be that in order to satirize ballet's romanticism and theatricality successfully, the would-be satirist has to present its technique, conventions, and aesthetic standards knowingly and accurately; and that requires either a deep personal familiarity with the art or the intelligent synthesis of insights and demonstrations by many, many observers and practitioners. Walt Disney himself was not in any way a balletomane, but he had an uncanny intuition for quality that a general audience would recognize as such. In the 1930s and '40s, classical ballet represented quality in the performing arts: its prestige was part of its identity, and Disney knew that the studio had to present it with much more sophistication than it had earlier in, for example, the 1934 short *The Big Bad Wolf*, in which the title villain tries to fool the Three Little Pigs and Red Riding Hood by dressing in drag as "Goldilocks, the Fairy Queen, the Spirit of the Wood," with high-heeled "pointe" shoes and suspenders for imitating the flight of a Romantic

sylph. To prepare his artists for the "Dance of the Hours" ballet, in addition to bringing Marge Champion, Louis Hightower, and an ensemble before the cameras and bringing other dancers into the studio for live-model sketching sessions, Walt Disney arranged for his crew to attend at least one Los Angeles performance in 1938 by Colonel de Basil's Original Ballet Russe. On that evening, they fell in love with the dancing of ballerina Irina Baronova, in what seems to have been an abbreviated production of *Swan Lake*, and they told Walt Disney about it. Disney himself attended another performance to see Baronova, liked what he saw, and sent the artists back a second time as well. The character for which they wanted Baronova to serve as a live-action reference was the ostrich prima ballerina, Mlle. Upanova, one of the characters for which Champion had already modeled. Champion had also sketched out some ideas on film of choreography for Upanova's accompanying ostrich corps de ballet.

According to a 1941 account by Robert Baral (a journalist known for his interest in the Ziegfeld Follies) in the magazine *The American Dancer*, Baronova was herself so enamored of Mickey Mouse that she had his figure embossed on her stationery and couldn't wait to serve as a live-action reference dancer. (Since Baronova doesn't

A drawing of the grand Twirling Blossom, just prior to her chute over the waterfall. Courtesy Van Eaton Galleries (Mike and Janech Van Eaton).

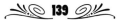

mention anything about Disney in her long autobiography, and Baral's story was published three years after the events it reports, we should take details like this with a grain of salt; however, photographs in the Disney archive do confirm that Baronova visited the studio.) According to Baral, on the ballerina's first trip to Burbank, her filmed improvisations and classical tutu suggested that the choreography for the "'Dance of the Hours' was more *Swan Lake* than anything else." Baral continues:

> It was not so hard though for Baronova to embellish certain movements with more emphasis for the sake of the drawing crew. But for the most part the dance was given in strict character. . . . Baronova danced the ballet three times. Next a film was shot, giving the staff free access to her famous technique. Parts were repeated time and time again to permit the characterization to seep through. The artists began to get the idea.
>
> A line of girls was imported for the ensemble work and the same procedure was followed.

Baral gives no clue as to whether these were the dancers from the Belcher studio with whom Marge Champion had already worked, or dancers from the Original Ballet Russe, or yet other dancers. Perhaps he didn't know for sure. He continues:

> By this time the Stokowski recording with the Philadelphia Symphony Orchestra had arrived, and the crew utilized the finished disk for final chores. Pencils turned into batons as the music sunk in. A rash of dynamic ballet broke out in the studio. It was nothing to see a sketcher leap from his working table, or another execute a tricky *arabesque* in between drawings.

One of these inspired artists was surely Jules Engel. In the event, Baronova returned, in street clothes, to the Disney studio on at least one subsequent occasion, and Baral describes how, in answer to the artists' entreaties to her to demonstrate more for them, she provided "a free and easy conception of the initial static calm of the 'Dance of the Hours.' No stiff deportment as laid down in the traditional annals by Cechetti [sic] and Petipas. . .[She] picked some worn ostrich feathers from an artist's table and then let herself go. Mlle. Upanova blossomed forth that afternoon. And it is this Mlle. Upanova a la Baronova which the public sees in *Fantasia*." In fact, the accuracy and aristocratic restraint of Mlle. Upanova's classical schooling in the finished animated film strongly suggests that both visits by Baronova were productive. The contributions of Marjorie Belcher and of the animators, such as Jules Engel, were crucial to Mlle. Upanova's deportment; yet

Between 1994 and 1996, Rusty Frank—author and self-described tap-dance preservationist—worked for the Disney studio, where she was the assistant in the Camera Department. One day, her colleague in the studio archives, Scott MacQueen, called her up: he had found some live-action reference film of two African American tappers in a can of footage marked DUMBO, and he wondered if she knew who the dancers were. Unable to identify the dancers, she mentioned to MacQueen that, on that very evening, she would be visiting Fayard Nicholas, one half of the immortal Nicholas Brothers (and the choreographer of many of their dances). MacQueen made her a copy of the mystery film, and she took it with her. As soon as Nicholas saw it, Frank remembers him saying, "That's Freddie and Eugene Jackson!"—ostensibly a team of brothers (half brothers, actually) who enjoyed decades of work on the West Coast as a tap "flash" act, featuring acrobatic maneuvers. Eugene had broken into the movies at the age of six, as Farina's elder brother, "Pineapple," in Hal Roach's Our Gang comedies. With his half brother, Freddie, whose real last name was Baker, he toured theater circuits, appearing once with the Gumm Sisters—including the sister who eventually took the name Judy Garland—with George Burns, and with other headliners. Both brothers worked in movies. Eugene appeared in some seventy-five films and television shows between 1923 and 1993 and Freddie in at least seven pictures between 1938 and 1942: their colleagues on the sets included Bill Robinson; Jeni LeGon (now Dr. Jeni LeGon), who was arguably—the formidable technique of Eleanor Powell notwithstanding—the most exquisite female rhythm tapper in Hollywood; and, in 1942, John Huston, the director of the Bette Davis film *In This Our Life*, in which Freddie Jackson had a small part. Both Jackson and Baker went on to extended careers in show business.

As it turned out, Fayard Nicholas had been in the army with Eugene Jackson and had a phone number for him. Frank told MacQueen this, and a subsequent call to Eugene Jackson apprised him of the discovery of the film footage showing him and his brother. An interview with him on the subject was arranged, with a cameraman and sound technician present. Prior to the interview, he and his wife were given the chance to watch the finished film of *Dumbo*, which he had never seen.

The next day, on November 21, 1995, the Disney studio sent a limo for Jackson and his wife to take them, as Frank remembers, to "someone's vintage Hollywood home" for the interview. Once they were comfortably seated at the interview location, Frank asked some questions and then screened for them a copy of the 16 mm reference film of the brothers from six decades before, and the cameraman recorded Jackson's visual and verbal responses to it as he watched. "What was so amazing," Frank remembered in a phone interview in 2008, "was watching Eugene see this footage of himself and his brother, for it was the *first* time he had ever seen them dance on film from this or any era in their career! That's what was so miraculous about the experience. Imagine having your whole career and never seeing yourself and your brother dance. I remember how he was absolutely dumbstruck. He just stared at that footage, smiling, not able to utter a word."

Jackson himself discussed his and his half-brother's experiences as live-action reference models for *Dumbo*'s crows:

> Our unknown big break came when I was around seventeen or eighteen, between 1935 and 1937. The reason I call this our unknown break was because we never received any big money for our contribution to *Dumbo*. . . . *[Jackson, of course, had no way of knowing that none of the dancers working for Disney in those days received much money. See the interview with Marge Champion, page 124.]* During that time, Walt Disney was just beginning, and he had acquired a loan for this film. Freddie and I did some dancing for Disney artists to go by in animating the crows for the film. The making of *Dumbo* wasn't easy for us as dancers. We didn't have all the modern technology of today. When it wasn't right, we had to dance over and over again. Sometimes even if it was right, we still had to do it more than once, because we didn't have the equipment of today.

Los Angeles producer and Disney aficionado Harry Arends volunteered to edit the resulting interview film, and, in 1996, Frank presented that edited version publicly to Disney animators as a lecture-demonstration, showing how the animators of yore at Disney had used dancing in the course of their work. (The footage was archived on DVD, but never commercially released.) Frank gave this program, called "Animation on Tap," twice at Disney's Burbank Animation Studio, once at its Florida studio, and once at its Paris studio. It was appreciated at all the venues, but the first presentation was a special success, as, following the screening of the reference film and then the film of Jackson watching it, Eugene Jackson himself came up to join Frank on the dais, where he

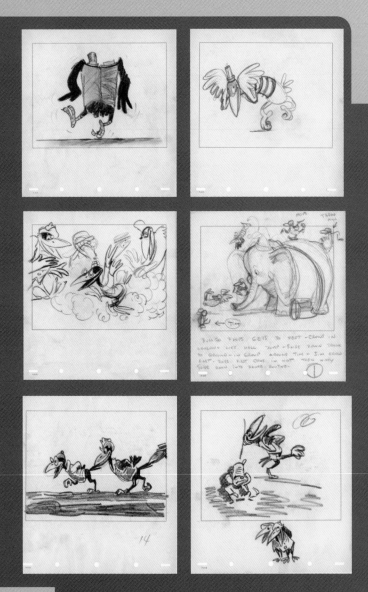

Story sketches of the sequence with the crows for Dumbo.

a "Southern-type" step called "Peckin'," and "stuff we made up." Eugene Jackson, born in 1916, died in 2001. Freddie Baker, born in 1919, died in 1995.

Although *Dumbo* was, with *Snow White*, one of only two Disney animated features released prior to 1943 that turned a profit—and re-releases internationally have maintained its popularity with audiences all over the globe—it has also incurred biting criticism for the alleged racism of the sequence with the crows, whose voices, language, and physical manner clearly suggest Hollywood's own industrywide racial stereotyping. There are five crows in the group, and all were given names by the Disney animators: the leader, Dandy (or Jim) Crow, and Fat Crow, Glasses Crow, Preacher Crow, and Straw Hat Crow. Although the voice of the cigar-smoking chief crow, called Jim Crow in production materials, was provided by white singer Cliff Edwards, who had also provided the voice of Jiminy Cricket in *Pinocchio*, the voices for the rest of the crows were provided by African American singers, members of the Hall Johnson Choir. For their dancing, though, the Jackson Brothers were the models for all five crows.

However, I agree with Disney historian John Canemaker that the crows' episode with the hapless Dumbo and his kind friend, Timothy Q. Mouse, uses racial stereotyping, familiar from vaudeville as well as the cinema, for a larger and generous purpose. As Canemaker writes in the chapter on Ward Kimball, the animator of the crows, in his peerless history *Walt Disney's Nine Old Men and the Art of Animation*: "One day in the studio parking lot, Walt told Kimball the plot of a new circus picture called *Dumbo*." (The film was based on the 1939 children's book *Dumbo, the Flying Elephant*, by Helen Aberson, with illustrations by Harold Pearl.) "'He went through the whole story in about five minutes,' Kimball recalls. 'I want you to do the dance sequence where the crows teach Dumbo how to fly.' And listening to him tell the story, I could tell that the picture was going to work.'"

Canemaker continues:

Actually, the crows sing and dance a song of derision, making fun of Dumbo and his friend Timothy Mouse for suggesting that an elephant might fly. Ultimately, the black crows empathize with Dumbo and his outsized ears, for they, too, are social outcasts because of their physical appearance; they teach him not to fly but to have confidence in himself. Besides Dumbo's mother and Timothy, the crows are, in fact, the only sympathetic and generous characters in a film full of cruel tormentors (Dumbo's fellow elephants) and selfish exploiters (the ringmaster, the circus clowns). Kimball's stylish animation gives the crows warmth, panache, and individuality. "The crows are stereotypical blacks," writes Michael Barrier in *Hollywood Cartoons: American Animation in Its Golden Age*, "but rescued from embarrassment by the immense good humor that suffuses Kimball's animation, the voices, and the crows' song, 'When I See an Elephant Fly.'"

played his ukulele, sang the Oscar-winning "Zip-a-Dee-Doo-Dah" from the 1946 Disney film *Song of the South*, and accompanied Frank as she tap-danced.

"We danced. They drew us. . . . Those cartoon artists—they were *geniuses*!" Jackson can be heard saying to Frank on camera as he watches the reference film, made in 1938 or '39. "They did everything! Seeing us, I could see what we were doing in the cartoons. You know, when you're watchin' those crows, you're watchin' Freddie and I."

A man's offscreen voice observes: "A lot of the moves you're doing are in the cartoon."

"Yeah, I see it," Jackson answers. Among the tap steps he identifies himself and his brother performing are the wing, the time step, trenches, a split, Truckin', the Charleston, the Mess-round,

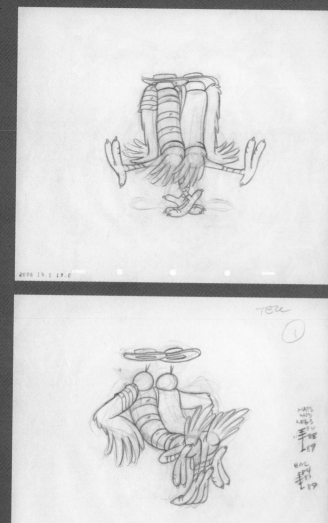

Animation drawings by Ward Kimball of the dancing crows, based on the dancing of the Jackson Brothers, in Dumbo's "When I See an Elephant Fly" number.

the particular blend of restraint, flirtation, and technical exactitude in the ostrich prima's dancing appears to be Baronova's, insofar as archival films reveal it.

Alas, the Disney film of Baronova's demonstration of *Swan Lake* that Baral mentions seems to have disappeared from the studio's various archives—a pity for any dancer of that stature, but especially for Baronova, for whom comparatively few performance films exist, at least in U.S. repositories. It is possible that it was one of the many historic live-action reference films at Disney that were thrown out by executive order during the 1980s. (According to some Disney aficionados in California, fans climbed into the Dumpster by night to retrieve as many as they could.) Although some archival films have been preserved and are available to scholars at the studio's archives and its ancillary libraries—I saw the complete Marjorie Belcher films for *Snow White* and "Dance of the Hours" there, as well as the heartbreakingly wonderful films of the Jackson Brothers for the *Dumbo* crows (see page 141)—and Disney historians have had the generosity and foresight to make available on DVD extras a great deal of what historic films remain, the losses to a dance fan are incalculable.

Perhaps some of the losses will be remedied, at least in small part, as materials are brought to light via the Internet. One treasure that has emerged in fragments, by way of photostats offered on eBay, is a legendary live-action reference film for "Dance of the Hours," directed by Disney artist T. Hee, of an African American actress whom you may not have heard of: she served as a model for the body of superstar Hyacinth Hippo, who takes her proper place center stage on the cover of this book. Her name was Hattie Noel, and, despite numerous attempts to find out anything about her in standard printed references, apart from occasional mentions by Culhane and a few other Disney historians, I wasn't able to discover as much as I wanted to know on my own from where I work in New York: even the catalogues of the New York Public Library of the Performing Arts and the Schomburg Center for Research in Black Culture (also a branch of the New York Public Library) came up empty. The Screen Actors Guild has no record of her, and there is no information about her in the Margaret Herrick Library of the Motion Picture Academy of Arts and Sciences. From some thirty pages on the Internet, I was able to put together most of the pieces of her career. Alexander Rannie, in Los Angeles, took up the search from there and was successful. Based on my long-distance research and his considerable efforts, along with a fortuitous contribution by an unknown IMDb (Internet Movie Database) contributor, I can offer the following mini biography.

Hattie Noel—actress, singer, comedienne, radio and cabaret personality,

OPPOSITE: *Three photostats of frames from the live-action reference model film that actress and singer Hattie Noel made at Disney, under T. Hee's direction, for the animators of Hyacinth Hippo in* Fantasia's *"Dance of the Hours." The identity of the Disney staffer in the middle frame is unknown; however, he appears either to be standing in for Ben Ali Gator, who has a similar moment of encounter with Hyacinth in the finished film, or to be helping Noel perfect a pose. Images courtesy Dug Miller, Robert Greskovic, and Alexander Rannie.*

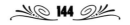

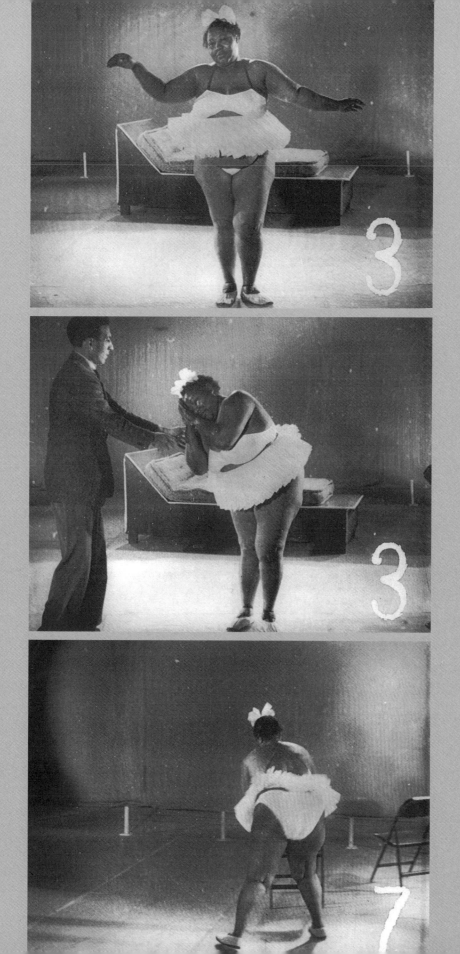

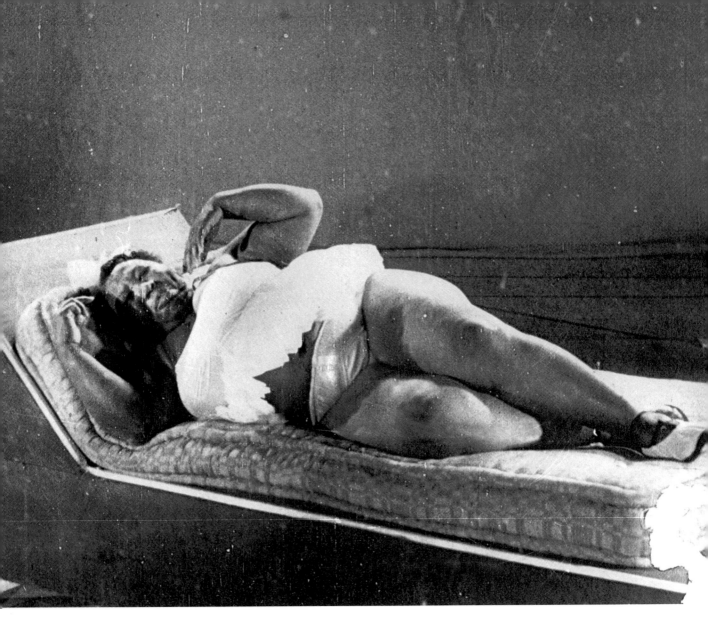

and sometime dancer—was born on February 2, 1893, in Logtown, Louisiana. She apparently broke into show business at the age of thirteen, when she ran away from home to join a carnival. (A sister, Anna Lee Anderson, with whom Hattie was close later in life, was either an infant or had not yet been born.) According to Bernard J. Peterson's 1993 encyclopedia of African American musical artists, *A Century of Musicals in Black and White*, Noel toured the South during the 1928/29 season in the vaudeville show *Midnight Steppers* starring Bessie Smith; also with the show were Lonnie Johnson, Lorenzo Tucker, and the Black and Tan Trio. (During her career, Noel would perform alongside Louis Armstrong, "Peg Leg" Bates, the Brown Sisters, Tim Moore, and four Smiths—Bessie, Clara, Trixie, and Mamie.)

In 1934, Noel appeared as herself in a Roy Mack live-action short starring Bill

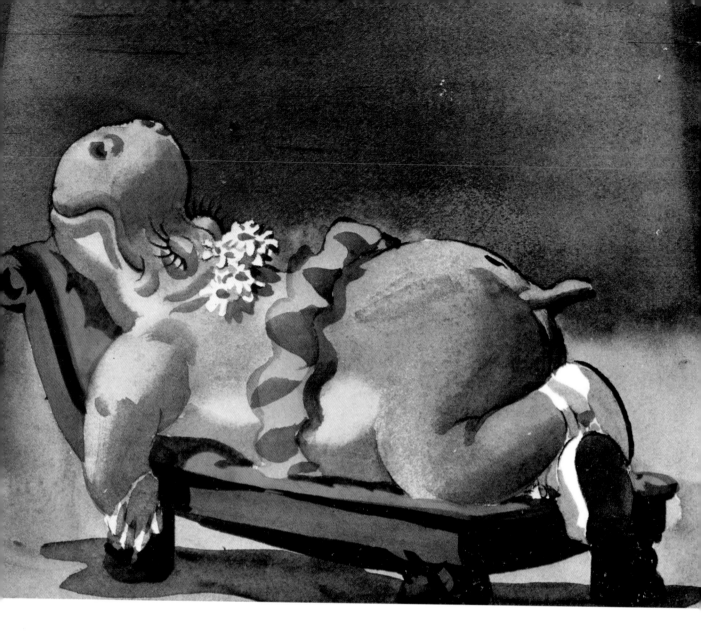

Robinson and called *King for a Day*; also in the cast were Muriel Rahn, Dusty Fletcher, Bebe Matthews (all three appearing as themselves), and Ernest Whitman. In 1936, the record producer John Hammond walked into the now-famous Club Reno at 602 East 12th Street in Kansas City, Missouri, and heard Hattie Noel performing with Count Basie's band and Jimmy Rushing. Shortly thereafter, Eddie Cantor brought Noel to Hollywood, where she worked in radio and the movies. By 1938, she was performing live in Los Angeles with Les Hite and his Black and Tan Revue of 1938, at the Orpheum: a review by Grace Kingsley in the *Los Angeles Times* treated Noel as the star of the show, calling her the "Sophie Tucker of Sepiaville" and singling out her "hot numbers" and her comedy. According to the review, Noel's "roguish wink . . . calculated to carry to the uttermost parts of the balcony, is a thing of joy." In 1939—which would have been just about the time she served as a live-action

OPPOSITE: *A photostat of a frame from Hattie Noel's live-action reference film for Hyacinth Hippo. Courtesy Dug Miller.* ABOVE: *An inspirational watercolor by Lee Blair of Hyacinth in a pose similar to Hattie Noel's. Lee Blair was married to Disney color stylist and designer Mary Blair.*

reference for Disney—she was one of several disappointed auditioners for the role of Mammy in *Gone With the Wind* (the part for which Hattie McDaniel won an Oscar).

However, Noel soldiered on, both over radio—performing on *The Eddie Cantor Show* seven times in 1939, with Gertrude Lawrence, Gene Autry, Betty Grable, and Benny Goodman—and in the movies, where she endured the industry wide racism that put African Americans into tiny roles or, if they had star turns, into sequences that could be easily cut for the films' distribution in Southern states. Between 1939 and 1943, she performed in bit or cameo parts in no fewer than seventeen Hollywood movies, including an uncredited appearance as a specialty dancer in the 1941 *Lady Be Good*. In *Irene*, from 1940, she can be found playing herself and sharing the scene with the big-band vocalist Martha Tilton and the Dandridge Sisters, where she dances a jitterbug to an up-tempo version of "Alice Blue Gown." In 1943, Noel played the secondary character of the maid Mignonette in the Broadway play *Try and Get It* (the last of some hundred shows to be produced in New York by A. H. Woods from the end of World War I), a risqué flop which survived only eight performances at the Cort Theatre; and she made an appearance, playing herself, in the Hollywood musical *Honeymoon Lodge* of 1943—a film packed with able performers, including Harriet Hilliard, Ozzie Nelson, and the bravura dance teams Veloz and Yolanda and Tip, Tap, and Toe. Noel continued to perform at live venues throughout the United States and, in 1956, made her first album for Walter "Dootsie" Williams, forging an alliance that lasted into the early 1960s. At first, Noel recorded her singing for his Blue Records company, then for his longer-lived Dootone (later Dooto) label. On these albums, she performed numbers that tended to be on the ribald side, including a "party" record with the comedian Redd Foxx on the theme of the embattled sexes. A photograph on a 1961 LP, *The Whole of Hattie Noel*, shows a large, very happy-looking woman who was clearly a fireball of energy.

Rannie picks up the story: "In her later years, Hattie Noel resided with her husband Antione Parker (1902–1966)—for twenty-two years a Santa Fe Railroad porter—in their home in the West Adams district of Los Angeles, one of the first integrated neighborhoods in L.A. as a result of a lawsuit brought by Hattie McDaniel and others. The area is filled with beautiful old homes, mainly built from the 1890s through the teens, and largely Victorian and Craftsman in design. By the time of Parker's death, Noel was for all intents and purposes retired, listing her occupation on public records as 'Housewife.' There is no record of children

from the marriage. After her husband's death, Noel was looked after by her sister, Anna Lee Anderson, and, after a brief bout with liver cancer, died on November 13, 1969. Hattie Noel is buried alongside her husband at Lincoln Memorial Park Cemetery in Carson, California."

It is important to understand Noel's role in the Disney live-action reference film—and the context of the film itself—in order to appreciate the significance of the stills from it, or that I'm presuming to be from it, that are reproduced on pages 145 and 146. I have not seen any of the actual film footage; nor do I know if any still exists. Presuming the pictures are, indeed, what they seem to be, first, and perhaps most crucially, it must be said that the film from which the pictures came was never intended to be screened publicly. None of the perhaps hundreds of live-action reference films made by the Disney studios were intended for the public. They served the animators as aides for their art—specifically, as visual references for how people, animals, and plants moved under certain specified conditions. It appears that Noel understood their purpose, although she reportedly worried about it, as in the following anecdote about something T. Hee told students during the 1970s at the California Institute of the Arts (the institution into which the Chouinard Art Institute—which supplied drawing instructors to the Disney studio during the 1930s—evolved). The story was told to me by special-effects animator Al Holter, a CalArts alumnus who has worked in commercials and on special effects in fourteen animated films, including *The Simpsons Movie* of 2007, for which he was special effects animator, and *The Prince of Egypt* of 1998, for which he was the 2-D–effects department lead:

> As a student in the CalArts Character Animation program in 1979 to 1981, I had a caricature class taught by T. Hee, who directed the "Dance of the Hours" sequence. When I met him he was a frail, thin old guy who advocated vegetarianism. By contrast, when he was at Disney in the late 1930s, he was a huge guy with a lot of weight. He once related how they shot live-action reference footage of a large dancer for the hippo. A lot of it was high-speed footage in order to capture the fleshy overlap of body mass. He said the dancer was very self-conscious about how the footage would be used. About whether or not it was being done in mockery. T. Hee said, "No, no," it was just going to be an aid to the artists. Then he peeled down to his shorts and, in his words, "danced with all my bulk in front of the cameras to show her that it was all in a light spirit."

Hattie Noel was *not* the live-action reference model for Hyacinth Hippo's ballet dancing: Disney went to classical dancers for that—the prodigious young Marge Champion and, later, the de Basil ballerina Tatiana Riabouchinska, who, like

149

Baronova, visited the studio and was sketched by the animators. However, Hyacinth and Ben Ali Gator do momentarily transform themselves into Lindy Hoppers, and the models for those moments would have needed a swing background. In the Disney studio's Animation Research Library, there is a music-mixing score for "Dance of the Hours" that contains notations of some of the live-action reference dancers for individual sections. For Hyacinth Hippo and the hippo dancers who bring her beauty implements, the names listed are: Hattie Noel, director T. Hee, Disney storyman Jack Caldwell, and Edith Jane, a dancer who went on to be professionally associated with the eminent jazz-dance teacher Luigi. (According to the score, Jane also modeled for the elephants in "Dance of the Hours"; and a dancer named Margaret Westberg—who danced for Ernst Belcher and Albertina Rausch—also modeled for the ostriches.)

Some of these performers—like the composer Oliver Wallace in the film of Dopey and Sneezy's dance with Snow White—were clearly serving the animators as models for proportion and the placement of figures in space, rather than dance technique. Disney's respect for ballet, noted in the "Dance of the Hours" by a commentator as tough as Lincoln Kirstein, extends to the respect accorded the character of *Fantasia*'s Hyacinth. She is made to appear as beautiful, charming, youthful, and adorably flirtatious as an animated hippopotamus comedienne can be; after sixty-eight years, she remains in every sense a great lady of the theater, a star with the prestige of Gertrude Lawrence or Ethel Waters; in addition, she is an irresistible comic ballerina, a Lydia Lopokova of her kind. Anyone who contributed to the glorious illusion of her life is honored to have been part of the process. It has been an unjust omission that Hattie Noel, the live-action reference for Hyacinth's physique, has been so little known, and it is a privilege for me to be able to recount Noel's participation, as well as what I've been able to learn of her larger career, in these pages.

That said, I do realize that some readers are going to look at the photographs—as some people who have posted comments on the Internet have—and see exclusively the unquestionable unhappiness in Noel's face, the unflattering costume that emphasizes her weight, the humiliatingly large child's bow in her hair, and the color of her skin. These aspects are going to add up to those readers as racism, possibly overlaid with sexism and disdain for someone considered overweight by social norms. Such readers are going to ask questions that I can't answer, because there don't seem to be any consultants living who know the answers. What was

she paid for her work on the film? Who else was on the set, apart from T. Hee, the cameraman and necessary technicians, and the unknown man in the suit who seems to be enacting a moment from Ben Ali Gator's pas de deux with Hyacinth? Why does Noel look so unhappy? Marge Champion has spoken of the heat on that un–air-conditioned set; might that account for Noel's sad expression? It is easy in 2008 to presume that, because the movie being made was a cartoon, Noel must necessarily have been an object of ridicule; however, even in no-holds-barred accounts of the behavior by some of the Disney crew during the 1930s, I have not been able to find any note of disdain on anyone's part for the models the artists drew. It is also possible to wonder why, for instance, Marge Champion's live-action reference films were saved and treasured by the Disney company while Noel's was not saved. However, you would then have to ask why the films of the Jackson Brothers were saved yet the film of Irina Baronova, one of the greatest ballerinas of the twentieth century, has vanished. Such films, like individual hand-painted animation cels, were considered disposable ephemera until quite recently; and if the films were of flammable nitrate stock, they could have been destroyed on purpose. There is no apparent rhyme or reason to what has been preserved.

Underlying all of this are the persistent charges against Walt Disney that he set a tone of racism and anti-Semitism in the studio that was reflected in his animated films; I've even seen the charge extended to anti-Asianism, as embodied in the wicked Siamese cats in *The Lady and the Tramp* of 1955. In fact, Neal Gabler, Disney's most recent biographer—who was given access to archives and papers unavailable to all other biographers—clinically analyzes both charges at great length, and, I believe, persuasively shows that, although Walt Disney could be accused of insensitivity, blindness, and plain foolishness in particular situations, he was neither a programmatic anti-Semite nor racist in any sustained political, commercial, or personal sense. I am not going to reproduce Gabler's extensive discussion here. However, I will say that Disney and some of his staff did evince coarse sensibilities on these subjects that, sixty or seventy years ago, were not as disturbing to the culture at large as they would be today. The tone of a passage in the admirable 1942 classic by Robert D. Feild, *The Art of Walt Disney*, which may contain the first mention in a book of Hattie Noel's contribution to *Fantasia* (although she is not named) surely seemed different to its early readers than it will to some readers today. "It was not easy to find an actress capable of reaching the heights attained by Hyacinth," Feild writes, in a section on live-action reference models, of the

moment when Ben Ali Gator hoists aloft the Hippo ballerina for "Dance of the Hours." "To lift the necessary hundreds of pounds even two inches from the ground required more than an airy playfulness. Eventually a Negress weighing more than two hundred pounds was found who tripped with lumbering grace over the live-action stage while the cameramen recorded the least quiver of her flesh, noticing those parts of her anatomy that were subjected to the greatest stress and strain."

And yet Walt Disney and his team treated individual performers well, given that many people who worked for the company felt underpaid. (The Jackson Brothers, who served as the live-action reference models for the crows in *Dumbo*, complained about what they were paid but not about the treatment they received at the studio.) And, in some cases, Disney went to great lengths to acknowledge a live actor's contribution. What mattered at Disney above all was roaring talent, which the studio could harness, and, after that, devotion to the studio's enterprise—that is, to the imagination and decisions of Walt Disney. One example is the African American actor James Baskett, who turned in a magnificent performance as Uncle Remus in the partially animated, partially live-action Disney feature *Song of the South* (1946), and for whom Walt Disney secured a special Oscar.

Unquestionably, there is material that is dislikeable or saddening about Disney in Gabler's account of this genius. And, personally, as a Jew, I was extremely disheartened to discover the first version of the 1933 *Three Little Pigs*, with its (since radically changed) episode of the Wolf dressing up as a caricature of a Jewish peddler—an illustrative stereotype that I recognized from German children's books and puppet theaters from the nineteenth and twentieth centuries, in which Jews were vilified. I also respect how decisively and fast Walt Disney changed that figure as soon as he received protests from Jewish organizations. Still, there was no live-action reference for the peddler in that cartoon—the models were other drawings. This is a different situation from seeing a real human being dressed as such a peddler: it is not quite comparable to what an African American reader might feel in looking at the pictures of Hattie Noel, even if she is lending her physicality to a "good" character who is a star. Whatever your response, it's worth remembering that, as a professional, Noel completed her assignment with honor. She brought more to the character than what the scholar Elizabeth Bell has called "prosaic strokes of cartoon corporeality": she brought her spirit—the femininity, humor, and deep feelings that animated the flesh the animators analyzed. These elements bespoke many experiences that the teenage Marge Champion would

A vigorous and exuberant Hattie Noel during a recording session around 1961.

have been too young to offer and the ballerina Tatiana Riabouchinska would have been too emotionally armored to reveal. They gave of themselves to the dancing of Hyacinth Hippo but not to her trademark vulnerability. That came from Hattie Noel, and she lives forever as one of the muses for the hippo in a tutu.

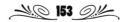

ABOVE: *A pastel inspirational sketch of the ostrich prima ballerina from "Dance of the Hours" taking a bow. This picture is a gentle parody of the pastel and gouache on paper* Dancer Taking a Bow, *circa 1877, by Edgar Degas. Degas was one of Walt Disney's favorite artists.* OPPOSITE: *A production cel on a non-production background of the pilgrims' procession in* Fantasia's *"Ave Maria." Courtesy the Cowan Collection (Jenny and Robert Cowan).*

AND **ENTERTAINMENT** OF *FANTASIA***

At least half the animated scenes in the original, 125-minute road-show version of *Fantasia* are set outdoors during daylight: most of "The Nutcracker Suite," all of the "Rite of Spring," nearly all of "The Pastoral Symphony," three quarters of "Dance of the Hours," and all of "Ave Maria," the second part of the last section, which is set at dawn. And yet, when you remember the film, it feels enclosed, dark. The orchestra, conductor Leopold Stokowski, and narrator Deems Taylor—who return between each section—shine forth from a nighttime surround; the underwater scenes in "The Nutcracker Suite" feel nocturnal, and the Russian thistles and Chinese mushrooms dance against velvety black; "The Sorcerer's Apprentice" takes place inside a dimly lit chamber deep within a stone castle. Although the "Rite of Spring" concludes with the extinction of the dinosaurs under a sweltering sun, the episode's absence of irony—an element that leavens the stylishly infernal "Night on Bald Mountain," for example—makes the Stravinsky piece the bleakest section of all emotionally—spiritually dark.

Furthermore, most of the films' component segments offer heroically proportioned figures whose power to bring about decisive change in a given situation, whether for good or ill, either cannot be affected by any other creatures around them or is so great that no other creature can exert any influence without a fight to the death: the Sorcerer of "The Sorcerer's Apprentice" (known to the animators as Yen Sid, or *Disney* spelled backward; he is also endowed with Walt Disney's famously arching eyebrow), the *Tyrannosaurus rex* of "Rite of Spring," Ben

Ali Gator of "Dance of the Hours," Zeus and Vulcan of "The Pastoral Symphony," and the demon Chernabog of "Night on Bald Mountain." All of these figures are reinforced by the Olympian position on the podium of the conductor Stokowski, and, to a lesser extent, narrator Taylor.

Fantasia also features ballerinas, sacred mothers, and female stars—even one or two superstars, notably the goddess Diana and Hyacinth Hippo; however, these female figures don't reign over entire societies. They represent the resources that warriors go to war to protect or that rapacious invaders upend and carry away. The virtual powers of the female characters in *Fantasia* are strong, yet they are not the ultimate powers in this universe: despite certain resemblances of the film's imagery to the worlds of the Romantic ballet or the ballets choreographed by Marius Petipa for the Imperial

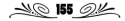 155

Theater in St. Petersburg, the dance element in Disney, even when caricatured, has been nourished by somewhat different sources.

If each of *Fantasia*'s sections were considered a ballet, then, taken together, the film's "repertory" might most closely resemble that of Serge Diaghilev's Ballets Russes, especially such works by Michel Fokine as *Schéhérazade* ("Dance of the Hours") or *Daphnis et Chloé* (portions of "The Pastoral Symphony") or *Petrouchka* ("The Sorcerer's Apprentice"). A few of Fokine's works remained in the repertory of one of the successor companies to Diaghilev's, the Ballets Russes de Monte Carlo, founded by choreographer René Blum and impresario Colonel Vassily de Basil in 1933, which toured extensively (under many variants of the company's name) across the United States throughout the 1940s and '50s. Among de Basil's leading dancers were Irina Baronova, Tatiana Riabouchinska, and David Lichine—who all served as live-action reference models for "Dance of the Hours."

One major dramaturgical difference between Diaghilev's Ballets Russes or any of its offshoot companies and the Disney film is the presence in the latter of characters who are in infancy or who are so childlike (Mickey Mouse, the dancing mushroom Hop Low) that children in the audience identify with them. The various Ballets Russes companies, both for artistic and pragmatic reasons (they all toured constantly, and seldom could maintain schools for training young dancers), largely neglected the traditional ballet repertory for, about, and including children as performers. Rather, beginning with Diaghilev himself, the Ballets Russes presented ballets performed by adults and about adults to primarily adult audiences. Disney's work, of course, was always intended for the whole family. The inclusion of child figures in his narratives affects the nature of the humor, which, in *Fantasia*, is broad as well as witty; it also represents a fundamental faith in the future. As *Fantasia* historian John Culhane notes, "All of Disney's best work is an allegorical representation of the triumph of life and hope over the powers of despair and death." Yet Culhane also comments that, although "the contrast of Moussorgsky's violent 'Night on Bald Mountain' with Schubert's tranquil 'Ave Maria' as the conclusion of *Fantasia*" was Disney's "most ambitious theme," the "defect of this conclusion is that the evil was expressed so much more effectively than the good, a frequent problem in all forms of art."

Considering Petipa's and Balanchine's choreography, however, I would change "all forms" to *most forms*. Petipa and Balanchine, neither of whom ever conceived their ballets in literal terms, extolled certain natural forces they associated with femininity through the steps and patterns they created for their ballerinas and female corps de ballet. For example, many choreographers today explicitly or implicitly contend that a male–female duet can never represent anything but sex—often with a distressing streak of cruelty and violence. Conversely, these

ABOVE AND ON FOLLOWING PAGES: *Animators' models (all painted by Mary Blair) of Mlle. Upanova, Elephanchine, Hyacinth Hippo, and Ben Ali Gator, from* Fantasia*'s "Dance of the Hours." Courtesy the Cowan Collection (Jenny and Robert Cowan).*

great Russian classicists assert that a pas de deux is essentially a ceremony between a man and a woman; while a given duet may for the choreographer in some sense represent, say, a rainstorm, if only for the purpose of providing an image to guide the process of the dance's construction, what matters is not what the choreography *represents* but what it *is* in terms of its dance quality.

To dance is to aspire to sacred perfection, and, usually, bliss. In Petipa's and Balanchine's masterpieces, good—which we inevitably associate with the youthful vigor of dancing, and which both men and women may embody—*dances*, while evil (together with old age and infirmity) is relegated to pantomime. Moreover, since women tend to be more physically flexible than men, their dancing offers more possibilities for nuance of tone. Thus in ballets by these choreographers and others rooted in the classical tradition, the ballerinas are featured in special ways.

Disney theoretically could have conceived *Fantasia* along these restrictive lines, but since Walt Disney was not, himself, a balletomane, who loved dancing for its own sake, he was naturally drawn to dancing in which the lyric impulse was subsumed to the telling of stories—to the choreographic tradition of Fokine, or of the Ballets Russes and de Basil choreographer Léonide Massine, in whose dramatic and allegorical works every little movement is meant to have a meaning of its own. And it is natural that, at the end of the 1930s, Disney would choose such an aesthetic path. Balanchine was respected by reputation, but, during those years, few of his ballets could be seen outside Hollywood films and Broadway shows: his concert work, the heart of his identity as both an artist and an entertainer, had too little presence in the public arena to be widely loved. On the other hand, Antony Tudor—a great ballet storyteller—was at the height of his career; Agnes de Mille was in the ascendant; Martha Graham, Doris Humphrey, and other modern dance choreographers who were still working with storyless patterns were considered overly intellectual, when they were considered at all; Fred Astaire, Hermes Pan, Eleanor Powell, and Busby Berkeley—all Hollywood royalty who were producing dances without demonstrable stories—were not looked at as concert artists so much as bankable entertainers and personalities. (Although a few dance writers, for example Arlene Croce and John Mueller, have had sufficient vision to examine some of these figures in terms of their formal achievements as early as the 1960s, it was not until the advent of videotape cassettes and DVDs—which permit the study of dance numbers independently of the films that contain them—that these

choreographers would be widely recognized as belonging to choreographic as well as cinematic traditions.)

Taken as a whole entity rather than as an anthology of separate pieces, *Fantasia* contains threads of lyric continuity—imagery that seems to connect for its own sake, according to a rationale that is separate, or more encompassing, than the stories related by the individual sections. One thread is that pervasive darkness and its associations with evil or death or seductive (and ultimately disabling) glamour; another thread is power and its incarnation in charismatic figures.

Yet another through-line in the film is purely a product of the dreamlike effects that animation can produce as a form of drawing. The climactic moment in "Dance of the Hours"—the penultimate section of the film—shows Hyacinth Hippo launching herself like a water balloon from a distant point in the background to sail to a perfectly targeted landing—*splat!*—on top of her (rather less massive) partner, Ben Ali Gator. Amusing in itself, and quite funny in the context of "Dance of the Hours," the leap and landing are hilarious if you encounter them after watching all of *Fantasia* up to that moment. The action and reaction have been anticipated in previous contexts, and their effects accumulate without the viewer's realizing the process consciously, until the great leap dramatically summarizes similar boldly physical moments that have come before. By the time Hyacinth makes her leap in the dark, we've already experienced the visceral feeling of it. In "The Nutcracker Suite," for example, a sequence for inverted blossoms on a rushing river—their petals invoking the silhouettes of long, Romantic-ballet tutus (such as those used in *Giselle*)—concludes with the largest of the ballerina-flowers going over a waterfall: she is seen from a perspective that puts the viewer hovering in the air, directly opposite her. Later, in "The Pastoral Symphony," which directly precedes "Dance of the Hours," the breathtaking swan-horses that represent a flying Pegasus family give us wonderfully elegant examples of flying as sailing and associate this soaring freedom with maternal femininity. So, when Hyacinth lands on Ben Ali Gator, the moment when she seems to suffocate him—a parodic exaggeration of an overprotective mother—is funny on its own and also because it releases the audience's ineluctable impulse to discover the flawed underside of idealized beauty. Indeed, in the last section of *Fantasia*—a diptych that links the midnight chaos and conflagration of hell with a soothing, devotional procession of hooded pilgrims at dawn—the dynamic is reversed, both in terms of moral themes and of the animation technology itself. The film's concluding six-minute procession at sunrise to Franz Schubert's "Ave Maria"—more than 540 feet of film—showcases

not the transformations of animated movement (so brilliantly emphasized in the preceding "Night on Bald Mountain") but rather the changes that can be effected by lighting, camera perspectives, editing, and the art of the background paintings. The sequence is a tour de force as much for what it plays down as for what it plays up.

The enduring criticism, in the pejorative sense, of *Fantasia* has been articulated principally by music critics. As someone who loves classical music—who goes to concerts and recitals for the sake of the music alone, without theatrical stagings—I agree with these detractors in theory. The adoption of Beethoven's "Pastoral" symphony as a support for *any* definite visual interpretation and the cutting of the climactic "Dance of the Chosen Maiden" from Stravinsky's *Rite* diminish those scores, as do various tweakings of the other musical selections (such as *The Sorcerer's Apprentice*). At first I thought the reasoning for the changes was, as in other Disney animated pictures, to give priority to the visual and narrative elements of the animators' contributions. And yet, as historians of music at Disney have observed, the animators of *Fantasia* were forced to work to Stokowski's "free" tempos, which represent the conductor's personal responses to the music, rather than to preset metronome markings, which would have made the process of animation much easier. If you don't know the scores independently from the film, of course, you may not notice anything amiss; and as Walt Disney explained often, with *Fantasia* he was trying to reach viewers like himself who were open to classical music but did not have the background or immediate inclination to appreciate it.

Still, such violations of the integrity of the musical scores expose a flaw in Walt Disney's vision, according to which story and art trumped certain aspects of the visions of composers, with long-term implications. On the other hand, in the case of *Fantasia*, Leopold Stokowski, known for his free hand with scores in concert situations, collaborated in all the musical selections, cuts, and changes. The film exposes the license that Stokowski took with even the greatest composers' music, and although Walt Disney and Stokowski apparently got along well in the collaboration, a music lover wonders what the resulting film might have been had conductor Arturo Toscanini, also a Disney fan and the candidate originally proposed by some of the Disney staff, been the project's musical guide. Toscanini was known for being temperamental, but he was also more careful and respectful of musical scores, which he conducted with debatably unparalleled brilliance; and, by extension, he might have been more sensitive to the animators' work as well. Up on Mount Olympus, where all of these geniuses surely reside, I imagine that, even now, they are pondering and revising and re-revising the possibilities.

In citing works in the notes below, short titles have generally been used. For full references, please consult the bibliography.

INTRODUCTION

15   *It was Walt Disney's feature* Peter Pan   Although my first memories of the film were most strongly governed by its palette and atmosphere, I recognize, having studied it, the importance to those impressions of the storytelling, characterizations, and the movement, both for the dances performed by the Indians and Captain Hook's crew and for the flying sequences, which have the quality of dance adagios. In a 2005 telephone interview, Kathryn Beaumont—the live-action reference model, as well as the voice, for *Peter Pan*'s Wendy—spoke of the actors and dancers whom the Disney studio directed to act out certain scenes so that their movement could be filmed for the animators to study and build upon. Her mission was to make the movements "look very liquid": "The scenes were sort of blocked out, and the director would work on what the position was to be, and we would work it out together," Beaumont said. "There was a lot of sweeping movement as simulation for flying, and leaping over things and looking as if you're ready to fly."

17   *(caption)   Disney, who hired Norman Campbell* See the biography by composer and lyricist Mel Atkey of Norman Campbell (1924–2004) on the Internet Movie Database: www.imdb.com/name/nm0132763/bio.

19   *(caption)   Ron Clements and John Musker,* co-directors of *The Little Mermaid*, discussed the influences on their work in the film during my interview with them at the Disney studio in Burbank in 2005. John Canemaker discusses the life and career of artist Kay Nielsen in detail in *Before the Animation Begins*, 74–83.

CHAPTER ONE

25   *some lessons in ballroom dancing* Gabler, *Walt Disney*, 191. Gabler quotes Disney as writing to the dance instructor, "[I]n spite of all your work, I'm still a lousy dancer."

25   *they made the man dance* Ibid., 482.

25   *knew very well why he did it* Ibid., 483.

27   *IT MOVES WITH THE TEMPO* Ibid., 409.

31   *cover girl Jinx Falkenburg* Rita Hayworth starred in the title role; however, Falkenburg herself also had a cameo in the film. Falkenburg was a great beauty and a woman of valor. For more on Falkenburg, see my "Letter from New York," *dance view times*, November 3, 2003: www.danceviewtimes.com/dvny/aloff/index.html.

31   *Alexander Rannie has observed* Telephone conversation with the author, spring 2008.

32   *his cavorting creation, Koko the Clown* A decade before Fleischer's Koko, who was an invention of the late 1920s, a handful of Bobby Bump cartoons by Earl Hurd mixed hand-drawn animation with live-action film of the animator's hand. Some historians of animation trace the origin of the mixed genres back to the 1911 Vitagraph film *Winsor McCay Makes His Cartoons Move*, a live-action short in which McCay—perhaps the greatest draughtsman in the history of animated films—demonstrates how he animates his still drawings. See the DVD *Popeye the Sailor 1933–1938*, vol. 1, for the outstanding documentary *Forging the Frame: The Roots of Animation 1900–1920*, co-produced by Greg Ford. (In 2005, Ford curated the multi-program I Love to Singa: Cartoon Musicals, a landmark festival of historic animated films, for the Film Society of Lincoln Center. This seems also to have been the model for the excellent 2008 cartoon festival at New York's Japan Society, Dawn of Japanese Animation, whose Music and Dance program included rare silent shorts made between 1929 and 1931.)

32   *We tried to take every idea* Kurtti, Interview with Dominique Monfery, 4.

35   *The importance of ballet for motion pictures* Balanchine, "Ballet in Films," 8. I discovered this essay in the superb dossier on Balanchine's work for *The Goldwyn Follies* that dance historian Beth Genné assembled for the Popular Balanchine

project, a research initiative of the George Balanchine Foundation documenting Balanchine's work in musical theater, revue, and film. The project's archive is deposited in the Jerome Robbins Dance Division of the New York Public Library for the Performing Arts at Lincoln Center.

37 *In an interview Taylor once spoke* In the 1990s, when I was the dance critic for *The New Republic*, I spent the better part of a year interviewing Paul Taylor for a thirty-page profile for the magazine, which I wrote but which was never published. Anna Kisselgoff, then chief dance critic for *The New York Times*, had already linked Taylor and Disney in her review "Freud Meets Disney."

39 *for his insolence is thrown into a "sweatbox"* Coincidentally, the animators famously referred to the various rooms in which Walt Disney would critique sequences of animated film in their presence as "the sweatbox," a term that originated in the early 1930s. It started as a noun that described the cramped, unventilated room under the staircase, where animators' pencil tests were viewed on a Moviola. It quickly evolved into a verb, however, as in "I'm sweatboxing my scenes this afternoon."

CHAPTER TWO

48 *he remains trapped in his own bubble* In a discussion about Goofy for a class in action analysis, conducted under the tutelage of Don Graham for Disney animators on June 8, 1937, Art Babbitt—a top animator who was especially sensitive to dance elements—told the students: "[T]he Goof is not the type of half-wit that is to be pitied. He doesn't dribble, drool or shriek. He has music in his heart even though it be the same tune forever and I see him humming to himself while working or thinking. . . . He is in close contact with sprites, goblins, fairies and other such fantasia. Each object or piece of mechanism which to us is lifeless, has a soul and personality in the mind of the Goof. The improbable becomes real where the Goof is concerned." Babbitt, "Analysis of the Goof," in Thomas and Johnston, *Illusion of Life*, 561.

60 *Minnie's physical injuries* This story point was recycled in more than one cartoon of the 1930s: a couple made for one another go out dancing, during which the guy awkwardly and accidentally tromps on his partner's foot, leading her to move on to a more physically imposing yet also more graceful rival. The Fleischer studio used the bit verbatim for Popeye, Olive Oyl, and Bluto in the 1934 short *The Dance Contest*.

64 *with* Pinocchio, *Disney reached* Maltin, *Disney Films*, 37.

66 *It's surprising what an effect touching can have* Canemaker, *Nine Old Men*, 207.

67 The Jungle Book *was the first picture* Thomas and Johnston, *Illusion of Life*, 414.

CHAPTER THREE

75 *Disney's Tiffany line* Merritt and Kaufman, *Silly Symphonies*, 4.

75 *routinely assigned his best artists* Ibid., 4.

79 *It was not an easy procedure* Thomas and Johnston, *Illusion of Life*, 288.

79 *If this close integration* Ibid., 288.

80 *Stalling built his score* In 1969 interviews and supplementary letters with Michael Barrier, Milton Gray, and Bill Spicer, Carl Stalling (1891–1971) noted that the foxtrot in his score for *The Skeleton Dance* is in a minor key. He also declared, "My music wasn't similar at all to the *Danse Macabre*" of Saint-Saëns. And he told his interviewers that he didn't remember using music from Grieg's *Peer Gynt Suite*. However, Disney archivist Dave Smith noted to the interviewers that the Disney studio had, indeed, been licensed to use Grieg's "The March of the Dwarfs" in the score for *The Skeleton Dance*. The two interviews and excerpts from the amplifying letters—the only extensive interviews ever conducted with Stalling, who is now considered a giant among composers for cartoons—were combined and first published in *Funny World* (Spring 1971), and republished in Goldmark and Taylor, "An

Interview with Carl Stalling," *Cartoon Music Book*, 39–41, 57.

83   *I did all the animation*   Iwerks and Kenworthy, *Hand Behind the Mouse*, 76.

84   *he reasoned that if he did only the extremes*   Ibid., 77.

84   *English satirist Thomas Rowlandson*   Ibid., 75–76.

88   *he used his assistant, animator Eric Larson*   Canemaker, *Nine Old Men*, 61.

88   *in another reference*   In a 1979 issue of *Funny World*, Dick Huemer recollected that Luske told him "that his wife acted the Goddess in that cartoon for him, but they didn't photograph and draw over it so it came out pretty terrible." Cited in Grant, *Animated Characters*, 73.

91   *Kirstein issues a call*   Kirstein, "Dance and Films," 101.

91   *The "cock o' the walk," a champion*   Merritt and Kaufman, *Silly Symphonies*, 169.

94   *version of 1728*   Fable CLXXXII, "The Fighting Cocks." The text of Samuel Croxall's popular *Fables of Aesop and others* . . . varies quite a lot in wording and anachronistic detail among its many British and American editions published during the 18th and 19th centuries. The first edition (1722) is the most laconic and martial in tone. I have used here the witty second edition, p. 330 (Gale Databases: Eighteenth-Century Literature Online, Gale document number CW3316592611). In other translations, this fable is titled "The Two Cocks" or "The Two Cocks and the Eagle."

98   *Silly Symphonies won the Academy Award*   Ibid., 4.

   she was already a professional   Merritt and Kaufman, *Walt in Wonderland*, 49.

CHAPTER FOUR

105   *Whenever we stayed too close*   Thomas and Johnston, *Illusion of Life*, 323.

105   *No one knows for sure*   Ibid., 323.

106   *Animators always had the feeling*   Ibid., 331.

107   *When you watch the thistle Cossacks*   Culhane, "Fantasia," 46.

107   *British Disney historian Robin Allan believes*   Allan, *Disney and Europe*, 117–18.

108   *dancer Joyce Coles*   Culhane, "Fantasia," 61.

110   *Les Clark was given the scene*   Thomas and Johnston, *Illusion of Life*, 329.

111   *Any dancing scenes in a story*   Ibid., 329.

112   *her distinguished father, Ernest Belcher*   For a full history of Ernest Belcher's extensive influence on dance and dancers in Hollywood, see Naima Prevots, "Ernest Belcher and American Dance." This historical essay was written with the full cooperation of Belcher's daughter, Marge Champion.

112   *From age eight, Marge spent*   Gilvey, *Before the Parade Passes By*, 24.

114   *Walt Disney's overall concept*   Culhane, "Fantasia," 60–61.

115   *In an essay entitled*   Engel, "Reflections."

115   *Miraculously, many of my original conceptions*   In Jules Engel, "Teaching Animation," *Millimetre* 14, no. 2 (February 1976): 30. Quoted in Allan, *Disney and Europe*, 120.

117   *For instance, the anticipation*   Culhane, "Fantasia," 53–54.

118   *Let's take these animals*   Ibid., 162.

119   *Culhane credits the head of layout*   Ibid., 166ff.

119   *Robin Allan quotes Jack Caldwell*   Allan, *Disney and Europe*, 151.

119   *Allan relates how, with the help of a scale model*   Ibid., 151–52.

120   *Ballet, of course, is an abstraction*   Culhane, *"Fantasia,"* 166.

120   *Balanchine may have made a comment*   A link between Balanchine's dances in *The Goldwyn Follies* and Disney was proposed as early as 1938—that's a year before Balanchine and Stravinsky visited the Disney studio for the first time—by the dance critic Edwin Denby: Balanchine's work for *Goldwyn Follies*, he wrote, "is particularly interesting because you see a number of dance phrases that were composed into the camera field—an effective and necessary innovation anyone could have learned from Disney, but which nobody tried till now. It is the only way dancing can make sense in the movies." Edwin Denby, "Balanchine's 'Apollon,'; American Ballet Caravan," *Modern Music* (March–April 1938). Reprinted in Edwin Denby, *Dance Writings*, 48.

120   *And is it also a mere*   Dance historian Sally Banes was the first to pose this question in her essay "Elephants in Tutus," *Before, Between*, 351. She also assembled the Popular Balanchine dossier on the 1942 *Circus Polka* (see note for page 35, above).

120   *During their animated conversation*   Tytla, *Disney's Giant*, 125.

123   *showed them the ostrich*   Ibid., 125.

132   *And those pictures did appear in LIFE*   The result was an unsigned two-page spread, "Snow White Sets Record/Here Is Her Model," in the April 4, 1938 issue. The photographer is not identified.

136   *an expert purveyor*   Prevots, "Ernest Belcher and American Dance."

137   *It is not difficult to parody*   Kirstein, "Mickey Mouse Joins the Ballet," 15.

139   *According to a 1941 account*   Baral, "Baronova as Mlle. Upanova," 13.

145   *Noel toured the South*   Peterson, *A Century of Musicals*, 235.

147   *In 1934, Noel appeared*   A list of Hattie Noel's films (incomplete) is available on the Internet Movie Database: www.IMDb.com/name/nm0633877.

147   *In 1936, the record producer John Hammond*   "Club Kaycee: Kansas City Jazz History": Club Reno (a.k.a. the Reno Club): www.umkc.edu/orgs/kcjazz/JAZZSPOT/clubreno.htm. Information contained originally in John Hammond, *John Hammond on Record* (New York: Ridge Press / Summit Books, 1977).

147   *Eddie Cantor brought Noel to Hollywood*   Logs of *The Eddie Cantor Show* can be found on Jerry Haendiges' Vintage Radio Logs: www.otrsite.com/logs/loge1005.htm.

147   *the "Sophie Tucker of Sepiaville"*   Kingsley, "Revue Tops New Show."

148   *the role of Mammy*   One of numerous references to Noel's audition can be found on the Internet Movie Database (IMDb): www.imdb.com/name/nm0633877/bio.

148   *In Irene, from 1940*   This clip is periodically removed and then restored on YouTube. The movie is not currently available on DVD.

148   *In 1943, Noel played*   From the Internet Broadway Database (www.ibdb.com). The IBDb also contains information about the producer and theater owner A. H. Woods. Review by George Jean Nathan reprinted in *The Theatre Book*, 21–23.

148   *she made her first album for Walter "Dootsie" Williams*   Dave Edwards, Mike Callahan, and Patrice Eyries, "Dootone / Dooto Album Discography," Both Sides Now Publications, www.bsnpubs.com/la/dootone/dootone.html.

149   *Presuming the pictures are*   The four images shown on pages 145 and 146 are photostats that are believed to be frames from the live-action reference model film of Hattie Noel, made by Disney's T. Hee for the animators working on the character of Hyacinth Hippo in *Fantasia*'s "Dance of the Hours." They were purchased on eBay from Dug Miller, a purveyor of Disneyana.

149   *The story was told to me by special-effects animator Al Holter*   Personal e-mail, February 27, 2008.

151   *It was not easy to find an actress*   Feild, *The Art of Walt Disney*, 214.

CHAPTER FIVE

156   *All of Disney's best work*   Culhane, *"Fantasia,"* 182.

157   *a given duet*   George Balanchine makes this point in one of the two poet-to-poet talks that Jonathan Cott conducted with him. "Cott: It's strange, though—when I see your pas de deux—especially those in *Agon, Stravinsky Violin Concerto, Duo Concertant, Pithoprakta*—I pay less attention, finally to the fact that there's a man and a woman dancing but rather start thinking of things like identity, personality, separation, reflections, duplications. Balanchine: That's right. Some people, though, see in these pas de deux only pure man–woman relationships: 'The woman didn't have any guts, the man wasn't sexy enough.' This isn't my business. And what you're saying is absolutely right. Strange things happen! In the Webern [*Episodes*] pas de deux, for example, it's like a roof . . . raindrops on a crystal roof." Kirstein, *Portrait of Mr. B*, 138.

BIBLIOGRAPHY

BOOKS AND ARTICLES

Acocella, Joan. *Mark Morris*. New York: The Noonday Press/Farrar, Straus and Giroux, 1993.

Aesop. *Fables of Aesop and others, Newly done into English. With an application to each fable. Illustrated with cutts.* 2nd edition. Translated by Samuel Croxall. London: Thomas Astley, 1728.

Allan, Robin. *Walt Disney and Europe: European Influences on the Animated Feature Films of Walt Disney.* Bloomington and Indianapolis, IN: University of Indiana Press, 1999.

Aloff, Mindy. "Disney kept the dancers real" (unsigned). *The New Yorker* (February 10, 1992): 5.

————. "Letter from New York." On animator Alexander Shirayev 1867–1940. *danceviewtimes*: www.danceviewtimes.com, January 10, 2004.

————. "Photography." *International Encyclopedia of Dance*, vol. 5: 175–188. New York: Oxford University Press, 1998.

————. (unsigned). "Stoki." *The New Yorker*, October 8, 1990: 37.

Balanchine, George. "The Ballet and the Film: The Making of the Goldwyn Follies." *Dance Herald* I, no. 6 (April 1938): 1, 7–8.

————. "Ballet in Films." *Dance News* (December 1944): 8.

Banes, Sally. "Balanchine and Black Dance." *Choreography and Dance* 3, no. 3 (1993): 59–77. Reprinted in Sally Banes, *Writing Dancing in the Age of Postmodernism*. Middletown, CT: Wesleyan University Press, 1994.

————. "Elephants in Tutus." In *Before, Between, and Beyond: Three Decades of Dance Writing* by Sally Banes, edited and with an introduction by Andrea Harris, with forewords by Joan Acocella and Lynn Garafola. Madison, WI: University of Wisconsin Press, 2007.

Baral, Robert. "Baronova as Mlle. Upanova." *The American Dancer* (January 1941): 13, 22.

Barrier, Michael. *Hollywood Cartoons: American Animation in Its Golden Age.* New York: Oxford University Press, 1999.

———. Interview with Joe Grant (Disney historian, storyman, head of model department). Available at www.michaelbarrier.com/Interviews/Grant/interview_joe_grant.htm.

———. "Making Walt's Music." In Goldmark and Taylor, *The Cartoon Music Book.*

Beck, Jerry. *The Animated Movie Guide.* Contributing writers: Martin Goodman, Andrew Leal, W. R. Miller, and Fred Patten. Chicago: A Capella Books/Chicago Review Press, 2005.

———, ed. *50 Greatest Cartoons as Selected by 1,000 Animation Professionals.* Atlanta: Turner Publishing, 1994.

———, and Will Friedwald. *Looney Tunes and Merrie Melodies: A Complete Illustrated Guide to the Warner Bros. Cartoons.* New York: Henry Holt and Company, 1989.

Bell, Elizabeth. "Somatexts at the Disney Shop: Constructing the Pentimentos of Women's Animated Bodies." In *From Mouse to Mermaid: The Politics of Film, Gender and Culture.* Elizabeth Bell, Linda Haas, and Laura Sells, eds. Bloomington, IN: Indiana University Press: 1995.

Berg, A. Scott. "Goldwyn's Folly." *Ballet Review* (Fall 1995): 53–59. Excerpted from *Goldwyn: A Bibliography.* New York: Alfred A. Knopf, 1989.

Canemaker, John. *The Art and Flair of Mary Blair.* New York: Disney Editions, 2003.

———. *Before the Animation Begins: The Art and Lives of Disney Inspirational Sketch Artists.* New York: Disney Editions, 1997.

———. *Paper Dreams: The Art and Artists of Disney Storyboards.* New York: Disney Editions, 1999.

——— and Robert E. Abrams. *Treasures of Disney Animation Art.* New York: Artabras, 1982.

———. *Walt Disney's Nine Old Men & The Art of Animation.* New York: Disney Editions, 2001.

Care, Ross B. "Cinesymphony, Music and Animation at the Walt Disney Studio, 1928–1941." *Sight and Sound* 46, British Film Institute (Winter 1976–1977).

———. "Making Walt's Music." In Goldmark and Taylor, *The Cartoon Music Book.*

———. "Threads of Melody: The Evolution of a Major Film Score." In *Wonderful Inventions,* Iris Newsom, ed. Library of Congress (1985): 80–115. A study of the film score for *Bambi,* based on relevant materials at the Library of Congress.

Champion, Marge. Oral history interview on her work for the Disney Studios (Mindy Aloff, interviewer). The New York Public Library for the Performing Arts, July 28, 2005.

Cott, Jonathan. "Two Talks with George Balanchine." In Kirstein, *Portrait of Mr. B.*

Croce, Arlene. *Afterimages.* New York: Alfred A. Knopf, 1977.

———. *The Fred Astaire & Ginger Rogers Book.* New York: Galahad Books, 1974.

Culhane, John. *Fantasia 2000: Visions of Hope.* Foreword by Roy E. Disney, commentary by James Levine. New York: Disney Editions, 1999.

———. *Walt Disney's 'Fantasia.'* New York: Abradale Press/Harry N. Abrams, 1983, 1999.

Denby, Edwin. *Dance Writings.* Robert Cornfield and William MacKay, eds. Gainsville, FL: University Press of Florida, 2007.

The Disney Bulletin: "Fantasia" Edition. (November 15, 1940). Posted on *Michael Sporn Animation.com,* www.michaelspornanimation.com/splog/?p=915. The Walt Disney Company's in-house newsletter.

Draganski, Donald. "Paul Hindemith Meets Walt Disney." *Michael Barrier.Com: Exploring the World of Animated Films and Comic Art.* Available at www.michaelbarrier.com/Essays/Hindemith/Hindemith.html.

Engel, Jules. "Reflections: Graphic Choreography." *New Magazine* 10. Available at www.Centerforvisualmusic.org/library/Reflections.htm.

Feild, Robert D. *The Art of Walt Disney.* New York: The Macmillan Company, 1942.

Finch, Christopher. *The Art of Walt Disney from Mickey Mouse to the Magic Kingdoms.* New York: Harry N. Abrams, 1973, 1999.

Fleischer, Richard. *Out of the Inkwell: Max Fleischer and the Animation Revolution.* Foreword by Leonard Maltin. Lexington, KY: University of Kentucky Press, 2005.

Gabler, Neal. *Walt Disney: The Triumph of the American Imagination.* New York: Alfred A. Knopf, 2006.

Ghez, Didier. *Walt's People: Talking Disney with the Artists Who Knew Him,* vols. 1, 2. Xlibris, 2006.

Gilvey, John Anthony. *Before the Parade Passes By: Gower Champion and the Glorious American Musical.* New York: St. Martin's Press: 2005.

Goldmark, Daniel, and Yuvel Taylor, eds. *The Cartoon Music Book: Interviews with Mark Mothersbaugh, Alf Clausen, Carl Stalling, and John Zorn; Writings by Chuck Jones, Neil Strauss, Will Friedwald, and Irwin Chusid; Drawings by Chris Ware and John Kricfalusi and much, much more.* Chicago: A Capella Books, 2002.

———. *Tunes for 'Toons: Music and the Hollywood Cartoon.* Berkeley, CA: University of California Press, 2005.

Gordon, Ian. *Comic Strips and Consumer Culture 1890–1945*. Washington, DC: Smithsonian Institution Press, 1998.

Grant, John. *Walt Disney's Animated Characters* (new, updated edition). With a foreword by David R. Smith; foreword to the revised edition by Roy E. Disney. New York: Hyperion, 1998.

Greskovic, Robert. "The Master and the Movies: Barbara Horgan on George Balanchine's Work with Television and Film." In *Envisioning Dance on Film and Video*. Mitoma, Judy, Elizabeth Zimmer, and Dale Ann Stieber, eds. New York: Routledge, 2003.

Heide, Robert, and John Gilman with Monique Peterson and Patrick White. *Mickey Mouse: The Evolution, the Legend, the Phenomenon!* New York: Disney Editions, 2001.

Hollis, Richard, and Brian Sibley. *Snow White and the Seven Dwarfs & the Making of the Classic Film.* New York: Hyperion, 1994.

Iwerks, Leslie, and John Kenworthy. *The Hand Behind the Mouse: An intimate biography of Ub Iwerks, the man Walt Disney called "the greatest animator in the world."* New York: Disney Editions, 2001.

Jackson, Eugene W., II, with Gwendolyn Sides St. Julian. *Eugene "Pineapple" Jackson: His Own Story*. Jefferson, NC: McFarland & Company: 1999.

Kaufman, J. B. *South of the Border with Disney*. Unpublished manuscript, forthcoming from Disney Editions, New York.

Kimball, Robert. *The Complete Lyrics of Ira Gershwin.* New York: Alfred A. Knopf, 1993.

Kingsley, Grace. "Revue Tops New Show at Orpheum." *Los Angeles Times*, August 11, 1938: 10. Review of a performance by Hattie Noel.

Kinney, Jack. *Walt Disney and Assorted Other Characters: An Unauthorized Account of the Early Years at Disney's.* New York: Harmony Books, 1988.

Kirstein, Lincoln, "Dance and Films." In *American Movie Critics: An Anthology from the Silents Until Now.* Phillip Lopate, ed. New York: The Library of America, 2006. "Dance and Films" was originally published in 1936 in the magazine *New Theatre*.

———. "Mickey Mouse Joins the Ballet." *Dance* 8, no. 5 (December 1940): 15, 32. This magazine, very rare, is not the *Dance Magazine* most readers will know. Its editorial offices were at the time at 30 Rockefeller Plaza in New York City, and it was edited by Richard Davis. Critic and historian Jack Anderson explains: "The present *Dance Magazine* is the result of the amalgamation of a magazine called *The American Dancer* and several previous magazines called *Dance* (including this incarnation). A good summary of all these magazines can be found in Doris Hering's anthology *Twenty-Five Years of American Dance*, published by *Dance*

Magazine (New York, 1954), especially Helen Dzhermolinska's article there, 'A Family Tree,' pages 198–99."

———, ed. *Portrait of Mr. B: Photographs of George Balanchine with an Essay by Lincoln Kirstein.* Foreword by Peter Martins. Includes "Two Talks with George Balanchine" by Jonathan Cott and "Three Sides of *Agon*" by Edwin Denby. New York: Ballet Society/Viking Press, 1984.

Kisselgoff, Anna. "Freud Meets Disney in Paul Taylor Works." *The New York Times*, Arts and Leisure, April 20, 1990: query.nytimes. com/gst/fullpage.html?res=9C0CE2D81F39F933A15757C0 A966958260&scp=1&sq=%93Freud+Meets+Disney&st=nyt

London, Kurt. *Film Music: A Summary of the Characteristic Features of Its History, Aesthetics, Technique and Possible Developments.* London: Faber and Faber, 1936.

Lutz, E.G. *Animated Cartoons: How They are Made, Their Origin and Development.* Bedford, MA: Applewood Books, 1920 (reprint).

Macaulay, Alastair, "An Appreciation of Movement and Dance in Walt Disney's Films." *The Dancing Times* (December 1989): 261–64.

MacMahon, Deirdre, "Disney's *Fantasia*," *Dance Theatre Journal* 9, no. 3 (Spring 1992): 10–13.

Maltin, Leonard. *The Disney Films* (4th ed.). New York: Disney Editions, 2000.

Merritt, Russell, and J. B. Kaufman. *Walt Disney's Silly Symphonies: A Companion to the Classic Cartoon Series.* Gemona, Italy: La Cineteca del Friuli, 2006.

———. *Walt in Wonderland: The Silent Films of Walt Disney.* Pordenone, Italy: La Cineteca del Friuli, Le Giornate del Cinema Muto, 1993.

Meyer, Susan E. *A Treasury of the Great Children's Book Illustrators.* New York: Abradale Press/Harry N. Abrams, 1983.

Mueller, John. *Astaire Dancing: The Musical Films.* New York: Alfred A. Knopf, 1985.

Nathan, George Jean. *The Theatre Book of the Year, 1943–44.* With a new introduction by Charles Angoff; originally published by Alfred A. Knopf, 1944. Madison, NJ: Farleigh Dickinson University Press, 1972.

The New Illustrated Treasury of Disney Songs (revised and updated). New York: Hyperion, 1998.

Peterson, Bernard J. *A Century of Musicals in Black and White: An Encyclopedia of Musical Stage Works About or Involving African Americans.* New York: Harcourt Education, 1993.

Potaznik, Reina. "Brothers Grimm's, Walt Disney's, and Ann Liv Young's *Snow White*." Unpublished term paper for the course From Page to Stage, Barnard College. March 15, 2007.

Powell, Michael. *A Life in the Movies: An Autobiography.* London: Faber and Faber, 2000. Originally published 1986.

Prendergast, Roy M. *Film Music: A Neglected Art.* With a foreword by William Kraft. New York: Norton Library, 1977.

Prevots, Naima. "Ernest Belcher and American Dance." *Dance Chronicle* 10, no. 2 (1987): 170–222. A slightly different version also appears in Naima Prevots, *Dancing in the Sun: Hollywood Choreographers 1915–1937,* Ann Arbor, MI: UMI Research Press, 1987.

Rylant, Cynthia (author), and Mary Blair (illustrator). *Walt Disney's Cinderella.* New York: Disney Press, 2007.

Smith, David R. "Ben Sharpsteen . . . 33 Years with Disney." *Millimeter: The magazine for and about film and videotape people* (April 1975): 38–45.

———. *Disney A to Z: The Updated Official Encyclopedia.* New York: Hyperion, 1998.

———, and Steven Clark. *Disney: the First Hundred Years.* New York: Disney Editions, 2002.

Solomon, Charles. *Enchanted Drawings: The History of Animation.* New York: Alfred A. Knopf, 1989.

Taylor, Deems. *Walt Disney's "Fantasia."* New York: Simon & Schuster, 1940.

Thomas, Bob. *Walt Disney: The Art of Animation: The Story of the Disney Studio Contribution to a New Art.* New York: Simon & Schuster, 1958.

Thomas, Frank, and Ollie Johnston. *The Illusion of Life: Disney Animation.* New York: Disney Editions, 1981.

Tytla, Adrienne. *Disney's Giant and the Artist's Model.* Deep River, CT: privately published (printed by Valley Press's New Era Printing Company), 2004.

Tytle, Harry. *One of "Walt's Boys": An Insider's Account of Disney's Golden Years.* Privately published 1997.

Waleson, Heidi. "When Balanchine Brought Ballet to Hollywood." *The New York Times,* March 13, 1988, Arts and Leisure: 24, 36.

Walsh, Stephen. *Stravinsky: The Second Exile: France and America, 1934–1971.* New York: Alfred A. Knopf, 2006.

Watson, Sonny. "Truckin'." Sonny Watson's Streetswing.com: www.streetswing.com/histmain/z3truck.htm.

Webb, Graham. *The Animated Film Encyclopedia: A Complete Guide to American Shorts, Features, and Sequences, 1900–1979.* Jefferson, NC: McFarland & Company, 2000.

West, Martha Ullman. "Making Dance Sing: Mark Morris's Choreography for Opera." *The Chronicle Review: The Chronicle of Higher Education* 53, no. 33 (April 20, 2007): B18.

Wondrich, David. "I Love to Hear a Minstrel Band: Walt Disney's *The Band Concert.*" In Goldmark and Taylor, *The Cartoon Music Book.*

Wright, Anita Peters, and Dexter Wright. *How to Dance.* Illustrated by Betty Randolph Bean. New York: Garden City Books, 1952.

Zorina, Vera. *Zorina.* New York: Farrar Straus and Giroux, 1986.

INTERVIEW AND LECTURE TRANSCRIPTS IN THE DISNEY STUDIO ARCHIVES

Canemaker, John. Filmed interview with Marge Champion, October 26, 1994.

Hubler, Richard. Notes from an interview with Wilfred Jackson, March 26, 1968.

Kurtti, Jeff. Interviews concerning the making of *Destino* with animator John Hench (March 25, 2002), Disney Archivist Dave Smith (May 2, 2002), filmmaker Dominique Monfery (May 29, 2002), and animation historian John Canemaker (February 26, 2003).

Jackson, Wilfred. "Music and Animation," lecture, December 8, 1952.

———. "Musical Pictures," lectures, January 26 and February 9, 1939.

———. "Musical Stories," lecture, January 12, 1939.

Story Meeting, "Dance of the Hours" (*Fantasia*), December 15, 1938.

Story Meeting, "Nutcracker Suite"—Overall Continuity (*Fantasia*), January 23, 1939.

THE JOHN CANEMAKER ANIMATION COLLECTION 1903–2003, FALES LIBRARY AND SPECIAL COLLECTIONS, ELMER HOLMES BOBST LIBRARY, NEW YORK UNIVERSITY

Various transcripts of Disney story conferences from throughout the 1930s; letters from artist Oskar and Elfriede Fischinger to conductor Leopold Stokowski concerning Oskar Fischinger's art for the Disney studio; undated art work related to the 1940 *Fantasia* and the unproduced Disney film *Don Quixote.*

INDEX

ACKNOWLEDGMENTS

Hippo in a Tutu exists because Christopher Caines, the editor at Disney Editions who had a vision of it, willed it into being, edited every word, buoyed me when I was overwhelmed, and lashed me on to the finish line, giving of his time and brilliance without respite. The text I supplied is a pale substitute for what he could have authored, were he not also a busy choreographer. It was an honor to be asked to write this book under his guidance and pure bliss to spend time with the material. Of course, none of us realized just how *much* time I'd be spending: a royal *révérance* to the staff of Disney Editions—its gifted editorial director, Wendy Lefkon, her most capable assistant, Jessica Ward, senior copy chief Monica Mayper, and copy editor Guy Cunningham—for their patience, kindness, and exemplary professionalism. The book's designer, Jonathan Glick, exhibited the same qualities, as well as creativity on the page. To work with this team is a privilege.

No chronicle of dancing at Disney could be written without the participation of the beloved Broadway and Hollywood star dancer Marge Champion, whose beauty, taste, and technical prowess also served Walt Disney's masterpieces of animation. Ms. Champion gave openheartedly of her time and memory to this book, contributed expressly for it an oral history of her Disney experiences through the oral-history program at the Jerome Robbins Dance Division of the New York Public Library for the Performing Arts at Lincoln Center, and provided unique photographs. I kneel to her in thanks. My enduring gratitude also to the library's Susan Kraft for arranging the oral history and to the Dance Division staff, who offered indispensable help, from the pages who located materials and the meticulous photocopiers to many librarians, beginning with Charles Perrier, Myron Switzer, and Pat Rader. Phil Karg, Alice Standin, and Tom Lasanti assisted with picture research. And my former co-interviewer on the Franklin Project, NYPL librarian emerita Monica Moseley, graciously entertained research questions.

A heartfelt thank-you is offered to choreographer Mark Morris for taking time from the creation of new dances to reflect on his relationship to Disney films in his foreword. Some thirty years ago, I first saw Mr. Morris dance like a Blakean angel with Hannah Kahn; I've been a member of the eager audience for his own company since the early 1980s; and I began to read his dance writing nearly a decade ago, when his account of a performance by the Kirov Ballet appeared in Wendy Lesser's *Threepenny Review*. He is a wonderful artist and a stimulating thinker, and his generosity in contributing a foreword here is deeply appreciated. William Murray, Mr. Morris's press representative, helped to make this happen, and I thank him.

John Canemaker—treasured New York University professor of animation, Oscar-winning documentarian, and revered historian of animated films—has assisted this book as a consultant, a reader, and a provider of rare source materials.

I quickly discovered that, regardless of whatever topic one addresses concerning Disney art, Mr. Canemaker has been there first, and always with wisdom, passion, honesty, tact, grace, and scholarship of the highest order. He took time from production of a film to write his foreword. I thank him with respect and joy. I also extend thanks to the librarians at the John Canemaker Animation Collection in the Fales Library and Special Collections of New York University's Elmer Holmes Bobst Library, where I was able to study historic Disney art and read transcripts of story conferences and the letters of artist Oskar Fischinger and Elfride Fischinger to Leopold Stokowski.

I am grateful to the staffs of the Barnard College Library and Butler Library of Columbia University, where some of the books I needed were housed, and to the staff of Media Services at Barnard, which assisted me with some of the films.

When I started my research, I knew a fair amount about dancing but almost nothing about how animated pictures are made. Along with my reading and study of the films, many of the individuals named here served as living tutors. However, one—composer and historian Alexander Rannie—proved to be a Virgil. Mr. Rannie's profoundly supportive and selfless contributions to this book in terms of background, fact-checking, e-mail brainstorming (he and I have never actually met in person!), and myriad revelations of both published source materials and rare Disney art made me feel as if I had wandered into Aladdin's cave. What he could not answer or effect simply cannot be magicked. At those points in the text where I have used his research and/or ideas without amendment, I directly cite him, although his learning and kindness light up many more pages than those where he is mentioned.

During the nearly five years I've been at work on the book, I made three visits, of one week each, to Disney's archives in California, where I pored over original art, films, transcripts of story conferences and interviews, photographs, and much relevant studio ephemera. Dave Smith, Chief Archivist of the Walt Disney Archives at the Disney Studio's Burbank campus and legendary sage, who more than lives up to the legend, oversaw an exactingly organized department, assisted by Robert Tieman and, when I was there, Rebecca M. Cline, both reservoirs of detailed information. A keenly knowledgeable college intern, Steve Vagnini, provided a Web site based in Russia that discussed the relationship of Disney cartoons from the 1970s to earlier films. At the Animation Research Library in Glendale, I worked with Disney devotees Fox Carney and Ann Hansen. I also consulted the Photo Library in Glendale, overseen by Ed Squair. These individuals love and thoroughly know the archives they serve, and most of them have continued to answer questions and provide information long-distance for years following my trips. Thank you to each and every one.

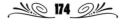

An affectionate thank-you as well to Disney researcher Jeff Kurtti, his partner Ken Martinez, and their family, for their extraordinary hospitality that made one of the visits possible. Mr. Kurtti, a Disney author and interviewer, also provided many leads and materials, particularly relating to the Disney–Dalí collaboration, *Destino*.

While at the archives, I was privileged to conduct contextual interviews with some of the finest Disney artists working today: the animator Andreas Deja and the hit directors Ron Clements and John Musker. And I was able to conduct a phone interview with Kathryn Beaumont, the exquisite voice and live-action reference model for Alice in *Alice in Wonderland* and *Peter Pan*'s Wendy. They all took the time from hectic schedules to help bring me up to speed about the intricate process of making a Disney animated film, and I am in their debt. These interviews were kindly arranged by historian and Vice President of Studio Communications for the Walt Disney Studio Howard Green, then working with assistant Beth DuMont. Thank-yous to all.

In California, I was able, as well, to meet in person or speak on the phone with some of the outstanding historians and connoisseurs of animation in the country, among them Charles Solomon, Harry Arends, and Les Perkins, who clarified intellectual issues and/or gave me rare DVDs of interviews or documentaries. Other historians and practitioners of animation have gone out of their way to offer assistance, either through phone interviews or e-mail conversations: composer and historian Ross Care; animator and historian Mark Kausler; distinguished Disney animator and storyman Burny Mattinson; special-effects animator Al Holter; animation historian J. B. Kaufman; peerless historian of the American musical, Miles Kreuger; historians Hans Perk and Stacia Martin; teacher and vivid historian of tap, Rusty Frank; and erstwhile Disney choreographer Naomi Goldberg. Michael Labrie at the Walt Disney Family Museum offered picture assistance. Booker White, Lisa Janacua, and Darren Otero of the Walt Disney Pictures Music Library provided musical manuscript support and scanned many images.

The discovery of the right picture, and then the securing of permission to publish it, occupied the time of many colleagues, and I am grateful to them beyond my ability to articulate it. First and foremost, I thank the Walt Disney Company for its magnanimous permission to publish the garden of beautiful art you see in these pages, as well as historic photographs. Jeff Kurtti was crucial here, as were Jonathan Heely, Director of Music Publishing at Disney, and Alexander Rannie.

Thank-yous, too, are extended for the many kindnesses related to imagery to the delightful Jerry Beck and www.cartoonbrew.com; photographers Johan Elbers, Beatriz Schiller, Bill Cooper, and Tom Brazil; the staffs of the George Eastman House Motion Picture Department Collection and of the Margaret Herrick Library at the Academy of Motion Picture Arts and Sciences; Jenny and Robert Cowan of the Cowan Collection (who, in fact, just for this book rephotographed Disney models they owned); Mike and Janeen Van Eaton of Van Eaton Galleries; the Disneyana specialist Dug Miller; the great choreographer Paul Taylor and his general manager, John Tomlinson, and the staff of the Paul Taylor Dance Company; editor and dance critic Robert A. Gottlieb; Jeff Seroy at Farrar, Straus and Giroux; Sue Carol Jackson Black; photographer Jack Mitchell and Craig High berger of jmphoto; Jeremy Lott, Clip and Still Licensing, MGM Consumer Products; Regina Feiler of the *LIFE* Gallery of Photography; Howard Stark of the Special Projects Department at RKO Pictures; Peter Kersten of Getty Images; Julie Heath and Jackie Pomales of Clip & Still Licensing at Warner Bros. Entertainment; Meredith Morris-Babb of the University Press of Florida; choreographer Lori Belilove and the Isadora Duncan Dance Foundation; composer Peter Lieberson and G. Schirmer, Inc.; and Joanna Ney of the Film Society of Lincoln Center. Dance critic Susan Reiter generously made it possible for me to afford the inclusion of one of the images from outside the Disney enterprise when I most needed such assistance.

Friends and colleagues in New York from the worlds of dance and literature extended considerable help with research in a variety of ways, and to them I am beholden: Robert Greskovic, esteemed dance writer for *The Wall Street Journal*; Nancy Reynolds, Research Director for the George Balanchine Foundation; James Harvey, critic and historian of American cinema; Phillip Lopate, anthologist and essayist; Mary Cargill, librarian at Columbia University; tap dancer and Barnard professor of tap Margaret Morrison; dance historian Claudia Gitelman; author and designer John Esten; dance historian George Dorris; dance critics and historians Jack Anderson, Barbara Newman, and Deborah Jowitt; and dance critic and editor Elizabeth Zimmer. Dance critic Alastair Macaulay and historian of Irish history and dance critic Deirdre MacMahon helped me to find their essays on a festival of Disney animated films put on in London by the British Film Institute. Dance bibliophiles Leslie Getz and Don McDonagh made life bearable on some bleak days: I thank them for being their intrinsically generous selves.

A tip of the hat as well for intellectual assistance to dance scholar Karl E. Toepfer, in Germany; Naima Prevots, Professor of Dance at American University in Washington, D.C.; and dance critic Lewis Segal, in Los Angeles.

My daughter Ariel's dad, poet Marty Cohen, expanded my thinking with the gift of a book on the social history of newspaper comics and some challenging questions that helped me sharpen my views. Film critic Dennis Grunes, a friend of nearly forty years, forced me to stay real through his many challenging essays on the cinema, sent from Portland, Oregon. Richard Bailey offered many kindnesses. Other friends provided moral support beyond measure. I offer them all loving thank-yous.

For my daughter, Ariel, the dedicatee here, this entire book is tendered as thanks.

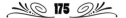

A pastel sketch (possibly by Jules Engel) of a little Orchid Dancer for Fantasia's
"Nutcracker Suite." Courtesy the Cowan Collection (Jenny and Robert Cowan).